"Did you buy anything?"

"No. Only tea and cake. Oh, and a raffle ticket."

"Who else was there? Everyone?"

I leaned back against the worktop. "A good turnout. That Amber from the café was there. She was full of herself as usual."

"There's something I don't like about her." Candy screwed up her nose.

"She was very dressed up," I said.

"She always is. She goes to the café in clothes you might wear to an opera!"

"She's new in the village, but she already seems to know everyone."

"I think she's only here for the treasure hunt. Mind you, the villagers always say that about people who are new."

"I suppose they said it about me when I first arrived," I said.

"But you come from here. You've returned to the village. That's different."

We spent a little time reminiscing about the treasure hunt. We talked about the most recent hunt. It was always good fun, even though this year's prize hadn't been one of the best.

"I wonder what it will be like next year. I'm not sure what's left of the family will be able to organize much," Candy observed. "It's a shame. Some people think there won't be a hunt at all."

From what she said, I imagined Candy knew little about the Lesters and the current situation, but then I thought all the locals were keeping their cards close to their chests. People had their own views and their own agendas, they certainly weren't about to divulge the contents of their minds. That went for me as well. I was planning to keep quiet, lie low, and wait.

# The Ultimate Village Game

by

Beth Merwood

This is a work of fiction. Names, characters, places, and incidents are either the product of the author's imagination or are used fictitiously, and any resemblance to actual persons living or dead, business establishments, events, or locales, is entirely coincidental.

**The Ultimate Village Game**

COPYRIGHT © 2022 by Beth Merwood

All rights reserved. No part of this book may be used or reproduced in any manner whatsoever without written permission of the author or The Wild Rose Press, Inc. except in the case of brief quotations embodied in critical articles or reviews.
Contact Information: info@thewildrosepress.com

Cover Art by *Diana Carlile*

The Wild Rose Press, Inc.
PO Box 708
Adams Basin, NY 14410-0708
Visit us at www.thewildrosepress.com

Publishing History
First Edition, 2022
Trade Paperback ISBN 978-1-5092-4229-0
Digital ISBN 978-1-5092-4230-6

Published in the United States of America

# Dedication

For rescue dogs everywhere, and their humans.

**Acknowledgments**

With thanks to my editor, Melanie Billings, cover designer, Diana Carlile, and all at The Wild Rose Press.

Chapter 1
Back In Steely, Moonstones

I opened my notebook and began to write. I could remember what I'd said, near enough.

*I'm a lucky person in many ways. I came back to Steely getting on for a year ago. I had a small amount of money saved up, enough to put down my deposit and cover a few months' rent. I moved into the cottage and allowed myself a little time to settle in. Soon afterward, I found my ideal job. I'm happy here. I lead a simple life, but it suits me. I wouldn't want it any other way.*

Yes, that's what I'd said to the man I'd met that morning, with Fergus.

"Hold on, Morsel, I'll let you out."

Things changed when I acquired Morsel. She's my rescue dog. She was part of my plan in a way—get a rescue dog, and people might think you give a damn; almost as soon as I had her, I realized how much I needed her. She came from the home in Weston Lee. She's her own person, dog person, that is. She's had it hard, same as me. We get along. Morsel and I go out and about together.

Prior to adopting Morsel, I would no way have been popular in the village, Steely Green to give it its full name. I've never been good at conversation. Throughout my life, now and then, I've made an effort, but generally with a complete lack of success. Morsel became my passport to friendship. The minute I took her out walking, I automatically seemed to become an accepted member of some select village club. I learned how to take part too. Other dog owners and dog walkers greeted me and stopped to chat. There was an excuse to speak, and also, I realized, very importantly, the perfect excuse to leave. *"Is that the time? I should be getting home,"* or *"I could talk all day, but I must give this one some exercise!"* We all did it. No one took offense. Through Morsel, I'd come to know a number of people, and I could communicate with them: there was George, there was Jenny, there was Charlie Harvey.

"Morsel! Morsel! Come back inside now. Good girl."

Another day was over. I thought again, but there was nothing more to write in the notebook. I'd eaten, I'd watched television, I'd read a little. I went upstairs to bed. As I lay amongst the sheets, my head swimming with thoughts, my mind was taken over by images of the future: the spoils I was to have, and the respect I would gain. I needed to be convincing, like an actor playing a part. I'd come back to the village with a plan and a bucketful of expectation, but I had to bide my time, weigh everything up, give the right impression, and make my moves with care. Morsel was right beside me, snuggled in, sleeping peacefully.

"You're my accomplice, Morsel," I whispered. "We'll make this happen together."

\*\*\*\*

The following day was Tuesday. I had to be up early. I dressed against the cold and headed out with my trusty companion. We arrived at the common.

"Oh look, the man with Fergus is here again,

good," I said to Morsel. "Hello, good morning," I greeted him.

"Hello to you," he said.

"How is Fergus today? Looks as though he's full of beans!"

"You mean Bones,"

"Bones?"

"Fergus is my name. The dog is Bones."

"Oh, I'm sorry. That's not the first time I've been guilty of such a faux pas! The Barratts' dog is called Wesley, and I always think Jenny is talking to me about her husband. Have you met them? He's a Labrador. Wesley, that is! How embarrassing. I'm so sorry."

"It's an easy mistake to make."

"I must rush. I have to be at work by eight. Perhaps I'll see you at the village hall on Saturday? There's a fundraising thing on for the church." I walked off hurriedly. "Come on, Morsel! Come on, girl!"

Once out of sight and earshot, I smiled, laughed, and told myself, "You're getting good at this, Lucy. You are sure getting good at this!" I said it in an American accent. I had no idea why.

****

"Stay there, Morsel, good girl. I'll be back by midday. You can watch the news channel. When I get home, you can fill me in on what's going on in the world." She sat in front of me, looking up with bright eyes. I bent down and rubbed her.

It wouldn't take long to get to work. It wasn't far: round the corner, past Charlie Harvey's house, on to the end of the lane, and up the hill. Moonstones was on the left-hand side, nearer to the top of the hill than the bottom. The manager's car was on the driveway, John's car too, both taking up their usual spaces. The mini-bus was also parked up.

"Morning," I said as I entered. I went to the staff room to put on an overall and buttoned it up on my way to the kitchen. I began to put breakfasts onto a trolley. Candy was late. Not unusual. She knew I wouldn't mind; she'd return the favor later.

"Been for a walk this morning?" John asked.

"Yes, chilly out," I said.

"I'm doing a special for You Know Who, but everyone else can have the same…apart from the ones I need to liquidize, of course."

"Thanks, I'll take these first."

There were ten residents. The home was full. We had three men and seven women ranging from seventy-eight to a hundred and one years in age. Moonstones was a rest home for the elderly, a good one.

To begin with, I delivered six breakfasts. Everyone ate breakfast in their rooms. I returned for the three that would be blitzed to a mush, and there was the special for Mr. Pickering. I'd deliver the meals; after that, I'd have to assist anyone who needed to be helped or encouraged to eat.

"What did you get up to last evening?" John asked. He was putting out a huge full English and preparing a separate plate piled high with toast. He handed me a dish of marmalade and another with pats of butter. "Mr. Pickering has an insatiable appetite. He rarely leaves anything."

"Not much. I was reading. I watched part of a crime serial. Part three, I think. I hadn't seen the first two parts, so it was quite confusing."

"Can't you get them on catch up?"

"I'm not sure. But I don't mind when the programs don't make sense. If you watch from start to finish, they're often just mumbo jumbo, aren't they? I really only watch for the images. There were some lovely houses in this one and some magnificent gardens."

John was using the liquidizer again, so we couldn't speak after that. He put some of the concoction into mugs with drinking spouts. I topped up the large teapot with hot water, loaded the trolley, and trundled away.

I knocked and entered. "Good morning, Mr. Pickering. How are you this fine morning?"

"Hello, Lucy. I'm very well, very well. I'm hungry. It smells delicious!"

"John's done you proud this morning. It's a super-looking breakfast."

Mr. Pickering was up and sitting in his chair in his dressing gown. I pulled the side table over and arranged the various breakfast items on top of it. "Is Miss Pickering coming to see you today?"

"Yes! Yes, she is. And I'm due to have a visit from our nephew this week! I think he's coming at the weekend."

"That's something to look forward to then." I told Mr. Pickering I'd come back shortly to pour him a second cup of tea. Miss Pickering was Mr. Pickering's sister. He'd moved into Moonstones recently, but up to that point, he and his sister had always lived together. I found Miss Pickering particularly interesting as she'd once been housekeeper at Steely Green Manor, the place the Lesters owned. I understood the nephew to be the son of another brother who lived elsewhere, though thinking about it, I wasn't too sure if that brother was still alive. Mr. Pickering was very much alive. He was one of the oldest residents but one of the best in terms of health. You might imagine there was little wrong with him aside from him being somewhat forgetful.

I returned to his room after delivering the liquidized breakfasts. "Did you remember to take your tablets, Mr. Pickering?"

"Yes, I did. I've taken them all." He opened his mouth widely and moved his tongue from side to side in case I thought he was hiding them.

"Good. Now, here's another cup of tea, and I'll clear these things for you."

"I'm due to have a visit from our nephew, Lucy. I think he's coming at the weekend."

"I'm pleased to hear that, Mr. Pickering."

Candy had arrived and was helping with the rounds. Once breakfast was over, we took a short break together in the kitchen. John had made fresh tea and more toast. The kitchen was a refuge for us when we were working. We used the small staffroom for storing our coats and bags but gathered in the warm kitchen, where food and drink were generally on offer, and the music station played cheerily in the background.

"Either of you like an egg? Piece of bacon?" John asked.

"Not for me, John, thanks," I said.

Candy gave in. "Ooh, I could fancy some scrambled if there's any going."

"I'll do fresh for both of us," John said, and he got on with breaking eggs into a bowl.

Candy and I checked our schedule. We'd go round together washing faces and cleaning teeth—most teeth were false, of course. Toileting came next, and the changing of bed sheets. After that, it would be time for a round of mid-morning drinks. There was a rota so that one or two of the residents had a bath or shower each day. We would see to this, and then we'd serve lunch. I had a half-hour break at midday and would dash home to let Morsel out. I'd return to Moonstones, cover Candy's break, and finish my shift. If I was a little late back, Candy wouldn't mind since I'd covered for her in the morning. Come two thirty, the shift would be over, and the rest of the day would be my own.

How it worked at Moonstones was there were two of us on duty from eight in the morning to two thirty in the afternoon. A new shift began at two thirty, and one person covered the night shift. Eight of us shared the workload, with the occasional agency worker coming in if necessary. John and Larry were the cooks, or chefs as they liked to call themselves. Joe and Lianne were the managers and owners of the home; one or other of them was always on duty as well. Joe and Lianne were a couple. They had separate accommodation on the grounds and had a large office downstairs at the back of the main building, originally a large Edwardian private residence.

\*\*\*\*

Later, at home, I took out my notebook and recorded the morning's conversation. I now knew the name of the new man. He was Fergus. I presumed from the name, and his accent, that he was Scottish.

\*\*\*\*

I was on morning shifts for the week. It was all go with duties on the early shift. It meant I didn't have much time to chat with the residents. However, on Friday morning, I went into Lolly's room in the late morning and found her in tears. Lolly was our newest arrival. She was a lovely soft bundle of woolens of a lady who'd lived alone in the village for years but had finally come to Moonstones after having a couple of falls.

"Lolly, what's the matter?" I said.

"I don't know, dear. I don't know," she said. "I just want to be back in my own home…making my own cup of tea."

"Shall I sit with you?" I asked.

"That would be nice. You're a good person, Lucy."

I went quickly to tell Candy that Lolly needed comforting. Candy would look after the others in the meantime. She could call on Joe or Lianne if need be. I shouldn't admit it, but one of my favorite parts of the job was helping people when they became a little down. I'd always had problems of my own with those sorts of feelings, and talking to someone miserable always cheered me up. That sounds wrong, I know, but I felt better in the knowledge that not everyone was happy and buoyant all the time. If someone was wretched, I felt at ease in their company. I handed Lolly a box of tissues. She took one, and I put the box down beside her. She was in her comfortable chair. I drew up the hard chair kept next to the wall and sat down.

"Lolly, I love making tea for you. Would you like more sugar?" I just wanted to get her talking.

"The tea is nice, and so are you, and so is having it made for me," she said. I waited for her to reveal more. "Will I have to stay here always, now? Am I never going to be able to go back to my bungalow?"

"I don't know about those things, Lolly. But while you are here, you should make the most of it. You can order what you like when you like, and we will fetch and carry it. Soon, when your leg is better, you'll be able to go to the lounge if you're fed up in your room. I'll take you there…and I can take you to the garden if it's warm enough." She dabbed the corners of her eyes with the handkerchief. "We have fun here, you know. All kinds of people visit. There's a lady who comes to play piano, and everyone sings along. There's a man who shows us exercises, and we join in. All sorts goes on."

She didn't speak, but I could tell I was making progress. I took her hand and held it. I would pay particular attention to Lolly until I was satisfied she was feeling better about life at the home.

\*\*\*\*

In the evening, I checked the notebook. The two entries about Fergus were the only things there had been to write down for over a week.

Chapter 2
The Church Sale

Morsel ran to the door bouncing and barking. It was Saturday morning, and Charlie had arrived on her skateboard.

"Hello, Charlie. Come in."

"Have you taken Morsel out? Can I come?"

"I haven't taken her yet, and yes, you're welcome to come. I need some shopping so you can look after her while I go into the grocery store. But we could go to the copse first if you like?"

Charlie was eight. To be honest, it took me a while to work out for sure that she was female. She was a right tomboy and something of a chatterbox. I hadn't known many children. I was afraid of them as a rule, but she was besotted with Morsel and regularly came to the cottage to visit her. Charlie lived nearby, just around the corner, and it appeared her parents let her do whatever she wanted. Once I'd managed to persuade myself she wasn't aiming to make fun of me or steal something from me, I began to accept her visits. I liked the fact that she seemed to think well of me. I needed people on my side, but I wasn't used to it. I'd made sure her mother, Belle, was aware she'd taken to calling on me, but I had nothing in common with the mother and could understand why her daughter liked to be out.

Charlie left the skateboard in my kitchen, and we

set off, the three of us.

"Do you have to work today?" Charlie asked.

"No, a day off. I'm not sure how I managed to get Saturday off!"

Charlie smiled.

"How was school this week?" I asked her.

"It was all right."

"What did you learn?"

"Oh, we never learn anything."

"Well, perhaps you're not paying attention?"

There were a few dogs and walkers in the copse. We let Morsel off her lead, and Charlie went with her, running in and out between the birch trees. That meant I could indulge in some weekend small talk. I sat down on the bench and waited for dogs and owners to come to me.

"Morning, Lucy."

"Hello, George. How are you? How is Helen?" Wotnot arrived, a young golden retriever. He put his paws on my knees and licked my face. "Hello, Wotnot. Good boy."

"Get down, Wotnot! She's well. She's gone to Melstow with Ange, so I've got Moose as well. Moose! Moose!" George called. "Where's he got to? Moose!"

"What's happening in Melstow? Just shopping?"

"Yes, just shopping. Get down, Wotnot! Here, Moose!"

"Don't worry, he's fine. Do you need a treat for Moose? He'll surely come for a treat. I have some in my pocket…here you go." I offered George a few small heart shaped meaty things.

"Oh, thanks. That should do it. Where's Morsel?"

"Over there, look, with Charlie."

"Ah yes. She loves Morsel doesn't she? Quite a little character, Charlie, don't you think?"

"Yes, I suppose so, not that I know much about kids. I've never had any of my own, as you know."

"Better off." George was looking into the trees.

"How is Daniel?" I asked.

"Football," he said.

"Right," I said.

Moose emerged, a huge gray, shaggy animal, and galloped in our direction. George steadied himself in preparation. Moose arrived sporting long, elastic drools of saliva that hung glistening from his jaws. He panted steaming, stinking breath.

"I'd better get these two home." George grappled manfully with collars and leads.

"Sure." The dogs began dragging him away.

"Will you be going to the church's autumn sale or whatever it is?" he shouted over his shoulder. "It starts at two o'clock."

"Oh, yes, I'd almost forgotten. I'll try to drop by."

\*\*\*\*

At the village hall, I scanned the room for Fergus, but there was no sign of him. Amber was on full show, however, and Martin was duly in attendance. I'd managed to send Charlie home to her mother and leave Morsel in the house; I was on my own. I bought a cup of tea and an enormous homemade chocolate chip cookie and went to sit at a corner table, with a good view out across the room. There were stalls selling all sorts of wares, from cakes and jams to homemade bird boxes. There was a second-hand hat stall, one selling various hand-knitted items, and someone selling homemade soaps; there must have been a dozen stalls.

Various people came over to speak. Between chats, I watched Amber, who looked as glamorous as ever, ostentatiously holding forth, in the main to a gathering of attentive looking men. I noticed Martin, with possibly his wife or girlfriend, mingling insignificantly and making his way around the hall.

Miss Pickering spotted me and came over. "Hello, Lucy. It's nice to see you here."

She was a petite, neat and tidy lady. She wore a royal blue suit, skirt and jacket, and an embroidered white blouse. A delicate gold cross hung at her neck. Her short, silver-gray hair still retained darker streaks and was permed into small tight curls.

"Hello, Miss Pickering. Can I get you a cup of tea?"

"You do enough of that at Moonstones!" She sat down next to me. I went to the stall and fetched her a cup of tea and a slice of sponge cake.

"Oh, thank you. You do like to spoil people! Bob feels like a king at Moonstones, he tells me. He was never pampered in such a way at home."

"I get the impression you looked after him very well, Miss Pickering," I said, "and I think you did more for him than he'd care to admit."

"Do you have a day off?" she asked.

"Yes, I'm off today. I'll be back on duty tomorrow afternoon."

"You'll probably meet our nephew. He's coming tomorrow."

"That will be nice. Mr. Pickering mentioned your nephew was due to visit." We both took a sip of tea. "Who's that man over there, Miss Pickering?"

"That's John Crane. He works at the manor,

gardening."

"I thought he was a Crane. None of the Lesters are here, are they?"

"No, no. I doubt any of them would turn up here. If Reg was still alive, he might have dropped in. If Nic lived in England, he might have come along."

Everyone knew about the Lesters, the notorious family who owned the nearby manor house. I'd certainly describe them as wealthy. It was new money. They were brash and showy. They'd spend, spend, spend, and whatever you did in the village, you couldn't ignore that they existed. They were a big part of Steely Green.

As she talked about the Lesters, Miss Pickering stared ahead of her, and I saw the hint of a smile on her lips. I imagined she was remembering some wonderful times she'd had while working as housekeeper at the manor. She went quiet for a few moments, wrapped up in her thoughts.

Amber came to speak to us.

"Where's that little girl of yours?" she asked me.

"She's not mine. She's a Harvey."

"I know, but she spends more time with you than with that mother of hers."

"She's home with her mum right now," I stated. Whenever Amber said anything to me, I felt she was judging me in some way, and there was an element of disapproval. I never felt any sort of warmth from her.

"What have you bought, Amber?" Miss Pickering asked. Amber had a paper carrier bag in her hand.

"A sweet little scarf from Mary Penny's stall," she said. "Have a look."

Mary Penny's stall consisted of a collection of

vintage jewelry and accessories. Amber took a very nice silk scarf out of the bag and showed it to us. It was the sort of thing I wouldn't have noticed, but Amber had picked it out, and I could tell it was going to look fabulous around her long elegant neck.

Back at home, I checked myself in the mirror. There was no full-length mirror in the house, and I supposed that for most of my life, I'd taken little interest in what I looked like. I did the minimum. I went to the local hairdresser's every six weeks or so for a cut and blow-dry; every now and then, I went to Melstow to buy clothes from the high street chain stores. I thought about Amber. What was her regimen in terms of her skin and hair, and where did she shop for her eye-catching clothing? Amber was another of those fairly new to Steely. She lived alone in a cottage near the old mill. She was a tall woman with long, red-brown hair and probably similar in age to me. She spoke with a well-to-do accent; however, she worked at the local café in a part-time role, serving at the counter and waitressing. I found this slightly odd, and it made me all the more cautious about her. Why would she work at the Wises' café? She didn't appear to be short of money. She drove a shiny sports car, and when it came to her wardrobe, which I admit was a particular fascination of mine, I'd go as far as to say it was elaborate. It seemed to me she was more of an office job type person or someone you might find working in an up-market shop of some kind or an estate agency.

I'd taken the mirror from the wall and positioned it as well as I could on the pillow to get the right angle. I looked into it. I don't know what other people thought, but I wouldn't be surprised if they used words like *'dumpy,' 'frumpy,' 'dowdy.'*

"Oh dear," I said to Morsel, "I should take more care. After all, if everything goes to plan, I'll need to look the part."

I opened the wardrobe and threw the contents onto the bed. Everything was plain, and most things were dark or dull in color. I had the odd item with some style: a nice coat; one nice dress I'd bought for a party at Moonstones but been too self-conscious to wear. All my shoes were clumpy, chunky, in no way refined. I had no stockings. I wore bare legs or woolly tights, that was when I wasn't wearing trousers. I put everything back in the wardrobe, went downstairs, and put on the kettle. Morsel followed all the while.

"Let's have a sit-down, Morsel. I'll write in my notebook." I tickled her behind her ears. I cut a few pieces of cheese for her and poured my tea into a mug. I sat in my chair and made notes about Amber and Martin.

*Saturday. The church sale.*
*Martin: Suspicious. Find out more about him.*
*Amber: Very suspicious. Keep an eye on her.*

I'd not said anything to Amber that would have any significance, and I'd not spoken to Martin at all. I'd never spoken to him, in fact. So far, I'd only been noting where I'd seen him and what he'd been doing. I had heard, however, from Helen Dean, that he was quite nosy and asked too many questions.

"Oh, Morsel, I'm not sure," I said. Morsel looked at me. She tipped her head to one side. "But I must remember that someone might be checking up on me. I'm sure whoever it is will have been planted here. It won't be one of the locals." I was convinced she knew what I was saying. I put the notebook away and rinsed my mug. "Shall we have another walk before it gets dark? I think you'd like that. Come on, girl."

On the way out, I made a point of looking in the hall mirror. I tidied my hair and put on a smear of lipstick.

Chapter 3
The Sunday Shift

I was working the afternoon shift on Sunday. After a lie-in, I rose and cooked a fried breakfast. There was a knock at the door. An angry-faced eight year old stomped in and sat in my chair. She folded her arms and pouted her lips.

"What's up, Charlie?" I asked. There was no answer, but I knew she wouldn't hold out for long. "Come on, you can tell me. Look, Morsel knows something's wrong."

She bent down and took Morsel up in her arms.

"Dad's come home," she said.

"Oh. Isn't that a good thing?"

"No, because Mum was going to take me to the skate park, and now she just wants to spend the day with him. It's not fair."

"Oh dear! I suppose she has to make a fuss of him. He's been away for a couple of weeks, hasn't he?"

"Yes. He's hardly ever here. And I don't care if he never comes home again!"

"You don't mean that. Anyway, are you hungry because my breakfast is ready and I've made way too much. We could share it?"

"Okay." She came over and peered into the frying pan. "I could have a fried egg…and some fried bread."

"Good, because I have to start watching my

weight."

"Why would you do that? You're not all that fat."

"Thank you, Charlie. It's nice of you to say so. But I would like to get a little trimmer, also a little fitter." I shared the contents of the frying pan between two plates.

We sat at the small, square table and ate. Morsel sat beside us, going through her repertoire of winning expressions until she managed to persuade each of us to part with a small piece of bacon. Downstairs I had two rooms: the front room, which was on the right as you came through the front door, and along the hallway, the kitchen. I hardly used the front room; I spent my time in the kitchen with the little dining area and the single armchair. There was a rather antiquated cooker, a sink, and a fridge, along with a few storage cupboards and shelves, the basics. The window looked out over the postage-stamp-sized garden behind the property that could be accessed via the back door.

"I have to work this afternoon, Charlie," I informed her.

"I'll go home then, but can I stay for a bit longer?"

"Yes, as long as your mum and dad won't be worried?"

"They won't be."

"Good. We can go to the copse again if you like?" I suggested.

A big smile spread across her face. It made me feel quite sorry for her. She was just a little girl, after all. She really only wanted someone to take a bit of notice of her.

"That would be super brilliant!" she said.

I was thirty-seven, and Charlie was eight, but I

enjoyed her company. Perhaps it was a maternal instinct emerging in me; I really didn't know.

We came to the trees and spent a good bit of time walking down the twisting paths and kicking up the leaves. We hid behind gnarled trunks and found each other again. Morsel joined in, skipping after one of us, then the other, trying to herd us back together. We walked to the far side and out to the fields beyond. We came to the footpath that ran along beside the river and carried on for a distance, spotting the ducks and swans. We threw a ball for Morsel. Sometimes she left us to run through the reeds and explore the bank beside the water.

"I wish I could come to work with you," said Charlie.

"I'm not sure you'd like it all that much," I told her. "The residents would like you, though."

"Would they?"

"Yes. They're very old, but they're incredibly friendly and love to chat. They want to know all about what's going on in the village. They like to hear about the villagers, and they have a soft spot for the youngsters."

"Am I a youngster?"

"Definitely!"

Charlie laughed.

"One day, if the right occasion arises," I said, "I'll take you to meet them."

We walked back to the village. I left Charlie at her gate in much better mood.

"Go in and be nice to your mum and dad," I instructed.

"I'll try," she said.

Reaching the cottage, I hurried upstairs and put on a black skirt and a purple jumper I'd forgotten about. I looked in the mirror, brushed my hair, and painted on a dab of makeup. I found a necklace and draped it around my neck. I looked okay, nothing special. At least I'd considered my appearance for once. It was a step in the right direction.

"What do you think, Morsel? How do I look?"

Morsel was holding a squeaky toy in her mouth. She eyed me.

"I don't think you care how I dress," I concluded. "I suppose I should be pleased about that."

\*\*\*\*

"Hello, all," I shouted as I entered Moonstones. I put my head round the kitchen door to see who was on, and it was John.

"Something smells good," I said.

"The Sunday roast. You've missed it. How are you?"

"I'm great, thanks."

"You look well. You have color in your cheeks. That day off's done you good."

"I'll say!"

"I'm knocking off now. I've left sandwiches and cakes for tea. If you and Candy want something later, there's chicken in the fridge, and there's good bread. There's soup too."

"Thank you, John. It all sounds lovely. Go and enjoy the rest of Sunday."

"I will, don't worry. I've got a new box set, sixteen episodes. I'll probably watch the lot!"

I made a giant pot of tea and prepared the trolley, putting milk and sugar, cups, saucers, and beakers onto it. I pushed it along the downstairs corridor to the lounge, a huge room with a large leaded bay window on the far side, draped by crimson velvet curtains that reached to the floor. Five residents were present, some with guests. I delivered two cups of tea to residents who had ground floor bedrooms and took the lift, with the trolley on board, up to the first floor. I served two more cups on that level. Mr. Pickering was missing. I supposed he must be out with his nephew. I'd check with Lianne. Candy arrived and was extremely pleased to find I'd already done a tea round.

"Everyone's happy," I said. "There are a few visitors in the lounge, and Lolly has a friend with her in her room. All in, I can report that things are nicely under control!"

"Did you get to the church sale?"

"Yes. I didn't see you."

"I didn't make it. Paul wanted to watch sport on TV. I ended up doing some cooking and then watching it with him. His team won, so he was in a good mood all evening."

We were in the kitchen. Candy was inspecting the various edible items John had left for us.

"I saw Miss Pickering at the sale," I said. "Mr. P must be out with her now, and the nephew presumably."

Miss Pickering still lived in their home in the village, a lovely old cottage called The Flower Pot. It had reached a point where she was unable to look after her brother as well as herself. He'd had a spell in hospital, and afterward, it had been decided he should come to Moonstones. She paid him a visit most days.

"Sometimes I wonder if Mr. Pickering needs to be

here at all," said Candy.

"He seems pretty good, doesn't he…but they say she had to do more and more for him before he came in."

"She's too old for that. Did you buy anything?"

"No. Only tea and cake. Oh, and a raffle ticket."

"Who else was there? Everyone?"

I leaned back against the worktop. "A good turnout, I'd say. That Amber from the café was there. She was full of herself as usual."

"There's something I don't like about her." Candy screwed up her nose.

"She was very dressed up," I said.

"She always is. She goes to the café in clothes you might wear to an opera!"

"She's new in the village, but she already seems to know everyone."

"I think she's only here for the treasure hunt. Mind you, the villagers always say that about new people."

"I suppose they said it about me when I first arrived," I said.

"But you come from here. You've returned to the village. That's different."

Several features made Steely Green attractive, but if you were to ask a stranger what they knew about it, if nothing more, they'd no doubt have heard of the village game. There was the annual event: music and dancing, eating and drinking, and the game—the famous local treasure hunt.

We spent time reminiscing, talking about the most recent hunt. It was always fun, even though this year's prize hadn't been one of the best.

"I wonder what it will be like next year. I'm not

sure what's left of the family will be able to organize much," Candy observed. "It's a shame. Some people think there won't be a hunt at all."

From what Candy said, I imagined she knew little about the Lesters and the current situation, but I thought everyone in the village was keeping their cards close to their chest. People had their own views, their own agendas, and they weren't divulging the contents of their minds. I had to keep quiet, lie low, and wait.

We were still chatting in the kitchen when Lianne came in.

"Afternoon, ladies!" she said. "Now, what's John left for tea? I have to have some of it!"

"There's quite a choice," said Candy.

"I've already had his marvelous roast, as well as the crumble dessert…with custard!"

"Sundays are that sort of day," Candy said understandingly.

"While I remember, Mr. Pickering is out with his nephew," said Lianne. "Nathan, he's called."

Sunday was a big day for visitors at Moonstones. We made many cups of tea every day, but on Sundays, we never seemed to stop. The atmosphere changed at the home, with younger voices filling the building and the news that they brought giving reason for more animated conversation. It was as if the home was being replenished.

Mr. Pickering was brought back by Nathan. I was introduced. Miss Pickering was with them. They'd been for a drive and stopped off for a somewhat unseasonal ice cream. They'd ended up driving near the manor so they could remind themselves of what it looked like, check for any new developments, and generally just for old times' sake. I had the impression this was a regular occurrence. They'd not gone onto the premises, but taken the wind-swept country lanes that weaved around the area and from which, at certain points, there were various views of the building.

"Is anyone there at the moment, do you think?" I asked. "Any of the Lesters?"

"It seems young Vicky's there most of the time," Miss Pickering said. "And Algie of course, poor Algie."

"Vicky's the one who's not very friendly, they say," I suggested.

"She hates to be called Vicky, you know. She insists on Victoria."

"She's a little so and so," stated Mr. Pickering.

Nathan laughed. "What do you mean by that, Uncle?" he asked.

"Well, she does nothing for herself," Miss Pickering asserted. "She gives the staff a difficult time, has no respect for them."

"Oh, a real bad lot," said Nathan cheerily.

"And supposedly she's worked up some debts," Miss Pickering added. "Keep that to yourselves, by the way."

"She's a little so and so," said Mr. Pickering.

"They're a real mixture, those children," Miss Pickering continued. "There were a number of wives, you see. The children of one wife don't tend to get on with the children of another. It was different when I was there. Mr. Lester's influence could always be felt, and most of the family couldn't have been nicer."

"I'm so intrigued by this family!" said Nathan. Nathan was probably in his late forties. He was well dressed, in casual but no way cheap-looking clothing.

He was taller than average in height and youthful looking. He was well built: rugby player sort of build rather than soccer player. He was affable and smiley faced.

"Now," I said, "Sunday tea? We have some lovely fruit cake and some lemon drizzle. I'll get some for you and a pot of tea. Where would you like it?"

"I think we'll go into the lounge, Lucy," Miss Pickering said.

"Good idea," I stood aside to let them pass. "Tea for three in the lounge coming up."

I'd be able to dash home at seven o'clock and let Morsel have ten minutes in the garden. Some of the residents would be in bed by then, and we could assist the few who retired later when I returned. Lianne and Joe were happy for me to take my short 'Morsel breaks,' as we called them. I was always prepared to be a little flexible with my hours, start a little early or leave a little late, and I was happy to cover the odd shift at short notice if they were stuck. Lianne said it should work both ways, I did a good job and they wanted to make it work for me.

Candy announced she needed a sit down, and we decided we could take a few minutes. We went back to the beautifully warm kitchen and sat in the corner, an area with benches either side of a sturdy pine table that the staff had made their own. Candy took off her shoes.

"Were you talking about the Lesters?" she asked.

"Yes, the Pickerings often talk about them."

"I wonder if they know what's going on with the will. I've heard Reg's will is being contested," said Candy.

I'd heard that too. "I wonder why, and by whom?"

I said. I was hoping Candy might have heard more, but she didn't expand on the statement.

"Did you ever meet any of them…" she said. "I mean, you know, when you were growing up here?"

"I sort of knew one of the sons for a while," I said.

"I never met any of them. I used to see them around the village now and then, in their fancy looking cars, and with their celebrity friends."

"The village wouldn't be the same without them, like them or loathe them," I said.

"No, and I would never have cared to live anywhere else. How drab and boring!"

A bell rang. It was Joan's.

"I'll go," I said.

Joan's room was on the ground floor. She was no longer able to get out of bed, and when she rang it was always for a reason. Some residents rang often, and on occasion they really just wanted to chat. I didn't mind that, but with Joan I always jumped up to attend to her because I knew she was likely to be in discomfort in some way and genuinely in need of assistance.

On leaving Joan's room I met Bert who was struggling along the corridor on his sticks, determined to get to the lounge for *Songs of Praise* on television. A group of the residents liked to watch it together.

"Are you all right, Bert?"

"Mustn't grumble. Don't help me. I want to do this on my own!"

"Did you have a visit today?" I knew he'd had someone in to see him or I wouldn't have asked.

"Yes, my daughter came, with a friend of hers."

"That was nice."

"She brought me some fruit and some sherry."

"Sherry? You'll be popular then!"

"It won't do any harm, will it?"

"I don't suppose so, as long as you don't drink it all at once!" We'd have to take the bottle and leave it in the kitchen for him. He'd probably be allowed a small glass in the evening. I'd check with Lianne.

Molly was also in the corridor, using her wheeled frame.

"Just popping to the shops," she told me.

She never went to the shops. That was just one of her regular statements. The front door would be locked so she couldn't go out, not that she was likely to try. The staff used a door code to enter and exit the building.

"Right, Molly." She was quite speedy with that frame, but had no idea where she was or where she might be headed. She opened Mrs. Cook's door on the way past. Mrs. Cook was sitting in her chair. I stepped into the room.

"Is everything all right, Mrs. Cook?"

"Yes, just watching television. Who's that outside?"

"It was Molly. She's gone off along the corridor now. What are you watching?"

"Oh, I don't remember. Something or other."

"The singing is coming on now, *Songs of Praise*. Shall I put it on for you?"

"Yes please, dear. Do I like that?"

"I think so. You can sing along. It's Sunday today, you know?"

"Is it Sunday?"

"Yes."

"Well I never."

Joan's bell had gone again and I rushed back. I could tell she wasn't comfortable. She was moaning, and I knew she must be in some pain. I rearranged her pillows and felt her brow, sat with her for a few minutes and stroked her hand until she seemed to fall asleep. She rarely spoke these days. I'd ask Lianne if we should get the doctor to look in on her in the morning.

\*\*\*\*

It would take me five minutes to rush home. I'd open the back door for Morsel and stay for ten minutes. I'd change her water and prepare her food, performing the tasks quickly so that, in general, I'd have about seven minutes to sit down in my own kitchen before returning to Moonstones. Believe it or not, it was a time I very much enjoyed. It set me up for the rest of my shift. Morsel went out and came back in. I sat peacefully in the armchair and she jumped onto my knee and curled up in my lap. I tickled and stroked her before gently putting her onto the floor and setting her bowl down beside her, assuring her I'd be home again in no time. She understood.

When I next arrived at the cottage, soon after ten, I'd be exhausted. I would let Morsel out for a last time and sit in my chair once again. Sometimes I would doze off, though I tried not to. The best thing to do was to get to bed and wake up early so I could make the most of the morning.

That night I needed to remember to write one important thing into my notebook. I'd told Candy I knew one of the Lester boys. She might not remember, but I had to be diligent.

\*\*\*\*

A week of afternoon shifts was coming up for me. I

usually worked alternate weeks of mornings and afternoons. The arrangement suited me, although it was probably confusing for Morsel. On the Sunday evening however, Lianne came to find me. She asked what I might think about doing some night shifts. Some people liked them because the pay was a little better and often there wasn't much to do except keep an ear out for anyone calling for assistance. Jackie told me she brought a book and sat in the kitchen reading for most of the night. There was a television in the office and Lianne and Joe were happy for the night duty staff to sit in there and watch it. It was away from the bedrooms and unlikely to keep any residents awake, those who weren't too deaf to be disturbed.

"I'm not sure," I said to Lianne. "I love my sleep."

"Well, have a think. I need another person to take on some night work, and if you did a few of the shifts, you could maybe take an extra day off?"

"It's worth considering," I said. "I enjoy doing mornings and afternoons, though."

"It's obvious that you love your work, Lucy, but I'm sure you also like your days off."

I suppose most people would go home and ask their husband, or boyfriend what they thought. I didn't have anyone to talk to about my choices. It was completely up to me. I sometimes wondered what it would be like to share my life. Naturally, I'd had parents once, but I was an only child and my mum and dad hadn't been the type to talk things through with me. I wasn't used to discussing my affairs with anyone.

Jackie was on that night. She was always early, I never had to wait for her. She arrived with a large shopping basket, and I could see she had books and magazines with her, and a thermos flask. There was a pair of slippers in the basket as well. I followed her to the staff room.

"Jackie, is someone leaving night work?" I asked.

"I have some holiday coming up, and I think Roger wants to cut down," she said. "Are you up for doing some shifts?"

"Lianne asked if I'd be interested."

"You should go for it. It's the best shift. You'd get used to it in no time."

"When do you sleep?"

"Straight away. As soon as I get home. I sleep until about two p.m. usually. On days off I catch up."

"And you do what, five nights a week?"

"Four or five."

"Do you think I could mix day shifts with night shifts?"

"I don't think I could…unless I had about a week off in between. I need a routine."

"I'm not sure it would suit me," I said.

"I'm away now if that's okay," Candy shouted.

"Goodnight," I shouted back. I found my coat and was soon on my way home too, to my lovely warm bed.

Chapter 4
Self-Improvement

It was a couple of days later when I next spotted Fergus. I was out walking Morsel in the late morning. I could tell he was headed for the common. I took a detour to make sure not to catch up with him. I didn't want to walk with him; a brief exchange would be far preferable. I took the cut through from Broad Street. There was a passageway between buildings that led to Bluebell Lane; from there I could get to the footpath and double back so I'd come to the common from the west side of the village.

It worked, and after a few minutes I saw Fergus approaching.

"Hello," I said. "How are you today?"

"I'm well. Very well, thanks."

"And Bones?" I stooped to rub the dog's neck. "Hello, Bones," I said. "How are you getting on?" I asked Fergus. "How is the village treating you?"

"Yes, fine. Fine, thank you." He was a difficult one to get talking.

"I only ever seem to see you on the common. But I suppose it's the same for you." I laughed, trying to get him to lighten up. "You only ever see me on the common!"

"Yes, I suppose so."

"I'm always at work otherwise. You too, I expect.

You've met a few of the other dog owners by now I imagine?" I carried on. "Everyone is very nice."

"Your name is Lucy isn't it?" he said.

"That's right."

"Well, good to see you."

I'd exhausted my small talk. I looked down at my watch. "Oh, is that the time? I'd better get on my way. Come along Morsel!"

We walked on to where the landscape turned into heathland and kept walking. Morsel was playful, running amongst the bushes and leaping over clumps of heather. We saw a number of birds and the odd rabbit, which she half-heartedly tried to chase. No one else seemed to be out, which was somewhat unusual. We stopped and sat on a grass bank. I felt hot with walking, but the air was chilly. There was some strength in the sun making it pleasant to sit for a few moments, the warm rays breaking through.

"He's an intriguing man, Fergus," I told Morsel. "It's hard to get him talking. I do wonder if he's the one. He might be. He might not be." Morsel was listening. "I'm sure, whoever it is, it won't be that obvious. I must make a good impression just in case…without him knowing I'm making an effort." The little dog was lying down with her belly on the cool ground, legs stretched behind her, pink tongue hanging out. "I did a bad thing, Morsel, but in return I'm supposed to get a reward, a big reward." Taking off a glove, I delved into my pocket to find a treat. I held one out for her to take. "The thing is, there are some rules. I'm not supposed to tell anyone for a start." She came for the biscuit, and I stroked her head. "That's easy enough…but I'm supposed to be nice, and good, and kind in order to get it…this reward…and someone is going to check up on me…that's what I was told." I pulled my glove back on. "I'm excited, but I feel bad about it at the same time." Morsel continued to concentrate hard on what I was saying. I stroked her again. "You are beautiful, Morsel," I told her. "I do hope you're not disappointed that you've ended up with me."

We turned back and walked until we came to the far side of the village. On the way home, I stopped at the newsagent's and selected some fashion magazines. I chose the most glamorous looking ones, not the ones aimed at housewives or stay-at-home mums. I could tell Mrs. Hughes was surprised I was buying them. She shuffled through them, entering the prices into the till, intermittently peering at me over the top of her glasses. I knew what she was thinking, but I said nothing. This is my new normal, I told myself. I buy fancy fashion magazines.

"How much is that, Mrs. Hughes?" I said matter-of-factly.

She told me the total, and I handed her the money. "Thank you, Mrs. Hughes." Back outside I rescued Morsel from the drainpipe I'd tied her to. There was a card in the window of the shop, advertising a garage sale at the weekend. It was to be at an address on Lark Lane. I made a mental note. It was to be from nine a.m. until two p.m. so it would be possible for me to go along. "Home we go, Morsel."

\*\*\*\*

That afternoon Lianne called me into the office. She wanted to have another chat about night shifts. She had a determined look on her face.

"Lucy, you'd be doing me a favor. I like to have the best staff on at night if I can. Nights are very important, and to be honest, if we have the right staff on duty, Joe and I don't get called so many times."

"I understand what you mean," I said. "But I don't think it's for me."

"Don't get me wrong, I don't mind being called when necessary. Really I don't, and neither does Joe. But we have had some staff, agency staff in particular, who are prone to calling us time and time again, night after night, for trivial reasons."

"That must make going to sleep very difficult," I said.

"I wish I could persuade you, Lucy. Do you think you might change your mind?"

"Are you really stuck?"

"Look, come round here, and I'll show you the rota."

I went to the other side of the desk. Lianne spoke to me like a colleague rather than an employee.

"This week is covered. Jackie and Roger are booked in until Friday. Joe says he'll do the weekend. He's happy about that. At the moment you're on afternoons every day including Saturday, and you're off Sunday. Perhaps you could cover nights on Monday, Tuesday, and Wednesday next week? Jackie has booked a week away but Roger can work the Thursday and Friday, and Joe might do the weekend again. If you did those three nights it would give you a feel for it. We could see how you get on. I'd make sure you had the Thursday and Friday off and put you back on mornings for the weekend." She paused. "What do you think?"

I wanted to please her, but I wasn't keen to do the

shifts.

"I forgot to say," Lianne continued, "Joe thought you could bring your little dog if you wanted to. We couldn't have a dog here during the day, I don't think, but if you brought her bed and put it under one of the desks in the office here, it wouldn't do any harm on the night shift." She paused again. "Well?" she said finally. She sat back in her chair, clasped her hands behind her head, and looked me in the eye.

"Maybe I should give it a go," I said.

"Is that a yes, Lucy?"

"So long as I wouldn't have to do any more nights if I didn't like it."

"Fantastic!"

"You won't sack me if I don't want to do any more, will you?"

"Don't be ridiculous! So starting next Monday, for three nights." Lianne busily entered my name into the system. "Yes! That's perfect. Another safe pair of hands to call on when required."

"I will bring Morsel," I said.

"We'll make Morsel very welcome." She looked up, and we had a good laugh.

\*\*\*\*

The garage sale was a good one. I browsed amongst the books, rummaged through the bric-a-brac, and crouched down to flip through the large stack of framed pictures.

"Hello, Lucy." I heard a voice.

"George, hello."

"I've tied mine up with Morsel out there. What have you found? Anything good?"

"There are a few things I wouldn't mind

buying…but I don't have room for them in the cottage." We were on the driveway. Fortunately it was a dry day, and the Partridges had been able to display some items outside on the concrete. "I haven't even been into the garage yet."

"Let's go in together," George suggested.

"Is Helen with you?"

"No, with Ange. They've gone for a spa day. They do that every so often. I have both dogs again!"

"So you do. Look at the three of them. They're being so good."

"There's a leaf blower here." George pointed it out. "I might buy that. You didn't want it did you?"

"No, no. My garden's hardly big enough for one of those!"

We walked slowly round the garage, checking out the interesting things that were all the more fascinating because someone else had chosen to buy them and previously made use of them.

"That's exactly what I need," I said, nodding my head in its direction.

"The mirror?" George asked. He seemed surprised.

"Yes, I don't have a long mirror." The mirror was full length, free standing with a pinewood frame. It could be tilted to achieve any angle required. "I think it would just about fit into my bedroom."

"Treat yourself then. It's sure to be cheaper than buying one on Broad Street."

"I'm not sure I'd be able to get it home."

"I could help you carry it."

"Would you?"

"Yes, why ever not?"

Twenty minutes later, George and I could be seen

walking awkwardly through the village, one of us at either end of a five-foot looking glass. George was at the front. We'd turned it longways and sideways, and he had the top end clutched under his right arm. Under his left arm was a boxed leaf blower and in his left hand a carrier bag containing two twelve-inch folk song collections. I took up the position at the back with the bottom end of the mirror under my right arm, part of the stand banging against my leg as I walked. In my left hand, I had three dog leads, with three dogs on the ends of them.

"Hold on. George, Wotnot has stopped. Come on, Wotnot."

"Come on, Wotnot!" George joined in with a masterly command.

We stumbled on.

"My arm is really hurting," I said.

"Not far now. Can you keep going?"

"Yes. No! I need to stop for a minute."

We stopped and stood the mirror up on its stand. Moose posed in front of it, and then started to bark loudly having realized he'd discovered Moose mark two. Still not happy, he howled in a high-pitched tone, and then began a series of deep growls.

"It's just you, Moose, your reflection," George explained. "I know it's hard for you to understand."

Morsel sat looking perplexed by all the fuss, and Wotnot tried to find something to eat within the short range allowed by his lead.

"I'm ready to carry on, I think," I said. We lowered the mirror onto its side again. "Whatever happens, don't let me drop it."

We made it to my gate and set everything down on

the pavement. I took the dogs inside and through to the back garden. George brought in the mirror and stood it at the bottom of the stairs.

"Is it going up?" he called.

"Yes, let me help." We managed to get it to my bedroom in one piece. "Thank you, George. You are very kind."

"It's my pleasure," he said.

George was in no hurry, he told me. I wasn't used to having people in my house. Apart from Charlie, it was rare for anyone to call. I didn't go to other people's houses either. I wondered if the place looked okay, but George seemed to feel at home. I made tea and we chatted. Then we decided to go to the copse, because although we'd both intended to walk our dogs, that wasn't what we'd actually done.

The minute the trees came into view, Moose and Wotnot strained to be let loose. I was so pleased I had Morsel and not a big, difficult dog. She looked up at me as if to say, *If you don't mind, it would be nice to be taken off my lead.* I set her free.

"Go and run with the others," I told her.

George and I sat on the bench. Jenny came over with Wesley, who was completely covered in mud.

"He found a puddle," she explained.

"Moose will be in it by now then," said George.

"Yes, Banjo's been in too."

"Right," said George. "I'd better go and see." He went purposefully in the direction of the excited barking sounds.

Jenny sat down. "Haven't seen you in ages," she said.

"Work takes over doesn't it?"

"Indeed."

"It's hard to imagine what it's like for you and Malcolm. You both teach don't you?" I said.

"That's right, for our sins. I'm art, as you know. He's science."

"So even when you're at home there's preparation, and marking?"

"Yes, we teachers are famous for our marking!"

"You've got everything covered, though, with art and science? You must be a wonder couple when it comes to the treasure hunt."

"What were your best subjects?" she asked me.

"At school?"

"Yes, school, university?"

"I was no good at anything, and I didn't go to university," I said.

"Well, everyone is good at something...and what I always say is it's our job, us teachers, to prepare everyone for life. The best thing we can do for our pupils is to help them to go on and be able to enjoy whatever it is they end up doing."

"I love my job, Jenny," I said.

"There you go then. Your teachers made a good fist of you."

George arrived back. "Look at me...paw prints on my coat. I've only just had it dry cleaned!" he said.

"How is Daniel?" Jenny asked.

"Football," said George. "Nothing but football. Do you know, I think I'll have to get going. I might have to give Moose a bath. I'm supposed to have him all day. Moose! Moose! Wotnot! Come! Come, Wotnot! Here, Moose!"

The dogs emerged from the trees, Moose in similar

condition to Wesley. Wotnot took a diversion.

"Oh, no!" said George. "He's found a sandwich. Get here, Wotnot!"

Morsel came running deftly behind, clean and food free. She sat down quietly at my feet.

"Thanks again for your help today, George," I said.

"Anytime, Lucy, anytime. See you both soon."

"George often has Moose, doesn't he?" said Jenny. "I'm not sure I'd want to look after him. He's such a handful."

"Helen and Ange are on a spa day," I told her. "They go on one every so often."

"Funny, I just saw Ange in the village. Perhaps they're setting off later."

"Perhaps. What a nice thought. I'll be at Moonstones this afternoon."

"I was going to ask if you'd used that new window cleaner?" said Jenny. "Martin is he called?…at home or at Moonstones?"

"No, I haven't."

"They tell me he also sweeps chimneys, and I need to get ours done. I should have had it swept in the summer. I always say that, but we never get round to it."

"I noticed his number's in the window at the newsagent's," I said.

"Oh, that's good. I have to go that way. I'll have a look for it on my way back."

\*\*\*\*

At home I spent a few minutes admiring my new mirror. It fitted nicely into the corner of the room. I dusted it and polished the glass. I put my stack of magazines on the chest of drawers, looking forward to spending a few hours lying on the bed reading through them. I wouldn't be able to afford a whole new wardrobe, but I'd get some ideas and begin to see what I should be aiming for. I'd given myself a strict ultimatum: I must no longer completely neglect my appearance. My life was going to change. I had to look the part.

I'd made some progress recently, in terms of my resolutions. As well as thinking about the way I looked, it was my plan to meet people and generally make a good impression. Imagine, today I'd had an adult visitor sitting in my house for at least half an hour, drinking tea! Not only that, I seemed to have made a friend who was prepared to help me, and as far as I could tell, with no ulterior motive.

Chapter 5
Executing the Plan

Monday came. I was to work my first night shift. The daylight hours had to be spent well; I walked on the common and alongside the river, enjoyed an afternoon nap, ate a nice evening meal. Digging out my large canvas shopping bag, I put the items I thought I might need inside it and pushed a large cushion into a separate carrier bag. I called Morsel, had a quick look in the mirror, and set off for Moonstones.

I rarely went out after dark as a rule, and that evening the village was like a new place to me. I took my usual route. On passing the inn, I noticed there were a few inside and wondered who in the village frequented the place. I climbed the hill, stepped quickly along the drive to the entrance of the home, tied Morsel to the hand rail beside the door, and went in. Candy and Mariana had been on duty and greeted me warmly. They could leave now I'd arrived. Lianne was in the office, waiting for me.

"Hello, Lianne. I'm here."

"Welcome to the night shift!"

"I thought I'd let Morsel in the back door, rather than walk her through the corridors."

"It's not locked. I'll get us some tea while you bring her round."

I fetched Morsel and put the cushion in a cozy

looking spot between the two filing cabinets.

"There, girl. That's your bed for tonight. What do you think?"

Lianne arrived with two mugs of tea and a dish of water.

"Look at her! She's so adorable. Hello, Morsel. Hello, Morsel." Morsel duly went to Lianne and sat down in front of her, lapping up the attention. Lianne tickled and patted her. "Well, usually," she began, "I only wait for the night shift worker if there's something in particular to pass on. There isn't anything tonight, really. Joan's not had a good day, so you may need to go to her. But that's nothing new, as you know.'

"I'm sure I'll be fine. I'll just stay in here, shall I, and respond if anyone calls? Do I need to do a walk round every so often?"

"You simply need to be vigilant. Some staff walk round. I'll leave it to you. If anything happens that you can't deal with, just call our number, and Joe or I will come."

"I'll do my best not to call."

"Don't worry about ringing if you feel you should. It's what we're here for after all."

Lianne soon went off to bed, and Morsel and I were left to get through the dark hours with the assistance of my canvas bag of entertainment.

It was a long night. Several times I went to the kitchen and made a mug of strong coffee. I was determined not to start snacking, though. I would reward myself with breakfast once the shift was over.

I read my magazines, and every so often, I walked along the corridors, listening for anything out of the ordinary. One or two of the residents were snoring loudly; most seemed to be sleeping peacefully. On my four a.m. walk round, I heard soft moaning sounds coming from Joan's room. I tapped the door and tiptoed in. The bedside lamp had been left on, and I could see Joan's face quite clearly. I sat with her for a few minutes, but although she gasped a few times, turned her head, and appeared to open her eyes on one occasion, I could tell she hadn't woken.

"Sleep well, Joan, sleep well. There's nothing for you to worry about," I whispered in a soothing voice in the hope it might help.

I returned to the office. Morsel was lying on the cushion, watching me. I opened the back door for her.

"Do you need to go out, Morsel? I know, it's a funny old night we're having tonight, isn't it? Poor Morsel." She didn't want to go out. She carried on lying on her cushion but kept a wary eye on me.

At seven a.m., I heard the front door and went to see who had entered. It was John.

"John, I'm so pleased to see you!"

"I can't relieve you, you know."

"I know. I'm just pleased to have someone to talk to!"

"Stay with me here in the kitchen while I start breakfast."

At that moment, Bert's bell went, and from then on, I was busy with the residents until Barbara and Camille arrived to start the morning shift. Lianne came to see how I'd done and congratulated me for having broken my night shift duck. She said I should have breakfast with her, but I made my excuses.

"I'll see you tonight, if that's all right," I said. "I'm tired now. I need to adjust to these hours."

"Of course. Off you go…and thank you, Lucy"

"I'll leave the cushion." I collected my possessions and swiftly clipped Morsel's lead onto her collar.

"See you tonight. Bye-bye, Morsel. She is adorable."

\*\*\*\*

After a long sleep, I woke hungry and went to browse through the food items in the kitchen. Having a feeling night shifts would test my resolve, I'd written a note and attached it to the fridge door. *Chubby! Stocky! Podgy!* That meant I cooked a modest breakfast: no fried bread, only one sausage, black coffee. Later in the day, after a good walk, I stood in front of my new mirror, tidied my hair and put on some foundation, then a dab of eye makeup and lipstick. I squeezed into the smart new trousers I'd bought on the internet. I didn't look so bad, I thought, not that I'd wear those pants in public just yet. I'd keep trying them on until I could wear them without having to endure pain.

The coming days were to prove eventful. It turned out there was nightlife of a sort in Steely. One evening, as I was passing the inn, I felt sure I saw Fergus sitting in a car nearby. I strained my eyes, trying to get a better view. I wasn't sure at first, but then I glimpsed the white bull dog in the back of the vehicle. What was he doing? Was he waiting for someone?

Another thing I observed, and that surprised me more, was Helen emerging from the establishment. She looked slightly drunk, tottering on high heels, being steadied by a tall man. I was too far away to see him in detail, but it wasn't George, that was for certain. Working nights was turning out to be rather interesting.

Time flew by. I agreed to cover Mondays,

Tuesdays, and Wednesdays for the coming weeks. At weekends, I would continue to work daytime shifts. My pay would increase, and Morsel wouldn't be left on her own so often. I started bringing my notebook to work, and once everyone was asleep, I spent an hour or so studying it and interpreting things. My mind seemed to work well in the early hours. My village notes were at the front of the book, and I started adding personal notes at the back: the date I'd purchased the mirror; how far I'd walked each day; what I'd eaten. Each night I brought a magazine with me and looked through it, meticulously scrutinizing the articles and advertisements. I needed to catch up in terms of my aspirations, not having been the sort to read magazines before now or knowing about the trends and subject matters a woman was supposed to immerse herself in. I had to get up to date.

\*\*\*\*

Charlie called by on Saturday morning. She wore what looked like body armor and a crash helmet.

"Would you like to come to the skate park?" she asked.

"Hmm, I'm not sure about that."

"Please?" She had large eyes, and they were looking up at me soulfully.

"Well, all right. Just for half an hour."

"Yes! Yes!" She punched the air.

I'd never been to the skate park. It had been built on some wasteland on the edge of the village, mainly to prevent the kids from causing havoc on the pavements, around the car park, and in the various other public places where they'd previously been trying to hone their skills. We brought Morsel with us. She seemed to take it in her stride, despite the constant sound of small wheels on concrete and steel and the deafening crashing sounds of daredevil landings being achieved.

Charlie seemed to be readily accepted by the mostly older male participants.

"Do you want a go?" she asked, after demonstrating her quite considerable talents to me.

"Yes, actually," I said, passing her Morsel's lead. I kept to the level area and pushed off. I scooted a couple of times, wobbled, and toppled off. I made another attempt, rolling along for a number of feet, even taking in a small slope. Charlie was jumping up and down, giving instruction and encouragement.

"Go on, Lucy! You're doing okay! That's right! Go down the ramp now!" she shouted.

"Oh no," I said. "That's quite enough for my first attempt." I picked up the board and turned to acknowledge clapping from five laughing teenage boys, one of whom I recognized as Daniel.

"Not playing football today, Daniel?" I asked him.

"Yes. On my way now," he said. "We have a match. We're at home. Come and watch?"

"I can't, Daniel. I'm working this afternoon…another time."

"Ok, I'll get Dad to remind you. See you," he said. He picked up his sports bag, hopped onto his board, and whizzed off across the park.

"How about a meringue at the café?" I said to Charlie.

"Really? Yes, please!"

"We'll take Morsel home first."

\*\*\*\*

"You're wearing makeup," said Amber. "It suits

you."

We'd arrived at the café and selected a table in the window. I decided that not responding was the best approach. She didn't mean it suited me. She meant I hadn't put it on correctly, and that I didn't look as good as she did. I didn't want to interact with her, just keep track of her.

"Two meringues, please, a pot of tea for one, and a glass of orange juice." I talked to Charlie about her home life. "Is Dad away?"

"Yes," she said.

"What's your mum up to today?"

"She's blogging."

"Oh, she has a blog, does she?"

"Yes, she blogs all the time."

"What about?"

"Herself."

"Perhaps she'll have time to take you out later?"

"I'd like to watch Daniel play football."

"I don't suppose she'd enjoy that. What about joining in with something she wants to do?"

"Here you are, ladies," said Amber, gracefully depositing the items we'd ordered onto our table. "Beautiful meringues, full of cream. Don't even think about your figures. These are far too enticing to forgo!"

She was always rude. She was suggesting we were both overweight. Well, I was going to show her.

"Mmmm," said Charlie.

Jenny came in. "Hello, Lucy. Hi there, Charlie."

"Come and sit with us," I said.

"I've only popped in for takeaway. We like the Chelsea buns. I often buy them. I know I shouldn't! The meringues look good, though."

"You could have a cup of tea with us?" I said.

"Yes, I will. A quick one." Jenny speedily made her order at the counter and came to join us.

"Did you find Martin?" I asked.

"I did, and he came to sweep the chimney on Wednesday. I left the back door open for him and rushed home at lunchtime to make sure all was well."

"Did he do a good job?"

"A very good job…and cleaned up nicely." I wanted to ask more about Martin, but I didn't want to alert Jenny to my interest in him. "Here comes my tea. Thank you, Amber."

"He lives over toward Melstow, I think," I said, to see if that might prompt her to give away any further information she might have come by. Charlie finished her meringue and sighed with satisfaction.

"Was that good, Charlie?" Jenny checked. "Yes, with his wife, and they have one small child. Her parents live in the area, I understand. That's why they came here, babysitters."

"Oh?"

"You know—young parents—they like to be near to grandparents to benefit from free babysitting services."

"Oh, I see."

"Your gran lives in Melstow, doesn't she, Charlie?" Jenny asked.

"Yes, but I don't see her much."

"She works at the hospital, doesn't she?" Jenny said.

"Yes, she has a very important job."

"That probably keeps her busy then. How's your mum? Is she well?" Jenny carried on.

"She's okay."

"Good. I'm pleased to hear it."

With that, Jenny gulped down her tea, excused herself, and headed back to the counter to pay. She was soon calling goodbye to us and hurrying out of the door with her bagful of buns. She was a human whirlwind. I felt jealous of that kind of person, with a lifestyle where you were always too busy to pause. There was an endless list of things that had to be done, and that had to be done straight away. There was no hesitation: you never thought about it; you just got on with it.

"I didn't know your gran worked at the hospital, Charlie," I said.

"She's a sort of nurse."

"She does sound important. Do you think you might follow in her footsteps one day?" Charlie folded her arms and focused on me but didn't reply. I felt sure I sometimes said the wrong things to her. She was probably too young to be thinking about her future in that sort of way. "Come on, we'd better get you home."

\*\*\*\*

Later, when I updated my notebook, I was able to conclude that Amber was still one of the most suspicious of the newcomers in the village. I made Fergus about equal to her, but Martin was less dubious. He seemed an ordinary bloke as far as I could tell, and what Jenny said added strength to that viewpoint. Even so, I wouldn't rule him out altogether just yet. I pondered over my entries for some time. It was tricky, but I needed to step up my efforts. More information was required. I decided to target Miss Pickering as a source; she seemed to know everything about the village…and I'd keep looking out for Fergus.

Chapter 6
Gossip

Sunday was always a good day for gathering information at Moonstones. I was starting at two thirty, just the right time for conversation. I arrived promptly, and John swiftly departed. Candy was on with me, which pleased me as I'd not seen her all week. She was on time for a change, and we were catching up in the kitchen. I told her my night work was going quite well but that I missed the busy daytime shifts. At least I was still doing a couple each week. Candy wondered if I was feeling tired, but I could tell her, honestly, that I'd easily adapted to the hours. Lianne did try to make sure everyone had a manageable workload. Candy, I thought, looked more tired than I. It transpired that she and Paul were going through a rough spell, and she was finding things difficult. He'd been sleeping in the lounge for the past two nights; she'd been lying awake wishing he'd come to bed, weighing up whether or not to go and climb onto the sofa with him. It might break the ice, she thought, but on the other hand, he might leave her there and go back and sleep in the bed.

"That's normal when you're married, isn't it, sleeping on the sofa for a bit and then making up again?"

"I don't know if it's normal. I know it's stressful. I find it very stressful."

"So is there any particular cause? There must be something you need to sort out if Paul's going to bed on the sofa?"

"He's not speaking to me. He's trying to avoid me. The last couple of nights, he's gone to work early and come home late."

"But what started it?"

"Work started it. I told him I didn't want him to work all the time, and that he needed to plan his hours around my shifts, at least some of the time."

"That sounds reasonable." Paul was a bar manager in Melstow. His hours were worse than Candy's, long and antisocial.

"Not if you're Paul."

"He'll come round, won't he?"

"I expect so. But you're right. We need to sort out the problem. He needs to listen. You're so lucky you live on your own."

I sighed. "I don't think many people would choose to live alone."

"Did you live with someone before? I mean, did you split up with someone? Is that why you came back here?"

"No."

"There must have been someone?"

"No."

"There must have been once?"

"Well, there was someone once, once or twice, but there was never anything all that serious. Fundamentally I'm a single person, and I can't imagine that will ever change."

"But you're happy with that, I can tell."

"I suppose I am."

"I wish I could be more like you, Lucy."

"Come on, let's forget about Paul and our problems for a few hours and go on a tea round."

"You're right, and we can see if there's any good Sunday gossip!"

Mr. Pickering and his sister were in the lounge, heads together, chatting away as if they'd not seen each other for months. I went to greet them.

"How are you both today?"

"Lucy, have you been on holiday?" Mr. Pickering asked.

"I've been doing nights, Mr. Pickering. I've been here, but while you were asleep."

"That's a nice thought. It's nice to know you're looking after Bob even while he's sleeping," Miss Pickering said. Her eyes were bright and mischievous. "I wonder if Lucy's heard you snoring, Bob?"

"Snoring? I don't snore, Pru, do I?"

"You have been known to," Miss Pickering teased. They dissolved into fits of giggles. They loved to tease each other, and I could tell this had for a long time been an important element in their friendship. I marveled at the understanding they shared. Being an only child, this was another type of relationship I would only ever observe as an outsider.

Miss Pickering beckoned me to come closer. I crouched and leaned toward her.

"I heard something else about Vicky Lester."

"Oh really?"

"She wants the house for herself."

"The manor?"

"Shhh…yes, so they're saying. There's this dispute over the will, you know, and it seems she's trying to get her hands on the manor house."

"Is this Vicky?" said Mr. Pickering.

"Shhhh, Bob. Yes."

"Surely there must be quite a few who'll get a share?" I said, though it wasn't what I actually thought or had pinned my hopes on.

"You'd think so, but who knows? It must be a large estate. There's other property, of course, and you could only guess at what else old Reg had to pass on. He was a very rich man."

"There are any amount of children, aren't there, and wives?" I said.

"Well, five children that we know of. I suppose it might only be the most recent wife who'd inherit. He was never married to her, in fact, Vicky's mother."

"Vicky's mother? Weren't they married?" said Mr. Pickering, looking quite shocked.

"No. You know that, Bob."

"So there was the first wife, the second wife, the third wife, and then Vicky's mother?" I questioned.

"That's right, and I'd be surprised if there weren't a few others along the way!"

I was aching to find out as much as possible, but I didn't want to appear over inquisitive. On top of that, I'd never understood the rules of gossip. Should I press for more information? I told the Pickerings I'd better make sure the other residents were all right and see if Candy needed a hand. I'd come back.

Reg Lester had enjoyed a good reputation in the village. Although outsiders often thought the Steely treasure hunt had been going on for centuries, it was actually Reg who'd started the tradition. It was true he'd been extremely well off. He was a highly successful businessman. No one had ever been sure what his business entailed, but he had a stream of high-profile clients. His offices were in the capital; he had no prior connection with Steely Green. He'd purchased the manor as a holiday home forty or more years beforehand. The locals didn't approve at first: he was too glossy and flamboyant, they thought, but Reg worked at that and gradually won them over. He spent a good bit of money bringing the building and gardens up to date, and where possible, he employed locals to carry out the improvements. He supported the area's proprietors and was enthusiastic about the annual event. Previously the event had been a sort of early summer fair, a modest occasion, but well attended. Local musicians might provide entertainment, and the local women would bake cakes and make tea. Others would set up stalls, and races were organized for the children. But Reg introduced the treasure hunt. It was an immediate success. Each year there would be a number of clues which the Lester family compiled, and Reg provided the prize, which was, in general, hugely generous. Each household in the village was eligible to take part. One clue was always connected to the manor, and that meant for a couple of weeks each year, the villagers were allowed to roam in the grounds in order to work out the answer. The winning family would be awarded the prize at the end of the fair.

Candy came to find me. Joan seemed disturbed. We went to her room together and concluded we should call Lianne or Joe. Joe arrived quickly and let us know Joan had endured another bad night. He tried to settle her. He'd already been planning to get the doctor in to see her the following day, it being Monday, he informed us, but her current condition convinced him he should try to raise him straight away. Lianne and Joe tried not to bother the doctor on Sundays, but we all felt concerned.

When a resident was distressed in such a way, it was hard to chat and joke with the others, even though the last thing we wanted was to let it affect them. Joe asked me to stay with Joan until he'd made the phone call and asked Candy to concentrate on keeping the other residents happy. He'd then come back and sit with Joan, and allow both Candy and I to set about creating the usual Sunday warmth, the general feel-good atmosphere of Moonstones.

"Poor Joan," said Candy. "My problems seem trivial when you see how ill she looks."

"You have such a kind heart, Candy," I told her. "You were made for this job. I hope when I'm a Moonstones' resident, there's someone like you to take care of me."

Candy went to prepare the large pot of tea, and once Joe had returned, I headed for the lounge to see if any more visitors had arrived. Most of the residents were present by that point. Bert, Lionel, Marcia, and Ethel were sitting together. Molly had positioned herself in a corner and was humming to herself. Mr. Pickering was still sitting with his sister. Mrs. Cook would be in her room, as would Lolly, and Mrs. Roberts had been taken out for a drive. I was hoping Lolly had a visitor. I would go to her room first with tea.

As I emerged from the kitchen, I saw the doctor arrive. Candy went to let him in. I left the trolley and moved quickly to close the door to the lounge hoping the others wouldn't be aware of his visit. Candy led him along the corridor to Joan's room. I'd deal with those in their rooms as quickly as I could and with luck get back to the lounge to distract those gathered there with drinks and conversation before they noticed the doctor's car in the driveway.

****

Morsel was getting used to our new routine, though I thought she'd been staying closer to me in recent weeks. If I went out without her, she would follow me around the cottage when I returned; that followed the initial greeting, which involved a lot of tail wagging and face licking. I tried to reassure her.

"You're such a special girl, Morsel. Don't worry, I will always look after you. We'll always be together."

I was convinced she understood most things. I chatted away to her all the time, and she listened intently. No person had ever taken as much notice of what I said. Morsel received plenty of exercise, but I realized I had often been sitting on a bench while she did the running about, or strolling while she energetically went exploring. I had to improve on that. I needed to walk farther and more briskly.

Several people had commented on my appearance. John said he thought I'd lost some weight while trying to ply me with custardy puddings. Lianne said people sometimes put on weight when they took on night work, but I seemed to have lost some, and George told me how well I was looking on a number occasions. He also said I was smiling more often. I took all the comments as compliments, not having previously been the sort of person who received positive feedback. It would be wise, I thought, to give out some encouraging statements in return because complementing might be a reciprocal type of thing.

It was a few days since I'd seen George, but he arrived at the cottage one evening when I wasn't on duty.

"You haven't seen Helen, have you?" he said.

"No, George. Come in, please come in."

"I don't know where she's got to. She left home a couple of hours ago to get a bit of shopping, and she hasn't come back."

It was unlikely that I would have seen her, but I was pleased to have a visit from George. It was funny; when I first met him, I'd never have guessed he'd be remotely interested in my company.

"Was she just heading into the village?" I asked.

"Yes, but there's only the one shop that's open at this time, isn't there, and she's not in there."

"She must have bumped into someone. Was she on foot?"

"Yes, on foot. I'm sorry, I shouldn't have disturbed you."

"Do you want me to come and help find her?"

"I don't know where to look."

"Is Daniel home? She's not gone off somewhere with him? Did you drop in at Ange's? She might be with her?"

"I phoned and left a message for Ange. Daniel's staying at a friend's tonight."

"Well, have a cup of tea with me, and then we can go to yours and see if she's back. If she's not, we'll have a ring round."

"That's a good idea. Thank you, Lucy."

"You're not worried about her, are you?"

"Not worried exactly, but she was only supposed to be popping out. We've not had dinner yet."

"Are you hungry?"

"No, no."

I made tea, and we sat in my kitchen, me on a hard chair and George in the armchair. Morsel walked around restlessly, sensing something was wrong. I'd like to have chatted to George in our usual way, had a bit of fun with him, but all he could think about was Helen. We drank the tea and set off to look for her. He lived a ten-minute walk away, which took in passing by the grocery shop. It was now closed. We went to George's house, a large homely property full of comfortable furniture. It disgorged the delicious smell of family life. The property was full of things a family buys: things bought by adults and things bought by a younger person, things which were amusing, or practical, or part of a new fad. No one was home.

"I'll try to phone Ange again," said George.

"What about the neighbors?" I asked.

"I don't think she'd be visiting any of them, not for this amount of time. She was coming straight back!" George was becoming less composed.

"I'll have another look outside," I said.

Of course, I remembered seeing Helen coming from the inn with a tall man a few days back. I had no idea who the man was. I was trying not to make a connection, and I certainly didn't want to tell George what I'd seen, but I wondered if I should dash over to the inn now and see if she happened to be there. I weighed my options. It would take nearly half an hour to get over to the inn and back. If I went off for that long, I might upset George even more. In the end, I didn't have to do a thing, as at that moment, Helen appeared, hurrying along, clasping a large shopping bag, a baguette sticking out of the top of it. There was no mistaking Helen: she kept her hair long and blonde; she was a bit on the plump side, but she owned it; she exuded confidence. Before she caught sight of me, I dashed in and shouted to George.

"Helen's coming up the road, George."

"She is?"

"Yes, I'll leave you to it."

I made a quick exit, not wanting to be involved in whatever might follow.

Back at the cottage, I put my feet up and told myself that Candy might be right. Maybe I was fortunate to be a single person.

Chapter 7
Dad

Reg Lester had been clever when he acquired the manor. He made certain moves to ensure the support of the villagers. The population of Steely Green soon fell for him. I didn't have anything against Reg, not at all, but I knew something about the family that meant, for a long time, I'd been less enamored than most. It was true, Reg himself had helped my father in a significant way, and I respected that. Dad made his living from painting and decorating. He was hard working and took on jobs when and where he could, but there were always spells when his income dried up, and our home life became difficult. My mother's only income came from taking in laundry, and there wasn't much to be made from that. There were times, even when I was very young, when I was aware of how desperately we needed Dad to find a job. Rent payments were missed, meals became plain and repetitive. When employment came through, the sense of relief was immense; it was as if our cottage itself had breathed a sigh of relief.

One winter, work dried up altogether. The weather was bad so that nothing could be started outside, and there were no interior jobs on the horizon. Dad went round the village, to the inn and various other businesses, offering a good rate, but no one took him on. Reg Lester must have heard about it. Dad wouldn't have thought of asking him, but Reg appeared one day, out of the blue, in his *Bentley*. He stopped right outside our door. I watched him pull up and get out. He walked up the path and tapped the knocker. He wasn't pompous; he was friendly and cheery. He'd heard that Dad was a decorator, he said. He had plenty of rooms that needed attention at the manor. Would Dad come and price up the work?

Dad was a proud man in some ways, but he'd come to the end of his tether. He didn't pretend to be busy; he didn't allude to being in a position to bargain. He offered to go with Reg straight away and take a look at what needed to be done. Dad told Reg he'd agree to a reasonable price and that he would be in a position to start immediately. He hopped into the *Bentley* beside his would-be employer, and they headed off up the hill, leaving Mum and me gazing after them. Once the car was out of sight, Mum was so overwhelmed she did a little jig. It was very out of character for her to do a thing like that.

\*\*\*\*

I would not enjoy my next shift. Joan had been taken to hospital; her room was empty. I was doing a night and kept walking to her door even though she wasn't there. On one occasion, I went in and spoke to her. I sat by the bed, beside the mattress that was no longer covered with sheets or blankets, and had a talk with her. I'm not sure if I'm religious, but I said a prayer for her as well.

In general, I had the night shifts sorted, splitting up the hours so the time didn't drag. The first hour would fly by. I'd say goodnight to the evening staff and receive any takeover notes, settle Morsel, and tidy up in the office. During the night, I would spend an hour with my magazines and an hour with my notebook. I frequently walked along the corridors, listening outside each resident's room, and made a drink for myself every two hours. By now, I had introduced an exercise regime, which I usually carried out around halfway through the shift. It woke me up if nothing more. After rolling out my foam mat on the office floor, I'd begin a series of press-ups, sit-ups, lunges, and stretches. I planned to add to this by perhaps bringing a skipping rope or some light weights along with me. By the time John or Larry arrived, I felt as though I'd had a workout, been educated, and broadly got on top of my situation in life. John commented that I was like no one else on finishing the night shift. He told me the others would be yawning, grumbling, and feeling cold, whereas I was full of life, informative, and wholly pleasant. Morsel and I had taken up having a walk before returning to the house to sleep. On waking in the early afternoon, we'd eat a delicious and thoroughly deserved breakfast.

\*\*\*\*

It wasn't long before I saw George again. He was out with Wotnot. I called over to him.

"George! Hello!" He was on the other side of the road. He held Wotnot back on his lead and waited for a few passing cars before crossing to speak to me. George, I thought, was quite an elegant man. In his late forties or early fifties, I'd guess, he was of above-average height and slender. He had a slightly rumpled look about him, but I was aware this was an important constituent of his character. His clothes usually seemed a little too large for him but were at the same time stylish and appropriate for his age. I could easily see what had attracted Helen to him. I imagined how the look had worked when they first met, twenty years or so back. Truthfully, what I thought was, I wouldn't want to swap him.

"How is Helen?"

Helen was the villager in the relationship. She and I remembered each other from years back, when I originally lived in Steely.

"Yes, she's fine. That other evening, she was round at Sue's. As we suspected, she bumped into Ange at the grocer's. They went to Sue's for a chat and lost track of time. I was daft to be worried. I'm sorry to have dragged you out for no reason."

"It wasn't a problem. You know that, George. It's always nice to see you, whatever the circumstance. If ever I can be of assistance, I'm only too pleased."

"You are such a good friend, Lucy. We must invite you over for dinner. I'll check with Helen about dates and call you. Which evenings are good for you?"

"How lovely! Well, any evening, really. I'm doing day shifts at the weekends, so I could come afterward. Early in the week, I'm on night shifts, but I could always come before work. On Thursday and Friday, the evenings are all my own."

"That gives us plenty of scope. I'll call you later." With that, George leaned over and gave me a kiss on the cheek.

"I'll look forward to that, thank you," I said. "Thank you very much."

He hurried away, his right arm stretched out in front of him, holding onto the taught lead as Wotnot pulled him along the pavement. He turned back, smiling, and waved goodbye over his shoulder with his free hand.

I walked on. For quite some time, I continued to grin widely. I was aware that if anyone set eyes on me, they would likely label me as completely mad. Luckily there was no one passing. In my old downtrodden world, I would never have had a friend like George. My dinner invitation would be recorded as part of my personal progress.

Chapter 8
Evening Wear

Looking back through my notes during my next notebook hour at Moonstones, I realized I hadn't come across Fergus for some time. I'd recorded seeing him outside the inn a few weeks back, but there'd been no sight of him since. I considered again what he'd been doing that night, and I wondered where he was living. Could it be that he wasn't living in the village at all? Several more days passed before I ran into him. He was on the common with Bones. He was striding along. He stopped, checked his phone, then began striding on again. I followed along after him, hoping to catch up with him. Morsel scampered playfully beside me. Fergus was headed to the path that wound through to the copse. I took my time, walking steadily, feeling sure we'd meet. Stepping over the style, separating the common from the trees, I carried on along the path. A variety of fallen leaves were strewn all over and softened the way underfoot. The trees were dark, bare structures now, standing against the pale late autumn sky. In stark contrast, the ground beneath was orange, and yellow, and red. Soon Fergus was in front of me; he'd stopped again and was now talking quite loudly on the phone. He was unaware of my presence as I progressed in his direction.

"Come on. Come on. What's the problem? I need

that information," he said, his strong accent unlike any other in our generally uniform-sounding community. "I can't get anywhere without your input on this." He didn't sound cross exactly, but he spoke forcefully.

At that point, Bones barked and came running toward Morsel, who deftly dodged him and ran in circles through the leaves. Fergus turned, his phone pressed to his ear.

"Hold on." As I approached, he pushed the handset to his chest, making sure nothing could be overheard from the speaker. "Hello, Lucy," he said before giving the other party a final rebuke. "Make sure you get it, and quickly!" He ended the call and adopted a pleasant expression for my benefit. "What a lovely day to be out of doors."

"Yes, my favorite type of day."

"You look very well," he said.

"Thank you. You look well too. It must be all this walking we're doing!"

"Do you want me to call Bones? He won't do any harm. He's just boisterous."

"No, he's fine. Morsel can look after herself. How is the village treating you?"

"Ah, not so badly…but I do need to find new lodgings if you know of anywhere?"

"What sort of place would you be looking for?"

"Something small, temporary."

"Let me think," I said.

"A holiday let perhaps, now that it's out of season…even a bed and breakfast at a push."

"Well, there is a B&B over near the church. I can't think they get many customers this time of year."

"Might be worth looking into."

"I passed by a day or so back. I don't think the vacancies sign was out. They may not be open, but they might be pleased to have a guest on a temporary basis."

"I'd need something flexible."

"I see," I said. His phone was vibrating with a new call, but he didn't answer. "Well, it's the large double-fronted house on the way to the church. It's called Hillside, I believe."

"Thank you. How is your work? You said you were busy?"

"Yes, always. I work at Moonstones, you know."

"It's a shop?"

"No, a rest home."

"Oh, really? That must be interesting," he said. The phone started to vibrate again, and he excused himself. "This is my work." He held the handset out in front of him, raising his eyes to the sky in resignation. He turned and began walking away from me. "Goodbye, Lucy. Take care of yourself. Bones! Bones, here!"

I stood and watched as his frame receded in the direction we'd both come from just a few minutes beforehand. Bones' heavy body passed noisily by me as he lumbered to catch up. More than anything, I wanted to follow Fergus, see where he was going, but I resisted. I had gained more information, and perhaps caught him a little off guard. I turned and continued on my way, calling Morsel and fixing my focus on the path in front of me. I pulled her ball from the pocket of my coat, threw it out ahead of me, and kept walking.

\*\*\*\*

"Is there any news about Joan?" asked Miss Pickering.

"I've not heard anything," I said. I'd bumped into

her in the street on my way through the village.

"She's still in hospital?"

"Yes, poor Joan."

"Do you know if she'll be coming back to Moonstones?"

"I'm not sure, Miss Pickering. I really hope so."

"I expect I will see you on Sunday. I'll look forward to that, Lucy. Bob is always talking about you. You've made a real hit with him."

"He's a lovely person, your brother," I said. "It's such a pleasure to do anything for him. I'll be working on Sunday afternoon, Saturday too."

"I'll tell him that. He'll be pleased."

"You can always ask me if there's something he needs or if he has any special requirements," I told her. "I'll do my very best to make sure he's happy at the home."

"Thank you, Lucy. It's not just a job for you, is it? You're always thinking about the residents and what you can do for them."

"Of course. Now we'd both better start walking before we get frozen."

"Yes. My goodness, is that the time? I need to go to the library and the grocery store before I set off to visit Bob…and I mustn't be late, or he'll soon let me know about it! I'll see you on Sunday."

She hurried away. A tiny, little old lady she might have been, but she had an energy level similar to Charlie's. She was forever on the go, and I'd never once heard her complain about an ache or pain, or anything else for that matter.

****

Joe was up when I arrived at Moonstones that

evening.

"Is something wrong?" I asked him.

"No, just catching up with paperwork. How are you, Lucy?"

"Fine, and quite enjoying these night shifts, to my surprise!"

"I don't mind them either. I seem to be able to think at night. Everyone else goes to sleep, the telephone stops ringing, and there's not so much peripheral stuff to deal with."

I asked Joe for an update on Joan. There was no change. She had breathing difficulties, added to various other long-term health problems. She wasn't likely to be discharged any time soon.

"Could I visit her, do you think?" I asked.

"In all honesty, I'm not sure she'd know you were there…but I don't see why not. She's in Melstow."

"I'd like to go. Will the family visit?"

"I've been on the phone to them today. They're trying to get down, but it won't be for a week or more. They live so far away, and they're both working."

At Moonstones, Joan received the odd visit from a distant relative and his wife, but I'd not been aware of them coming recently.

"Everyone else is well?"

"Yes, fingers crossed those flu jabs do the trick this year."

Joe had an hour or so's work to get on with, so I left him and went for a walk round the building. In the kitchen, I found a thoughtful note from Larry about having left a large slice of chocolate cake for me. I made a strong black coffee and had a look at it. I turned it, inspected it from all sides, knowing I might be forced to give in to it later. I could always do extra sit-ups. I walked along the corridors, then went to the residents' lounge and watched part of a Scandinavian detective drama with subtitles. It meant I didn't need the sound up and wouldn't disturb anyone. Back in the office, Joe was packing up.

"What should I wear to a dinner party, Joe?" I asked him.

"Depends whose, I suppose."

"Friends have asked me. It's at their house. I don't usually get asked to those sorts of things."

"I don't go to many. I think, if it's friends of yours, smartish casual wear would be acceptable. Nothing too formal."

"Black?"

"You can't go wrong with black, can you? You should ask Lianne, though, not me. I'll tell her to find you in the morning."

"Good night, Joe."

Morsel was happily curled up on her cushion. I took out the night's magazine and began flicking through the pages for evening wear ideas.

****

I had to take the bus to Melstow to visit Joan. I combined the visit with a trip to one or two shops to look for a sparkly upper garment that would appear more expensive than its price tag. The hospital came first. I found the ward where Joan was one of eight patients. Her bed was in the far corner, and a nurse brought a chair for me. I told the nurse I was just a friend. There'd been no other visitors.

"How are you, Joan?" I whispered. The woman in the next bed seemed keen to chat. Her eyes were drilling into me, but I made certain not to turn my head; this was Joan's time.

"I've missed you...we all have. Your room at Moonstones is waiting for you. Joe is ready to collect you as soon as you feel well enough." Joan was very still. Her eyes were closed, but I thought her breathing seemed good. I held her hand, stroked her arm, and told her some pieces of news. "John and Larry can't get used to not having to cook for you. They've put your dinner out a few times! Miss Pickering has been asking after you. Mrs. Cook wanted me to send you her love, and Lionel and Bert are really looking forward to having you back."

She seemed comfortable. Better than she'd been at the home in recent weeks. I supposed she was getting additional medication now. I enjoyed being with Joan and stayed for almost an hour. Fortunately, someone turned up to visit the woman in the next bed, so I didn't have to interact with her.

I left satisfied with how I'd found Joan and was able to turn my thoughts to the trivialities of my party costume without feeling sadness, not that I made a purchase. I found a number of items that could work: several black options, a deep blue colored jersey in a mohair type wool with sequins and a ruff, a daring bright red figure-hugging garment. That one might need to be worn with a jacket in order to disguise my current, still rather lumpy physique. I would take another trip to Melstow and make my purchase the next time, after some further homework. Dinner at George and Helen's was to be on Thursday evening.

## Beth Merwood

I timed the bus departure perfectly and headed home, opening the front door to a warm welcome from an excited small black dog.

Chapter 9
Dinner

Sunday afternoon shifts were the shifts I most enjoyed, and I honestly thought I might cover them even if I wasn't paid at all. The following Sunday, I arrived early. John was finishing up and evidently in a good mood. I could hear him singing away in the kitchen as I entered. The rota confirmed Candy was on with me, so I had an additional reason to be cheered.

"Hello, Lucy," called John over the sound of the running tap, a flow of water crashing into the deep stainless steel sink.

"Hello, John. Lunch over?"

"Yes, thank the Lord!"

"You sounded in good form there!"

"Thank you. I was inspired by the thought of walking out through that door, getting home, putting my feet up, and watching the match!"

Candy joined us, rubbing her hands to warm them. "I can't get away from it. Paul's been getting ready for the match all morning."

"Big match."

"Yes, so I understand."

"Now, ladies, I have made some lovely gingerbread and also shortbread for today. A bit of a change. If that doesn't go down well with anyone, there's a small Victoria sponge in this container here."

"It all sounds good to me," said Candy.

"There's plenty. No one will go hungry." John arranged the tea towels and untied his apron. "I've no further interest in food. I have a fridge full of beer, a large sofa, and a football match waiting for me. There's no more a man could ask for."

"Go and enjoy yourself," I said as he headed off. "How have you been?" I asked Candy.

"Not so bad."

"Are things sorted with Paul, then?"

"Better than they were. But he has the afternoon off, and I'm working!"

"You'd have to watch the football if you were home by the sounds of it!"

"True. I'm trying to get him to take an evening off in the week. We could go into Melstow for something to eat or a film or something."

"Good. Keep working on him, I say."

Candy went to put her things in the staff room, and I followed her as far as the lounge. I put my head round the door to discover a room full of residents and a number of visitors, including Miss Pickering, Bert's daughter, and some friends of Lolly. Lionel and Mrs. Cook also had guests; the room was full of chatter and laughter. Candy and I got on with the afternoon chores. Soon we began the usual ritual of preparing the large pot of tea and arranging the cakes on a series of white porcelain plates.

"What should I wear to a dinner party, Candy?"

"Ooh, who's is it?"

"George and Helen have invited me."

"Ooh. I'd say wear the best thing you have in the wardrobe. You must have something hiding away in there? Wear a bit of jewelry?"

"Are trousers acceptable?"

"Yes! …with a fancy top and some good shoes."

"I have no shoes. Well, only the practical type."

"You're not a six, are you?"

"Yes, I am in most footwear."

"Same as me. You can borrow a pair. I have loads. I'm obsessed. I'll bring a couple of pairs for you to try. I'll leave them here for you during the week."

"That's so kind. It would save me splashing out." Without thinking, we were both munching our way through sticky squares of gingerbread. "Oh no! Look at me! I really shouldn't eat this stuff, but it's just too nice."

"Shortbread!" Miss Pickering said. "I adore shortbread, and so do you, Bob."

"Yes," Mr. Pickering said.

"John must have a secret recipe. It's so crumbly," I told them.

"Such a treat. It always reminds me of when our brother was married. It was a long time ago, of course. He went to Scotland for the honeymoon and brought us back some shortbread. Bob, do you remember the shortbread Geoffrey brought back from Scotland that time?"

"He went to Scotland on his honey spoon," Bob stated.

"His honeymoon, yes," said Miss Pickering.

"Scotland is famous for it, isn't it?" I said.

"Yes, and they went back a few times on holiday, and we were always brought a tin of shortbread on their return. A tin with a tartan pattern, full of lovely shortbread."

I left two plates of cakes for Mr. Pickering and his sister, seeing as they were particularly keen and knowing Mr. P's appetite was never in question. Candy was serving the others. Bert was a huge fan of gingerbread, it turned out, and couldn't remember the last time he'd eaten any. It was remarkable, but you could easily win the hearts of a roomful of people with a couple of hours of cake baking.

"I'm just popping to the shops," Molly informed me.

Lolly had become more robust. She had a string of regular visitors who came in from the village. She'd been much liked in the community, and as opposed to the experiences of some of the residents, people who said they would visit did actually turn up. She had three friends with her that afternoon, and they were busy playing cards. It was the way things should be, I thought. Some things about the home and the realities of old age could really get you down, but on Sunday afternoons, when we were plying the residents with favorite foods and cups of steaming tea and making their visitors welcome, I always felt a warm glow of pleasure.

****

"I just hope," I said to Morsel, "I've done enough sit-ups." Standing in front of my long mirror, I pulled on my new trousers. They fitted. I'd put stockings on underneath, a low denier, and I slipped on the ostentatious black high-heeled shoes Candy had left for me in the staffroom. I'd spent plenty of time trying on the various options she'd provided but kept coming back to this same pair. In Melstow, I'd chosen the blue top with the ruff and sequins. I pulled it on and turned a few times to admire my look. I couldn't help but smile. I thought I looked passable. I took everything off again. Later, once I'd walked Morsel, I would bathe, dress, and apply some makeup. I'd bought a beautiful bouquet of flowers to take as a gift for Helen and had my good coat dry cleaned for the occasion. Determined to make the most of my night, I'd taken no shortcuts in carrying out my research. I'd read a number of articles about dinner parties and taken note of the information and the tips included.

\*\*\*\*

I set off for George and Helen's wearing my boots and carrying Candy's shoes in a plastic bag. It was impossible to walk in the heels. I'd change into them just before I arrived at the house and shove my boots into the carrier. It was cold but not raining, so I would look fine on arrival. I had thought of a few conversation pieces I could start in case everything went quiet. I was as prepared as I could be.

George opened the door. The cozy warmth of the family house wafted out. He put his arms around me and shouted to Helen that I had arrived. He took my coat, and Helen came to greet me, Wotnot following her before being sent back to his bed.

"You look lovely," said Helen, "…and what's that perfume?" I wasn't wearing perfume. That was another thing I needed to learn about.

"Perhaps you can smell these; they're for you." I handed her the flowers, and she received them in one arm, embracing me with the other.

"Now, a drink," said George. "What can I get you?"

"Oh, anything at all," I said before realizing I

should probably have some sort of an idea.

"We have everything. I've opened a beer. Helen will have a glass of wine, but I can offer you vodka, gin, a whisky?"

"I'd like wine, please, the same as Helen."

"She's drinking red."

"Yes, red is fine, thank you."

I was pleased to find I was the only guest. I'd half expected there to be a houseful. Daniel was nowhere to be seen either.

"Come and sit down," instructed Helen. She may have had one or two drinks already, I observed.

We went into the comfortable lounge and sat. George began telling various stories. Helen sat one minute and darted to the kitchen the next. She joined in with George's stories for a moment, then disappeared. George was in the middle of a tale about a man they'd met on holiday, who constantly photographed every possible thing. Helen returned and joined in.

"And do you remember his wife?" she interjected. "The way she dressed? Unbelievable, Lucy. Her clothes were inconceivable!"

George continued on without acknowledging the interruptions. They were a practiced double act. He concluded with the very funny ending. Helen had again been to the kitchen and back by that time.

"Is there anything you don't eat?" She said to me. "George forgot to ask."

"No, I eat everything."

"Try these. I admit I bought them. I didn't make them." She put a big plate of small savory pastries with various fillings in front of us. "Tuck in."

Soon we were summoned to the table where I

opted to stick to the red, and my large glass was replenished. An ornate-looking starter involving salmon, prawns, and cucumber sculptures was put in front of me.

"This looks amazing, Helen," I said.

George told more stories. Helen told one about the neighbors. I realized I wouldn't need to talk much at all, which suited me well. George had a glass of wine with the meal. He sipped it now and then, I noted, while Helen topped my glass up generously several times, as well as her own. George was reserved in a way, whereas Helen was flamboyant and spoke loudly, laughing often. It was interesting to study them in their home environment.

The main course was served, a chicken dish with various vegetables.

"Are you sure you're still fine with red?" George checked again. "Let me open a bottle of white?"

"No, no. Red is lovely, really."

"You're like us," Helen stated. "We nearly always drink red."

It was nice to be like other people. George began a story about the dogs, and on this occasion, I felt confident enough to join in.

"I'm rather lazy when it comes to walking Wotnot, I'm afraid," admitted Helen. "I adore him, though. I spoil him, don't I, George? He's had his chicken already!"

"But you miss out on the dog community. Isn't that right, Lucy?"

"Yes, there's quite a gang of us, not to mention our four-legged friends," I said.

"Wesley and Banjo," said George

"Marty and Mimi," I said.

"Smudge, Polo," said George. It was almost as if we had a competition going on—who could remember the most dogs.

"Bones," I said.

"Whoever is Bones?" George looked bemused.

"You know, the bull dog. Fergus's dog," I said.

"Who is Fergus?" asked Helen.

"I don't think I've met him," said George, "or Bones."

We became distracted as Helen had been clearing the table and then produced three tall glass dishes containing all sorts of layers of sweet-flavored enticements.

"Dessert!" she pronounced.

"My favorite part of the meal!" George smiled.

We took the long spoons and began to work our way through the different colored stripes.

"This is gorgeous, Helen," I said.

"It's an old village recipe," she said. "I have a book of them. I bought it a couple of years back at one of the sales in the village hall. Mrs. Wilkinson collected them all up and produced the book to raise funds for the church. I'll lend it to you, Lucy."

"What a village we live in!" George stated.

"Like no other," said Helen. "This dessert came from one of the housekeepers at the manor."

"I wonder if it was Miss Pickering," I said. "Her brother is at Moonstones now. I see her most days."

"The book must give the housekeeper's name. I'll have to check."

"I will imagine I'm eating mine sat at a huge table in a magnificent room overlooking the grounds," joked

George, keeping his eyes tightly shut.

I had anticipated a conversation about the game, or the Lesters, the manor, or all three.

"There is a room like that, a great big dining room. I saw it through the window one year when we were looking for clues," Helen said. Her eyes sparkled. "The best game of all was 1996. Do you both agree?"

"Don't ask me," George said. "I've only lived here eighteen years, don't forget. I still count as a new boy."

"And we'd moved away by then," I said. "Who won?"

"The Cranes—one branch of the family. The prize was a holiday in a private villa in the Caribbean. Can you imagine? I've dreamed about having a holiday like that ever since!"

We went back to the lounge and sat drinking coffee and tots of brandy. The conversation had become intermittent. We were warm, well fed, and drowsy.

"Those pastries were nice," said George. "Any left?"

"You're not still hungry?"

"I was joking."

"They serve something like them at the new restaurant in Melstow," Helen said.

"How do you know that?" asked George.

Helen may have made one little slip in an otherwise immaculate performance.

"Oh, Ange must have told me," she said, and neither George nor I asked anything more.

It was a good deal later that, feeling relaxed, I changed back into my boots in the hallway and fought off George's offer to escort me home. I was nicely under the influence of the alcohol and enjoyed my short walk in the cold night air. I thought about some of the conversations we'd had and all the lovely food we'd eaten as I went. Morsel was at the door the moment I opened it. She danced around me. I picked her up and cuddled her.

Chapter 10
A Lapse

The dinner party went down as a milestone in terms of my personal achievement. Nevertheless, in the days that followed, as I knew I would, I agonized over what I'd said. Again and again, I tried to go over the whole evening in my head, remember what we'd talked about, and analyze my contributions. Had I said anything stupid? Had I said anything wrong? I was reasonably comfortable in the company of George and Helen, but I wasn't used to being in a situation such as that, where I needed to interact, to have a point of view, and tell a joke or two. One thing I could congratulate myself on was that I'd offered no opinion about the Lesters or the manor.

The villagers were all of the same opinion as far as I could tell. They wouldn't hear a word said against Reg, and they held the rest of the family in high regard because of the village game and also simply because they were glamorous and wealthy. The villagers wallowed in a form of reflected glory. I'd experienced it once or twice. Someone would find out I was from Steely and become extremely interested in me. They would ask question after question about the Lesters, purely because I was a Steely person. They believed I must know them and everything about them.

Knowledge of any member of the family was of

value, although Vicky seemed to be the exception. She wasn't popular; she was seen as a bit of a nuisance, a bit of a madam. Even so, I thought the villagers would be prepared to forgive her: she was young, she'd lost her father, and after all, she would always be a Lester.

I must have been eight or nine when Dad first took me to the manor. It was during one of the school holidays, and Mum had a busy washing day ahead of her. Dad told her he'd take care of me for a while. I clambered into the old blue pickup truck. I sat on the passenger end of the single leather-covered seat that stretched the width of the cab. The seat felt hard as we bounced along on it through the village. We carried on into the countryside until Dad swung the truck past the grand gate posts and onto the long gravel drive that wound round the grounds of the estate. I'd heard talk of the Lesters and the manor, and I'd had a few encounters, including when Reg had come to our cottage, but it wasn't until that day that I realized what being well off was really all about. The house came into view. To me, it was mammoth: a very old stone-built property from another era, with a grandeur I immediately understood, even though I had no references to work from. Part of the building was turreted like a castle; another section had tall, twisting chimneys. Gardens stretched out before me, lawns and paths, paved areas and ornamentation, trees with wide, wide trunks that reached to the sky. Dad drove slowly to the back of the building. I gazed out of the vehicle, clinging onto the handle above my head as we rocked from side to side. A number of outbuildings came into view, and we finally stopped in a yard area. An elderly man came out of a back door to meet us.

## The Ultimate Village Game

The man was a staff member, and he said it would be all right for me to be with Dad as the family was away. Dad was underway with decorating the whole top floor of one wing. We went in through the back entrance and crossed a huge old-fashioned kitchen to a staircase that led up at the side of the house. We climbed to the top floor, to the room Dad was working on, and he began to prepare his paints and brushes and re-spread his dust sheets. The room was empty of any furnishings. Dad explained that everything had been moved into other rooms so he could work efficiently. He said, if I didn't touch anything, I could walk along the landing and look into the other rooms. He had already decorated the ones to the left; the ones to the right were still to be completed.

The building was in two sections, with one section at right angles to the other. Dad told me one part was much older, that I would see how the ceilings were lower, the windows smaller, and the walls thicker. I roamed from room to room. The enormous wooden doors had big metal latches, the types of which I'd never seen before. I spent time in each room, looking at the stonework, the light fittings, the leaded windows, and the fireplaces. In the rooms that hadn't been emptied, the furnishings were, again, unlike any I had ever seen. Everything seemed much bigger than I was used to—great wardrobes and bedsteads, tables with intricate inlay, heavily carved trunks. The bathrooms were ornately tiled, with roll-top baths that sported ancient taps and clawed feet. I looked out through the windows of various rooms. You could see for miles over the land and sometimes across the village. The village looked very small.

Dad came to find me. He couldn't believe how long I'd been gone, but as soon as he set eyes on me, he could tell I had been put under the spell of the place.

"Isn't it something else?" he said. He took me back down to the kitchen, and the elderly man, whose name was Peto, brought me a glass of chilled milk in a thick glass beaker. It was the best glass of milk I'd ever tasted.

The experience never left me. At home, I asked Mum for paper, and I drew and painted pictures of the manor. I tried to draw the furniture and the gardens, the tall trees, and the outhouses. I could recall every detail. I remembered the smells of the manor, so different to our house or the school. I could remember everything Peto had said to me and the snippets of the building's history that Dad had recounted.

****

Miss Pickering asked after Joan again. I'd made another visit to the hospital. There seemed to be little change, and I hoped that was a good sign. She wasn't any worse. The woman in the next bed had been discharged, and another lady, who appeared frighteningly frail, was in her place. The new lady had kind, watery eyes. She smiled at me as I passed, but she didn't speak. A different nurse brought me a chair and returned to check some readings on the surrounding equipment, noting her findings on the card at the end of the bed. Joan's poor body had a maze of tubes to deal with. The nurse whisked away, and I began my conversation, telling Joan everything I could think of. I told her about what had happened at Moonstones since my previous visit, who'd had guests on Sunday, what had been for lunch. I told her I'd been to a dinner party, and that I'd given Morsel a bath before I'd come out that day. Joan looked peaceful; she looked almost content. The nursing sister noticed me and came to speak. She asked if I was family. I told her no, just a friend, I worked at Moonstones. The sister knew Moonstones and commented that it had a good reputation. I said I hoped we'd soon have Joan back with us, but from her expression, I could tell perhaps that might not be the most likely of outcomes. She offered me tea, but I turned it down.

"How did she seem?" Miss Pickering pressed me.

"To me, she seemed better than on my first visit."

"That's good."

"Yes, I thought that too."

"I do hope she's able to return soon."

"So do I, Miss Pickering. It's not the same without her."

I asked Joe if he'd heard from the hospital in an official capacity. He hadn't.

"You'll keep her room for her?"

"I will," he said.

But I knew he wouldn't be able to keep it indefinitely. The home was a business. The income would be missed. And there was a list of people waiting to come in. I didn't like the thought of someone new in Joan's room. She'd been at Moonstones for years, a long time before I started at the home. When she'd first arrived, she was one of the fittest residents they told me, like Mr. Pickering was at the time, I supposed. Even when I first took the job, Joan would sit in her chair in her room during the day and read the newspaper; she would chat away to the staff at every opportunity; her hairdresser would visit every fortnight and maintain her well-groomed appearance. Gradually that all changed.

"The shoes were perfect. Thank you so much, Candy."

"Which ones did you wear in the end?"

"The black patent leather pair. I've never worn such high heels!"

"Was it a good evening?"

"A lovely evening. I had a bit of a hangover the next day!"

"You're coming out of yourself, Lucy."

"Do you think so?"

"Yes. It's great to see."

Candy was getting to know me quite well, this new person I was struggling to be, but I wasn't always comfortable with it. She probably saw me shrink at the suggestion that I might be coming out of myself. I wanted to be more confident and join in with things: that fitted into the plan, but my natural instinct was to do the opposite, to hide behind other people or my job, not to get noticed. In effect, my whole life was an act, I was deceiving everyone, and sometimes I was confusing myself.

Two bells were rung, one just after the other. Candy and I both had to attend to residents. It was the Saturday morning shift, and it would be full-on. The residents were in high spirits because there was to be a game of bingo in the afternoon. Joe was to be the caller, and Jackie was coming in to help him. Before we finished that day, we would bring as many of the residents to the lounge as wanted to join in. The afternoon staff would be taking over quite a party. A few of the residents had also told their visitors about the bingo, and some were coming along especially for the occasion.

"I think I might stay for it," Candy told me in a moment when we'd both arrived back in the kitchen.

"I'll have to get home to see to Morsel, but I suppose I could hang on for a couple of games."

Late morning, before we served lunch, Candy, Joe, and I went to the lounge and rearranged the tables and chairs, and in front of them, we set up two trestle tables which were to be where Joe and Jackie would sit. We covered the tables with black drapes. Joe brought in his equipment, which consisted of a professional-looking cage and set of bingo balls, a large pile of score cards, and some fake bank notes to be given as prizes. Whoever won the most money was to receive a real prize.

By two-thirty, our usual leaving time, Candy and I had gathered the residents into the lounge: Mr. Pickering had chosen his table and was keeping a seat for his sister; Lolly was set up with two extra chairs for friends who were coming from the village; Bert and Lionel were sitting together; Marcia, Ethel and Mrs. Roberts were seated right at the front. Molly was wandering the corridors, but she'd probably come to the lounge once everything started. Even Mrs. Cook, our oldest resident, was to make an appearance. She'd be brought in at the last moment, as she wouldn't be capable of taking part for long.

Barbara and Mariana were on duty for the upcoming shift.

"Oh my Lord!" exclaimed Barbara when she set eyes on the lounge. "It's everyone, isn't it? Everybody is going to play!"

"Mrs. Cook is *en route*, and there are a few friends still to arrive," I said.

"Count me in," said John, who'd taken off his apron. "I'm ready to help out or play, either thing." He brought a jug of water and a couple of glasses for Joe and Jackie and placed them on the draped trestles.

"This is going to be so much fun," Candy said. I could tell she genuinely meant it.

Joe had dressed in a smart black jacket with a white shirt and a bow tie. He took on the role of MC and welcomed everyone to the afternoon's extravaganza. Jackie was also dressed for the occasion, in a sparkly dress and wearing plenty of makeup.

"My lovely assistant here will hand out the cards," Joe announced. "You must cross off each number on your card as you hear it called. There will be one card per game for each participant. The winner of each game will receive a hundred-pound note!"

"Oooh!" we all cried.

'Bingo!' shouted Molly, who'd arrived on her frame and was standing contemplating the room from the doorway. Jackie went to help her to a table.

"I'm afraid the hundred-pound notes are not legal tender, but if you have more than everyone else at the end of the game, you will win a fantastic Moonstones' prize!" said Joe.

"What do they win?" whispered Candy. She, John, and I were sitting together at the back.

"It's chocolates, wine, or fruit, depending on who the winner is," John whispered back. "Some of them aren't allowed to eat chocolate. Some wouldn't be allowed the wine or the chocolates."

"Joe's thought of everything," I said.

## The Ultimate Village Game

All the visitors had arrived by that point, and Jackie gave out the first cards. The staff were to play one card as a team but wouldn't be allowed to win a prize, she stated authoritatively.

Joe began calling out numbers.

"Two and six, twenty-six."

"Shout a bit louder," Lionel instructed.

"I'll repeat each number I call," said Joe. "Put your hand up if you can't hear me."

Joe knew a good bit of bingo lingo, and what he didn't know, the residents were able to help with.

"Knock at the door, twenty-four."

The room was quiet as everyone scanned their card.

"Half a dozen, number six," called Joe. More silence. "All the threes, thirty-three."

"Pardon?" Ethel shouted. "Did you say that twice?"

"Bingo!" Molly cried out.

"Can't be!" Lionel roared. "We haven't had enough numbers yet."

"I'll come and check your card," Jackie said in an attempt to keep the peace.

I gave Candy and John a knowing look and went to sit with Molly. "Can I join in with you, Molly?" I asked her. The number calling continued for some minutes.

"Bingo!" shouted Lolly.

"Aaaah!" said everyone. Jackie confirmed the card was full, and Lolly received the first hundred-pound note. Mariana and Barbara had arrived with the tea trolley, and more score cards were handed out. The afternoon continued. I crossed off Molly's numbers.

"Number forty-five," called Joe.

"Halfway there," shouted one of Lolly's friends.

"Garden gate, number eight," called Joe. I helped Molly with her tea. Joe carried on. We all concentrated on our cards. Then…

"Two fat ladies—"

"Bingo!" I shouted, "Molly has it!" Jackie came to check, and sure enough, the card was correct, and Molly received the next hundred-pound note.

"Bingo!" said Molly. "Bingo!"

"Yes!" I hugged her. "Bingo indeed!" She took the note and stroked it with obvious satisfaction.

The eventual winner turned out to be Bert, who accepted a nice bottle of red wine. Lolly and her friends were given chocolates for coming a close second, and another box of sweets was opened and passed round, as was the lovely bowl of fruit.

I realized I was still at Moonstones; I'd become totally immersed. Poor Morsel. I had to get back to her.

"See you for more fun tomorrow," said Candy as I left.

I found out later that Joan died on Saturday afternoon while we were all playing bingo. Lianne received the call.

\*\*\*\*

It was a relief when Sunday was over that week. I had created a convincing new world that people seemed to have fallen for. It almost seemed easy to live in it, but my head knew otherwise. Morsel was once again my sounding board.

"I'm not this person I'm showing to the world, Morsel; I'm a mean woman with a selfish plan. I'm role-playing at being nice. I could easily come unstuck. Nic Lester must have someone watching me. If I drop my guard, if I don't stick rigidly to my agenda, the real Lucy could emerge. I'd have blown it then. The whole thing would have been a waste of time."

But the feelings I'd been experiencing in my new, make-believe life surprised me. I had empathy when it came to the Moonstones residents, and I couldn't help liking the staff. When I started out with my plan, I didn't think I'd feel a thing. I'd chosen to work in a care home because I had to demonstrate that I was a nice person, a kind person. That was what everyone had to think. All my interactions were about presenting this false persona. It was based on distant memories and behavior I'd learned by watching soap operas and dramas on TV. I'd study the kindest characters and mimic their behavior. The real me was very different. Even so, Joan filled my thoughts on my next series of night shifts. Her old room seemed more empty. I didn't go in, but each time I passed the door, I was saddened.

As the days went by, my notebook remained unopened. I didn't bother with my exercises. I ate the large slab of coffee cake and the buttery scones that Larry left for me, accompanied by mugs of sweet milky coffee. At home, alone, I drank red wine, and white wine, and cream liqueur. Lianne noticed a change in me. She was in the office.

"Are you okay?"

"Yes, fine, Lianne, thank you."

"You don't seem your usual cheery self."

"No? Probably the cold weather."

She shuffled her paperwork and put some documents into the tall filing cabinet. "Joan was in the best place, you know."

"I know."

"We couldn't have looked after her here at the end."

"No, I know."

Before Lianne went off to bed, she brought me a bowl of soup with a big chunk of bread. She opened two large bags of brightly wrapped chocolates and poured them into a dish beside me.

"There, we must make sure you're looked after. You can talk to me, you know…if you want to…about anything."

"I know. Thank you, Lianne."

Chapter 11
Looking After George

What happened next was just what I needed. I left Moonstones soon after eight the following morning, and there loitering outside, waiting for me it turned out, was George.

"Hello, George," I was surprised to see him. Wotnot was with him.

"Are you walking Wotnot?…at this time?"

"Not exactly."

"Are you looking for me?"

"I was hoping to see you."

"What is it?" He looked unsettled and as if he'd rushed out without giving much thought to his appearance. It was cold, but his jacket wasn't fastened, his hair wasn't combed. This wasn't his usual fashionable untidiness; it was proper neglectfulness.

"Helen," he said.

"Helen?"

Helen had come home extremely late the night before. She'd been drinking and had gone straight to bed. He'd waited up for her during the evening, but all she'd done on her arrival was proclaim she was tired, sing goodnight at the top of her voice, and proceed upstairs in an unsteady manner. She'd had no reason to be out late; there'd been no discussion about it beforehand.

"She's having an affair," said George.

"She's what? No, George, I don't believe that."

"It's obvious. She went missing for hours that other night…and now this."

"There must be an explanation. Where is she now?"

"Still in bed, as far as I know. I slept in the spare room."

"Perhaps she was with Ange and Sue again, like last time."

"There's been other things as well. Phone calls where she glances at the number and then cuts off the call…and I've caught her hiding behind the tree in the garden, talking on her mobile. There's someone she wants to keep a secret."

"She's not being that discreet if that's the case." Morsel and Wotnot stood beside each other, their breath visible in the chill morning air. "Shall we go to the copse?"

It was beautiful amongst the trees. A watery white sun, low in the sky, strained to break through wispy mistiness. George finally fastened his coat and wrapped his scarf more carefully around his neck. I turned up my collar, and we sat on the seat, watching the dogs expend their energy.

"Things aren't right," said George. "I sort of knew already, even before the signs that made it obvious."

George carried on, and I listened. This was what I was good at. Having a person with problems to support was going to be a great help to me, and it would put me in a better frame of mind. I thought George was right; after all, I'd also seen Helen coming out of the inn with a man. I could feel his pain, the cramp in his stomach, the ache in his head, but I didn't give away my thoughts.

"When you get home, be careful. I don't think you should accuse Helen. There's probably a perfectly good explanation. If you accuse her wrongly, you'll upset her and make a real mess of things."

"I hear what you're saying, Lucy, but I don't think you're right this time."

"Well, I'll be at home for a few hours if you want to drop round or anything."

We parted. George struck a miserable figure as he disappeared along the road. He looked hunched, defeated. Wotnot seemed to have picked up the mood, walking languidly behind him, head down.

"We're so lucky," I told Morsel, meeting the eyes of the small dog who sat patiently waiting for me to set off in the direction of our own home. "George and Helen, Candy and Paul…we're lucky we have each other, and we hardly ever fall out."

I took out the frying pan. "One large fried breakfast coming up, including some extra bacon for you, Morsel." In due course, I would write a new notice for the fridge—to replace the one I'd torn down and stamped on. Helping George would inspire me. I'd get back on track with my plans, but for the moment, I was in dire need of comfort food.

\*\*\*\*

I often asked Dad if I could go to the manor with him. He usually turned me down: the family was at the residence, or he had too much to do that day, or the housekeeper would disapprove. I became used to being disappointed, but I wasn't discouraged. One late summer morning, I asked him again, and he consented.

It transpired he could do with someone to look out for Reg. Reg was due to come to the manor that day, and Dad needed to speak to him. He didn't want to miss him.

Dad was working at the rear side of the building. Reg always parked at the front and sometimes only stayed for an hour or so. I was to watch for him. I opened the doors to several rooms and chose the window with the best view, overlooking the gardens and the graveled area beside the main entrance. That was where Reg would leave his car while he carried out his business.

I had a wonderful morning. In my head, I had a list of rooms I wanted to revisit and pieces of furniture I'd like to view again. I wanted to take another look at some of the carvings: there were chairs with all kinds of patterns and crests; I'd seen fierce-looking birds and evil-looking faces incorporated into the stonework. I'd also seen angels blowing on horns and animals that might have existed in fairytales. Becoming so wrapped up in the magic of the house, I almost forgot my purpose and had to run back to the room with the selected window. No car was parked. I stayed for a while, gazing out, kneeling on a silk-upholstered chaise lounge, my chin resting on my hands, my elbows lodged on the deep window sill. I stared out across the land, and in time, a black car came into view, winding along the driveway. I thought it must be him, but I waited to make sure. Dad would have to stop work and clean up, and he wouldn't be pleased if he did all that and someone else was in the vehicle.

The car drew up outside and stopped. I could see Reg inside. He always drove himself. I expected him to be alone, but once he'd stepped out, he moved to the rear and opened the door. The back seat was revealed. Out tumbled two boys, perhaps a little older than I. They were similar in looks, though one was slightly taller. They were dressed in a type of clothing I'd never seen real people wearing: suits with waistcoats, white shirts, and cravat-type neck ties, shiny boots. Both were fair-headed, their hair brushed and arranged to perfection. They trotted after Reg into the manor.

\*\*\*\*

Charlie arrived at the door on Friday morning. The school was closed for the day, for some reason I never managed to get to the bottom of. We took Morsel out and returned to the house. Not long after, George arrived. I sent Charlie up to the front bedroom, where there were a number of old suitcases I used for storage. She was to look for Morsel's coat. I'd been given a few items for Morsel when I adopted her, and somewhere, there was a little knitted garment she could do with, given the continuing inclement weather conditions. Charlie was pleased to have the task and took Morsel with her.

"How are you? What's happened?" I asked George. He looked tired, and his facial expression was one of going through endless torture.

"I had a long talk with Helen. I tried not to accuse her outright, but I did say she was acting as if she was having an affair. She laughed it off. 'Whoever with?' she asked me."

"So there was another explanation?"

"She became more serious. Then she told me it's Ange that's having the affair. Well, she's not exactly having one, but she's interested in someone. There's a sort of will we or won't we thing going on between her and some bloke. Helen says she's been covering for her, even though she doesn't approve."

I was trying to work out if the argument rang true. It would be such a good thing for George if this really was what was going on.

"I don't actually believe it," George continued. "I want to, of course." We could hear Charlie rummaging noisily upstairs, talking away to Morsel. "Is she all right up there?"

"Yes, she'd be sure to shout otherwise. Where did you say Helen was that last evening?"

"She went to Ange's to meet her…so Ange could tell Will they were off for a girly night out. Then she went with Ange to Melstow and had a drink with her while they waited for Ange's new man…I mean the one she's interested in."

"She was quite drunk, though, when she came home?" I checked.

"Yes, and came back very late. How long would they have waited for him?"

"Who is this new man?"

"She wouldn't say. She said Ange would never forgive her if she told me."

"Poor Will!"

"Yes, but Ange and Will are supposed to be splitting up. That's been going on for a while."

I went to check on Charlie. "Are you okay up there, Charlie?" I called up the stairs.

"Yes, I've found lots of things!"

George raised an eyebrow, and we both smiled. We could enjoy each other's company even in this unwelcome circumstance.

"So you don't believe Helen?" I said.

"No, Lucy. It doesn't make sense."

"Give her the benefit of the doubt?" I said.

"What, and just wait for the next betrayal?"

"There may not be any more occasions like that. You could lay down some rules. She at least has to tell you if she's out covering up for Ange?"

"I'm not sure. I never thought I'd have to deal with this kind of thing. I'm not equipped for it!" He was almost shouting.

"I think you should take your time. Remember how long you've been together," I told him. "In a few weeks, everything will be back to normal. I've never been married, but that's what I've generally observed."

"Or, I could go and talk to Ange," he suggested.

There were loud footsteps on the stairs. Charlie appeared in front of us with a small knitted dog coat, Morsel scampering behind. She held it up, very pleased with herself.

"Great, thank you, Charlie! She can wear it on her walk later, but right now, Morsel needs sleep, and the three of us…what about we go to the café for meringues?"

We set off for the café, George trudging along next to me, Charlie out in front skipping, and intermittently walking backward, trying to persuade us to hurry. Charlie wore baggy-legged jeans with the bottoms turned up and a thick check-patterned shirt. George was huddled into a long overcoat. I wore my down jacket. It made me look huge, but my only care was that it was keeping me warm.

Amber was on shift. "Good morning," she enthused in well-bred fashion as we entered. At least

Charlie responded.

"Hello." Charlie chose a table and slipped into a seat while George and I maneuvered ourselves into position next to her.

"What can I get for you?" Amber asked. "I say, Charlie, your hair is growing. It looks lovely a little longer."

I was annoyed I'd not noticed, but it was true. Charlie's dark, straight hair used to be cropped short, but it had grown somewhat, and she'd begun to look more female.

"Mum wants it to grow."

"Well, Mum is right!" Amber declared.

"I'd like a meringue, please," Charlie said to her.

George wasn't hungry but needed coffee. I ordered tea, juice and asked for three meringues anyway because I knew a bit of sugar would do George a world of good if we could get it into him.

"How nice to have a day off," I stated. I had to strike a balance between my respective companions' misery on the one hand and ebullience on the other.

"Yes, I think we should always get Friday off," said Charlie, "...and Monday."

George smiled. "I work from home a fair amount, so it can be all too easy to take time off. I do endeavor to be disciplined."

"What are you working on at the moment?" I asked him. Amber brought our order, and Charlie dived straight in.

"An environmental report for the government."

It sounded far beyond my comprehension. I didn't really understand what George did. I knew he had a connection with the geological department at the university.

Charlie looked interested while grappling with her disintegrating cake. "Eat your meringue, George. They're very good," she said.

He couldn't resist Charlie. He picked up the third meringue, took a big bite, and began to make exaggerated noises of satisfaction that pleased her no end. "Yum, yum, yum! Yum, yum, yum!" he said.

"You have cream on your nose." She giggled.

\*\*\*\*

We went to Joan's funeral—Joe, Lionel, Mr. Pickering, his sister, and I. Joe drove us in the minibus. It was a small affair. We did our best to get through the hymns, none of us being gifted when it came to singing. The vicar asked us to the vicarage afterward, where we all accepted a small glass of sherry and recounted our memories of our departed friend. Joan had been a dress maker, a skilled seamstress who'd made a good living from her village home. She'd had a thriving little business, and people had come from far and wide to order wedding dresses and other garments for their various special occasions. She'd been married but was still young when she lost her husband. They'd had no children. It seemed the only remaining family members were on her husband's side. The young couple who'd occasionally visited her at Moonstones attended the funeral, but no other relations. The two of them learned a lot about Joan that day, they confessed. Joe and Miss Pickering were determined to keep spirits up and passed on their memories with real warmth. Joan was to be buried with her husband, Alfred. They'd died more than fifty years apart.

"She's at peace now," Miss Pickering told us.

"Yes," Joe confirmed. "She's with Alfred, and they have a fair bit of catching up to do."

I felt better on the journey back to Moonstones. We were quiet on the bus, but everyone had achieved some sort of contentment. There was a feeling of togetherness between us. We'd brought each other through an important event, and we knew we'd done the best we could for Joan. We'd shared a life experience. As individuals, we would grapple with so many thoughts, but with each other, we had reinforced the shared meanings of our lives.

\*\*\*\*

I was getting back on track. I resurrected my notebook, packing it into my evening bag before summoning Morsel.

"Come on, girl, we need a bracing walk before work."

We strode to the common and on along beside the river, a good hour's walk. We visited the newsagent's on the way home to buy a fresh stack of magazines. Mrs. Hughes had become more used to my fashionable choices. I think she was even ordering additional titles, especially for me. She was also noticeably more polite than she had been on some previous occasions as I handed over my money.

"Thank you, Lucy. How are you keeping?"

"I'm well."

"You don't mind the cold weather?"

"Walking keeps me warm. Walking and working."

"Ah, not if you do my kind of work! My hands are like a box of frozen fish fingers."

"It's never cold at Moonstones."

"I suppose not, you're lucky there. Enjoy your

reading."

"I will. Thank you, Mrs. Hughes."

"Do call me Linda. You make me feel old otherwise."

"Thank you, Linda."

Morsel and I returned home. I picked out two of the magazines, pushing them into my bag with the notebook. We'd have to leave for Moonstones in half an hour. There was time to write a fresh sign for my fridge. *Lumpy! Bumpy! Blubbery!*

"Yes, that's good." I wrote each word with a different colored pen for emphasis and put the notice on the side of the fridge, held in place by the frog magnet. At the side there, no one would see it but me. I had to think about those kinds of things now that I seemed to be receiving frequent callers to the house. I was sharing my world more than I had for a very long time. It was part of the plan, though something I hadn't been sure I'd achieve, and I had to admit, I liked the company.

"Time to go, Morsel. Are you ready?"

It was a quiet night at Moonstones. The evening staff left for home minutes after my arrival, and Joe and Lianne seemed to have already retired to bed. I went on a walk round, and all was peaceful. I settled in the office. Having had a break from my diet and from my village study, I was ready to resume. I took out the notebook and allowed my mind to begin to puzzle away at the facts before me once more.

I'd been back in the village for long enough now to believe that I again knew it well. Few people remembered me from back when I was growing up in the area. I had hazy memories of some of them, and by now, I was coming to know once more, who the major players were, which businesses thrived and which struggled, who played straight, who ducked and dived, and not least, who was new to the area. I saw it as a puzzle I had to solve, like a drawn-out board game or a complex card game. Where did I stand, I wondered. I saw myself, as usual, as an outsider. I wasn't mistrusted, as I'd been brought up in Steely. However, I hadn't yet spent enough time back in the village to acquire much of a position. What I was aiming for was along the lines of trustworthy, reliable, steady. I couldn't say it didn't appeal, the life I was creating. I was enjoying my lie of a life to an extent, and under different circumstances, I might have been happy to accept it to be my lot. But beyond this temporary persona, toward the later stages of the game, I believed things were going to change. If I could get it right, and luck was on my side, my world would change radically and forever. In effect, I was playing the ultimate game, the ultimate village game. How to get from A to Z was the conundrum. At that particular moment, I gauged myself to be at about G in the alphabet. There was a long way to go, but I'd made a start; I had to stay focused and keep working to achieve my goal.

I'd pretty much struck Martin off my list. I'd seen him one more time, dressed in his workwear, dropping a child at the school entrance. The news that he had relatives close by gave him a reason to be in Steely. I turned the page of the notebook. Amber. Who was Amber? I still couldn't answer that. She didn't seem to have any connection with the area. Why would she come to live in Steely? She surely wouldn't have come for the treasure hunt alone, and besides, the future of the treasure hunt was somewhat up in the air. Everyone knew that. I pondered, turned the page again. Fergus, who was he? Equally as suspicious, certainly. Whatever was he up to? How was it that George had never come across him? Where was he living, and why had he turned up in the village out of the blue? I contemplated some more. He wasn't in need of long-term accommodation, he'd indicated. Were there any projects underway where an expert might be required for a short time or a freelancer? I would ask a few people about that. I would ask Linda. She'd know about that kind of thing, standing there the whole day behind that counter. I felt sure she read the local paper from cover to cover, and her customers probably passed on every bit of local gossip.

"Goodness! The time is flying, Morsel! I'll have another walk round, and then you can go outside for a few minutes."

I supposed I should congratulate myself on my progress. Maybe I should have returned to the village sooner, but I'd made my mind up about that a long time ago. I'd always known I would move back, but I'd resolved to return only after Reg Lester had died.

****

I thought about those two blond-haired boys as I drew my next pictures of the manor. I based my works on my new observations. I revised some of the previous drawings, taking on board my latest studies of the carvings. I worked away at them until I felt satisfied. All the time, I was wondering what it would be like to have a sister or a brother to run around with and what it would be like to live in a big house. I wondered about the other rooms. I'd been into the kitchen, a staff area really; I'd climbed the back stairs and seen all there was of the third floor, but I longed to walk into the grand ground floor rooms that looked out over the gardens.

Who were those boys? I asked my dad. He told me they were Reg's sons, that they went to a boarding school, and they'd been dressed in their school clothes when I'd seen them. Now, aren't you lucky, he said, that you can walk along the road to school and back and that your uniform is plain and straightforward? He ruffled my mousy brown hair. Though I smiled at him, I wasn't so sure that I was fortunate. I tried to draw the boys, using a yellow crayon for their hair, and mixed the white with the brown for their tweedy suits. They looked nice. I stared into their eyes and longed to speak to them.

\*\*\*\*

I didn't get round to my exercises, but otherwise, the night had been well spent. There'd been no one to see to. Larry was on in the morning. He made a fresh pot of coffee and poured some out for me.

"I mustn't drink too much of this stuff," I told him. "I'll never get to sleep."

"I could do you a decaf?"

"No. I'll add more milk to this."

"Quiet night?" he enquired.

"Very. Probably the quietest I've had."

"That's good."

I took a seat on one of the benches. "Have you heard any mention of a new resident?"

Larry was busy emptying the dishwasher. "I think someone's due to come in before Christmas."

"A difficult time to be starting a new life."

"Yes, that's true, but we'll make them welcome. We're going to have a ball. So many activities that time of year." He stopped and turned toward me. "It's your first?"

I nodded. "Yes, my first Moonstones' Christmas."

"You'll enjoy it, honestly."

"Will I need to buy presents or anything like that?"

Larry resumed his work, taking a series of stainless steel bowls out of the machine. "We all do Secret Santa, even the residents. Lianne and Joe buy a few presents as a rule, and the staff usually give each other cards. John and I are getting going on food already. We order some stuff in, but we make plenty of it too. Be sure to be here for Christmas dinner. It's not to be missed!"

I so admired John and Larry. They put terrific energy into the home. It was true that if people were well fed, a lot of gripes and grumbles would be averted.

"I'm really looking forward to it all now, Larry," I said. "I imagine we'll decorate the building, and everyone will be singing carols."

"Yes, definitely, and it will all start very soon. In fact, are you working on Sunday? I'll make sure there are mince pies. Then Christmas can officially begin!"

Morsel and I went home feeling fortunate and positive. Perhaps what I had was enough. Did I really need to fill my life with aggravation and dispute?

Chapter 12
Football

George was becoming a frequent visitor to the cottage, but sometimes we met in the copse. We had the same conversations again and again. He was still convinced about the affair, though there was no evidence.

"You've been together how long?" I said. We were walking along a familiar path with the dogs.

"Twenty years."

"Is Helen really going to start an affair after twenty years?"

"It happens. She was quite a flirt when she was younger—when I first met her. She was a manizer. Is that a word?"

"But she chose you."

"She did all the work. I would never have had the confidence to pursue her."

We came to the river and carried on walking.

"Do you talk about things like that?" I said. "I mean, about when you first met and so on?"

"Not really."

"I was thinking, that might be a good idea? Remind her about when you first got together and how much you wanted to be with each other. It would be romantic."

"Would it?"

"I think so. I realize I'm no expert."

"I wasn't questioning your expertise, Lucy. You're the only person I can speak to about this. You understand me somehow." George seemed so vulnerable. "I'll see if I can start a conversation along those lines."

Shouldn't he just hug her and tell her how much he loved her? I knew he half wanted me to intervene, to ask Helen or Ange what was going on, but my instinct told me that could be disastrous. I could cause a rift that wasn't there, and it could certainly put paid to my newfound friendships.

George finally changed the subject. "Did you say you lived in one of the railway cottages when you were young?"

"That's right, the second one along."

"I was reading about them recently. There are plans to improve them. They're going to get a makeover."

"They're sweet little cottages," I said, "but not the most comfortable. Little more than basic. I doubt they've changed a lot since we were there. We rented, of course."

"I expect they could do with modernizing," George said. The railway closed a long time back, but the cottages still stood. The old track was now just a grassy path that had come to be used by walkers and cyclists to reach the nearby villages. "There are a few places in the village that have become run down. It would make a difference if the cottages were improved. Old Reg Lester did a wonderful job with those cottages on the site of the fire, I understand."

I always tried to avoid any talk of the fire. Years ago, a fire had raged through another row of cottages beyond the church. They were slightly off the beaten track, so you would only see them if you went to look for them, a four cottage terrace. They'd belonged to Reg Lester. He'd acquired them at the same time as the manor, and after the fire, he promised to spend whatever it took to put them back together and make them habitable again. They were more than habitable by the time he finished. They went from low-rent housing stock to sought-after rural retreats. It was one of those cottages that Amber was currently residing in.

"They were completely different by the time he'd finished with them," I said. Then it was my turn to change the subject. I started telling George about Moonstones and all the things that went on there at Christmas. By the time I was working my Sunday shift, it would be December. I told George I intended to throw myself into the festivities and hopefully help the residents truly enjoy themselves. It would give me so much pleasure, I insisted.

We'd completed our circuit and arrived back in the village. We stopped.

"I nearly forgot," said George. "Daniel asked me to let you know they have a home game on Thursday night. I told him I didn't think you'd be interested."

"Really? I might go along. I did say I'd try to attend one."

"Well, if you were to go, I would come with you. I hardly ever go these days, and he says no one cares. It's not that. It's just not much fun standing out in the cold on your own for all that time, and the games aren't generally that riveting."

"I'd like to go. What's more, I will ask Belle if Charlie could come along. What time does it start?"

"I think six p.m. But be warned, you must wear your thermals, your warmest coat, a scarf, a hat, and a thick pair of gloves."

We parted company and headed off in different directions. On my way home, I knocked on the Harveys' door. Belle answered. She invited me in, Morsel too, and offered me wine, which I politely turned down. It was late afternoon, and to me, it seemed rather early to be drinking alcohol. Belle obviously didn't think so. She poured a large glass for herself. I asked if it would be convenient for me to take Charlie to the football match on the coming Thursday, that was if Charlie wanted to go. Belle said she was sure Charlie would be delighted at the suggestion and added she was very pleased Charlie had discovered me because, sadly, there was no way she would ever be taking her to something like that.

"We are the most different mother and daughter there's ever been," she declared.

"I'll call in on Thursday, just before five, to collect her. You'll let her know?"

"Of course. I'm sorry, Lucy. Were you hoping I'd come too? I just wouldn't be able to conjure up any enthusiasm, I'm afraid."

"By the way, she must dress up warmly," I said.

"I'll look out her duffle coat. Are you sure you won't stay for a glass of wine?"

"No, thank you. I'm working this evening, you see."

I most certainly hadn't been hoping Belle would come to watch the football team. It hadn't crossed my mind. I would feel awkward in her company, I thought. I supposed I should take notice of her, though. She was effortlessly feminine, with her painted nails and perfectly made-up face. I'd been aware of her perfume as well, probably a well-chosen, famous brand. I was fairly sure she wouldn't have left the house all day, so I had to assume she'd prepared herself in this way purely for her own satisfaction, or perhaps on the off chance that someone might call round. It was baffling to me, but I could learn something from it.

What was I to do about George? I'd like to find out for him if he was right about Helen, but did he really want to know? If I found out she was seeing someone, I wouldn't want to be the one to tell him, but neither would I want to see him made a fool of. Perhaps I'd suggest we go to the inn after the football. It wasn't that I thought we'd find Helen there, but I could check the expressions on the bartenders' faces. Did they know something about Helen? Would it be obvious in the way they behaved with George?

Thursday came. I'd phoned George to tell him I was bringing Charlie, and I'd see him at the ground if he was still planning to go. He said to bring Morsel, and he'd bring Wotnot. We could walk about with them at halftime, and also if the game was boring. Charlie was excited. Belle had at least dressed her up in plenty of layers of warm-looking clothing, although she didn't come to the door to see her off. We walked through the village to the fields beyond the church. There was a good pitch in Steely, thanks to the Lesters. The family had paid for some leveling to be carried out so the team no longer had to play one half of a game uphill and the other half down. They'd put in some lighting and a three-sided wooden shelter which the supporters used in bad weather, not that it helped much in terms of the cold. Even so, the facilities were better than those of most clubs they played against; other teams enjoyed coming to play Steely Green FC. It wasn't a boys' team. Daniel was probably the youngest player. The age range was quite extreme. Though most players were older teenagers, or in their twenties or thirties, at least one was in his sixties.

Charlie and I arrived at the gate. George was on the far side of the field with Wotnot. We waved vigorously and walked round to meet him. We were all dressed according to George's instructions, including Morsel, who wore her knitted coat. Wotnot was in a jacket that looked as though it would be appropriate on a horse, but he was quite a big dog. We greeted each other, and George offered us both a boiled sweet.

"Daniel is on the wing," he told us.

"Do you think he'll score?" Charlie asked.

"Hmm, well, Foxly is a good team, I'm told, but he has scored a few times this season. You never know."

The teams were on the pitch now, and the referee was tossing a coin. I realized not everyone in our team was local, but I recognized a few faces. Martin, the window cleaner, was playing, also a couple of the Cranes and a Hughes.

"Who's in goal?" asked Charlie. "I like to play in goal."

"It's Brian Partridge. I'm not sure if they've ever had a female goalie," George told her. He pretended to kick a ball, and Charlie made a make-believe save. She held the imaginary ball and laughed. She really got George's sense of humor.

The whistle went, and we kicked off. The pitch was quite muddy, and there was a lot of falling over. It looked as though it was going to be a hard game. Charlie was engrossed.

"Come on! Come on, Steely!" she shouted, jumping up and down and waving her arms. "Ah, ref! Come on, Steely! Free kick! Free kick!"

George was impressed with Charlie's enthusiasm.

"If there was a prize for best supporter, she'd get it, wouldn't she? Look at the rest of us, huddled up, hands in pockets."

"Ah no! No! Ref! Come on, Steely!" She stood between us, and whenever Daniel had the ball, she grabbed us both by an arm and went silent. It was as if she was playing for him in her head.

I looked around at the rest of the small gathering: about a dozen fans, stepping from foot to foot to keep warm. Two younger boys were sporadically chanting for Foxly, but they weren't in the same league as Charlie. Half time arrived with the score still at nil-nil. Daniel came to have a quick word.

"Hello, all," he said. "Thanks for coming."

"You're doing well, Daniel," Charlie told him. "I think you'll get them in the second half."

"I hope you're right," he replied, seemingly bemused by the extent of Charlie's football knowledge. "That lad I'm marking's a tough cookie, though. I'm going to have a few bruises to show for my efforts."

He went back to join the rest of the team, and George asked us if we wanted anything from the van. There was a van outside the ground selling hot snacks and drinks.

"I'll surprise you," he said, handing me Wotnot's lead.

"You're a bit of an expert, Charlie," I said. I

needn't have worried about her getting cold, she was all action, and I could tell she was, in fact, probably almost overheating in all those layers.

"It's a good game," she told me seriously.

George returned with three hot dogs and three polystyrene cups full of steaming tea. "I wasn't sure if you'd want tea, Charlie, but it seemed a bit cold for cola."

"Thank you, George. Tea and a hot dog are so perfect."

"Good girl," he said. "Here, Wotnot, you can have this end piece."

The second half was just as muddy and tough. I could see what Daniel had meant about the bruises. There would be twenty plus extremely sore men later. What a way to spend an evening! I tried to keep up. One minute Craney had the ball, and Charlie was shouting to him to kick it to Hughes. Then Foxly tackled and ran off with it. They had a player called Marco, who their young supporters and subs cried out to the whole time. At one point, Daniel was in a heap on the floor, but the ref whistled and finally awarded him a free-kick. The other Crane, known as Crinkle, took it, and the ball went in the direction of the goal. Everyone tried to head it, but everyone missed, and it went out. Charlie groaned. There was a goal kick.

I leaned over to George so that Charlie wouldn't hear. "We could pop to the inn afterward if you wanted, once I've taken Charlie home."

"Yes. I'd like that," he said.

"Get it. Get it, Hughes!" shouted Charlie.

Hughes got it and passed to Daniel, who went on a run. He twisted and turned with the ball. Even I could tell this was good, and soon I was shouting too.

"Go on, Daniel! Go on!"

Daniel stopped and then skillfully crossed into the box. The tall defender, called Davey, headed it in. Charlie, George, and I jumped up and down, and the team ran round celebrating in very professional fashion. Not long after, the final whistle blew. Steely had won, one-nil.

"What a game!" Charlie declared.

Later at the inn, I examined the clientele. It was relatively busy, I thought, though this was the first time I'd ever been inside. George had bought me a glass of red wine, after warning it might not be all that special. He had a pint of bitter in front of him but didn't seem to have much interest in drinking it. The dogs were brought a bowl of water, and they settled down under the table. We talked about the match, how good I thought Daniel had been. George said he'd captained the school team for as long as he could remember.

I analyzed the barman. He was one of the Peters family who'd run the inn for generations. I'd checked his expression for any signs as he served George but not spotted anything. I'd half expected to find Helen in the bar, or Ange, or both, but that didn't happen. George was in a fairly cheery mood, and there'd been no further incidents in terms of Helen in recent days.

The inn became more and more full as the evening progressed. Some of the footballers arrived, fortunately having first gone home to bathe. Martin, Crinkle, and Davey drank at the bar, receiving frequent congratulations from other drinkers. The vicar turned up. I overheard him saying he'd seen the goal from an upstairs window at the vicarage. The doctor turned up and sat with the vicar.

"It's popular here," George said.

"So I see."

"They're a nice family, the Peters. It makes a difference in this sort of business."

"Yes, I'm sure."

"They won the village game this year, remember, the huge food hamper?" George continued.

"Yes, I remember."

"They shared it out with everyone. They gave the best items to the people who could least afford to buy them for themselves."

"That was nice of them." I felt slightly woozy.

"Another?" George asked.

"No, not for me. Shall I buy you one?"

"No, I'm fine."

"I'm not much of a drinking companion tonight," I admitted, "but I'm enjoying the atmosphere."

"A soft drink?"

'No. I'm okay, really.'

Just then, the door clicked, and I noticed Will coming into the bar, Ange's partner. I realized how tall he was. He was tall and willowy. He wore a long coat. I thought back to the night I'd seen Helen leaving the inn with a man. Could it have been Will?

"Hello, Will," George greeted him.

"George! Don't usually see you in here."

"No, we were at the football. You know Lucy, don't you?"

Will went to the bar. He didn't ask after Helen. I would have to go over all the information I was gathering the following day because I knew I'd stopped thinking clearly by that point. I needed to sleep.

In my mind, my life was all about gaining points; it had been that way for a long time. I needed points to trade for the bad things I'd done…and the bad things I was about to do. It was the only way I'd be able to live with myself. That day I'd carried out a few good deeds. Belle, Charlie, and George, Daniel also, would think well of me. During the week, I'd worked hard at Moonstones, and I'd made a plan to put in every effort over Christmas. I'd gone back to my fitness regime, though that was purely for me and my future. I wanted to get on with the other things I had to do but knew I must bide my time. It was important to make sure there was balance. The rewards were going to be enormous, but I had to prepare. I had to play the game expertly and manipulate my way into the ideal position to be able to make off with and properly enjoy the winnings.

Chapter 13
An Unwanted Visitor

Almost a year passed before my first encounter with the Lester boys. I'd seen them on a couple more occasions. During the Christmas holiday, I'd caught sight of them in the back of the big black car as it drove steadily through the village. At Easter, I'd spotted them playing on the riverbank, and a few weeks later, Dad took me with him to the manor. I was going along for the ride. Dad had to meet Reg. I was to stay in the truck. He parked up at the back of the house, and I waited. I wasn't aware of anyone else as I sat patiently, enjoying being at least on the grounds of the magnificent property. Then…

"There's a girl in there," I heard a voice say, and the two boys, Reg's sons, were standing beside the vehicle looking up at me.

"Come and see the fish," one of them said. My heart was beating fast with excitement. I wanted to go with them, but at the same time, I felt apprehensive.

"I'm supposed to stay in the truck," I told him. They looked at each other and laughed, but not in an unkind way.

"No one will mind…and the fish are only just here," the other boy said, and he pointed.

I looked for Dad, but he was inside the manor. I opened the door and jumped down. The boys led the way to the side of the house and down a wide set of steps. I'd never noticed it before, but surrounded by stone pillars and grand containers accommodating tree-size plants, was a pond. Giant-size carp were swimming amongst large-leafed water lilies. The boys knelt and leaned over the edge, peering in. I stood behind them.

"Do you have fish?" asked the bigger boy, glancing back at me for a moment.

"No," I said. "We don't. We're poor people."

The younger boy straightened up. "Algie!" he said. "People don't usually have fish!"

"I didn't know that," said Algie. "I thought maybe they did in the country."

"What's your name?" asked the younger boy, getting to his feet.

"Lucy."

"I'm Nic. He's Algie."

Then Dad was at the side of the building telling me we were leaving. I ran back up the steps and clambered into the cab. I looked out at the boys as we traveled along the driveway, and although Algie was still studying the pond, Nic turned and waved to me as we passed.

****

George and I had left the inn and parted company at the point where my road led off from Broad Street. George would have walked on through the village toward his home. As we approached the cottage, Morsel began to bark. This wasn't normal. I tried to hush her, but she was unusually agitated. There were no street lights, and though I'd left a light on upstairs, it didn't help much. It was a dark evening, and hard to make anything out. I could only think Morsel had spotted a fox. She'd barked at foxes before, and you did see them out at night on occasion, hunting for food, even right in the middle of the village. I restrained her as we approached the gate. Suddenly a dark-clothed figure sprinted out through it and away. It all happened so quickly I hardly took any of it in. I saw very little. I couldn't tell much about the figure. I felt nervous.

"Thank God I have you, Morsel. I mean it."

I went to the door, opened it tentatively, put on the lights, and found a torch. Standing inside, shining the beam out into the garden, I checked every nook and cranny. I inspected the area near the door for anything that had been left or dropped. Nothing had been put through the letter box. After testing the windows—all were tightly sealed—I made my way to the back door and hesitantly examined the rear of the house for anything out of the ordinary. I wasn't drunk, not at all. George and I had only had the one drink each, and though we'd taken our time to finish them, it wasn't late; it wasn't long after nine p.m.

Inside I shut all the curtains but left on the lights. I made a mug of coffee and sat in my chair, listening in case the intruder returned. I racked my brains, trying to think why someone would be in my front garden. Was there a plausible explanation? I couldn't think of one. If they'd been delivering business cards or some such, why run off without leaving anything? Why run off instead of just saying hello and handing me a business card? Perhaps Morsel had startled them? I wondered about that, but it still seemed odd that they would have gone off in quite such a hurry. What if the intrusion wasn't so innocent? I didn't want to think along those lines. I'd only frighten myself even more. I kept Morsel close. She was still disturbed, but by that point, she was probably picking it up from me. Grabbing my notebook, I wrote it all down: how Morsel had reacted, what I could remember seeing, and some of the possible explanations.

A little time passed, and then I opened the front door again and shined my torch around the garden once more, checking under the hedges and over the flower bed. There was no one there. I gradually calmed down. I made another drink and turned up the heating.

My initial thought was that I mustn't tell a soul about the event. At Moonstones, they'd tell me to inform the police. I couldn't do that. The police might start asking questions. I didn't want to draw attention to myself, and if someone was actually intending to frighten me, even do me harm, I had to show I wasn't to be messed with. I had to be strong, but perhaps I should tell somebody in case it happened again and I needed help. George was the obvious choice. If anyone, he'd be the best person to talk to because he was wrapped up in his own predicament and would be unlikely to pay much attention to mine. I could tell him in passing, so that if nothing more, I could call on him to vouch for me, to confirm it had happened.

Before I went to bed, I checked carefully to make sure the exterior doors were both securely locked. I left the light on in the hallway. Morsel was with me. That night I told her several times how lucky I was to have her. In the morning, we would check everything again.

\*\*\*\*

I rose at daybreak and headed straight out to inspect the garden. As I was making breakfast, there was a knock on the door. I nearly jumped out of my skin. It was Charlie. She'd come round before school with some exciting news.

"Lucy, our choir is coming to Moonstones to sing carols."

"Really? That's wonderful news. Do you know when?"

"I can't remember. It's not yet. I think it's on a Saturday."

"I usually work on Saturdays. I expect I'll be there."

"You have to be there!"

"I'll do my best. I promise."

"Hello, Morsel." Morsel put her paws on Charlie's knees, and Charlie bent down to pat her. She received a lick on the nose in return, which made her laugh. "I'm going to school now." She turned and ran away down the path.

"I'll see you soon. Be good," I called after her.

\*\*\*\*

Morsel and I were in the copse when I noticed George walking in our direction.

"Hello, Lucy." He arrived beside us. "Hope you got home safely last night."

"Well, after a fashion."

"How do you mean?"

"Just a silly thing, probably. There seemed to be someone in my garden when I arrived back. They ran off, though, no harm done. You get home, okay?" I was hoping to make my remark a passing comment, but I'd underestimated George's concern.

"Someone in your garden? Doing what? What happened? Have you told the police?"

"Oh no, George. I'm sure it was nothing."

"It doesn't sound like nothing to me," George said. "Tell me exactly what happened."

I explained what I'd seen, trying not to show how frightened I'd felt.

"So you didn't see their face. A burglar, do you think?"

"I have nothing to steal. Why would they choose my place?"

"I do think you should report it. What if they come back?" He added a proviso to the last comment because he could likely see I was worried about that possibility. "They probably wouldn't come back to your cottage, but they might go to other properties."

"I'm not sure it was a burglar."

"Why else would they be there? …Perhaps it was someone who knows you work night shifts? They thought you'd be out." He appeared to have already forgotten about trying not to worry me. He carried on with questions and advice for several more minutes. There was a pause.

"Is everything all right with you?" I asked, trying to move him on.

"Shall I pop round later? I don't like the thought of you being on your own tonight?"

"I'll be fine."

He gave me a doubtful look, before finally beginning to speak about his wife. "Helen. I haven't seen much of her! But her work's keeping her busy at the moment. She was pleased we went to Daniel's match…as was he, of course. Thank you for coming."

"I had a good time, and I'd say Charlie enjoyed herself!"

"What an enchanting child she is."

It was a cold morning. There was frost on the ground. We opted to walk beside the river rather than sit.

"I just don't know with Helen. I listened to your advice. I'm trying to give her space. She'll either prove me wrong or hang herself."

\*\*\*\*

Moonstones was like a refuge to me. I would never have thought it in advance of taking the job, but I felt comfortable there. John and Candy could make me laugh, Joe and Lianne made me feel wanted, and the residents gave me purpose.

"Good morning, Mr. Pickering. Here is your Saturday breakfast."

"Good morning, Lucy. How good it is to see you!"

"There's a boiled egg for you today and toast dippers. Larry thought you'd like a change. He's taken the top off."

"Lovely. Can you sit with me for a few minutes?"

"Yes, I can stay for a little while."

I pulled the table across his chair and arranged his breakfast in front of him.

"There's a new resident," said Mr. Pickering.

"Yes, Agnes," I said.

"She's very nice. I spoke to her yesterday."

"Do you know her from the village?"

"She's not from the village."

"Of course, that's right, she's from Weston Lee. Mr. Pickering, are those new slippers?"

"Yes, Pru bought them for me. Aren't they smart?"

"They are smart, and they look nice and warm." The slippers were in a plaid fabric and had a fleecy lining.

"She sent off for them. She has one of those carrot cards, you know. She sends off for all sorts."

"Credit cards. I have one. They're too easy to use sometimes. I often send for things."

"You'll have to get yourself a pair of these!"

"I will." We both laughed at the thought of me wearing the slippers.

"Agnes," said Mr. Pickering, "I believe she's from Weston Lee."

The Christmas decorations had started going up in the lounge. There was an inordinate amount of tinsel. Joe was bringing in the Christmas tree that afternoon. Lianne had purchased an oversized advent calendar, which was to be opened at lunchtimes. A different resident would open the window each day, and the calendar would be left in their room until the day after. I calculated each resident would get to open at least two windows during the month.

By Sunday, all the decorations were up, the tree looked fabulous, and Larry had made enough mince pies to feed the whole village.

\*\*\*\*

I was back at home, having thoroughly enjoyed my weekend shifts. It was pitch black outside and freezing, and I was trying to take my mind off my intruder. I picked up my notebook and leafed through it again, making a final note about Martin. I crossed him off my list. I was now fully satisfied he was just an ordinary villager. He'd never taken the slightest notice of me. He was on the football team. He'd come to the inn after the match the other night and seemingly enjoyed a good few drinks. He'd sung a few victory songs with the others, and I'd heard him, more than once, describing the goal in great detail to the poor barman. He was loud, but the other players obviously liked him. I concluded that he wasn't suspicious in any way. He might be a bit of a clown, but there was nothing wrong with that.

I'd eaten so many mince pies during the day, I wasn't remotely hungry. I put some food down for Morsel and made a pot of tea. I found a magazine article on travel ideas for the following year and settled down to read it. Having never been anywhere, it would be good to read about the places people liked to go to on their holidays and what they might like to do during their stay. The room was warm and cozy, and the article was lulling. I was imagining being on a sun lounger on a tropical beach. I almost dropped off to sleep but was suddenly brought back to reality and sat bolt upright. I felt sure I'd heard something. I looked at Morsel, but unusually, she continued sleeping. There was another small sound, and my heart began to pound. I pulled down the window blind so it wouldn't be possible for anyone to see into the house, found my long coat, and pulled on a woolen hat. I had selected a large piece of wood—a fallen tree branch—on my walk earlier and brought it home with me. I took it and crept to the front door. There was another rustling sound. I took a deep breath, held the branch high above my head in one hand, and swiftly opened the door with the other. I let out a terrifying yell, expecting to find the dark figure in front of me and planning to clunk him soundly on the head. There was a scream.

"Lucy! Lucy! It's me, Belle!"

"Oh my God, Belle! I'm so sorry! I thought I had an intruder." She looked startled, quite afraid.

"Whatever must you think of me? Please come in."

"I have an invitation for you. I didn't expect you to be in, actually. I thought I'd slip it through the letterbox. It was supposed to be a surprise."

"You did surprise me," I said.

She came in. I'd rarely seen Belle away from her own home. Tonight she reminded me of a comic book heroine. She was slender but big busted and looked sporty in a way. Her long hair fell down in waves as she removed her stylish cap. I wished I had wine to offer her, but I didn't. I could only offer tea, instant coffee, or malted milk, all of which she declined. It turned out it was going to be Charlie's ninth birthday in a few days and she wanted to invite me. Belle handed me the homemade card. Charlie had drawn a skateboard and a dog on the front, and inside it said:

*Come to a party*
*Charlie is nine*

The party was to be on the eleventh of December at the Harveys' house, at four p.m. after school.

"This is so thoughtful, Belle," I said.

"I can make an excuse for you if you like?" She sat down, perching on the edge of a hard chair.

"No, no. I'd like to come," I took a seat at the opposite side of the table, "even if I can't stay for long." I wondered if I was supposed to politely decline. "Would you rather I didn't?"

"Not at all. You're very welcome, of course. But the other parents will drop the kids off and vanish…make the most of the time they'll get to spend without them, while I arrange games for them all."

"Oh."

"I'd like you to come if you can bear it."

She then began to complain about Charlie's dress sense. Belle wanted to buy her a pretty dress for the party, but Charlie wanted to wear her jeans and check shirt as usual. She currently regarded those to be the best items in her wardrobe.

"She sounds a bit like the way I was as a girl, but then I don't suppose you'd want her to end up like me!"

"Why do you say that, Lucy? You make a great role model. She looks up to you, you know."

"I'm not worthy of that, Belle, really I'm not."

"Well, you have a good job. You're kind and caring. Everyone speaks well of you."

I didn't know how to respond to all these compliments, so I talked some more about clothes.

"I had no desire to wear pretty clothes as a girl, but sometimes now, I would love to dress in the most beautiful of garments. Obviously, they wouldn't suit me."

"Don't be silly. Everyone looks fabulous in good clothing," Belle told me. "You only need to see the photos in those society magazines. Well-chosen clothes make the grimmest looking daughters appear acceptable…and you're attractive to start with," she added hastily.

"Will Charlie's father be able to make the party?" I asked.

"I think so, but you never know with him. He has so much work on. He's on a project in the north. It's overrunning, and the bosses are trying to get more and more hours out of everyone. It's good money, but it's not much fun for either of us."

"It seems to be the way these days. If you work, it takes over your life altogether. I'm lucky. At least I love what I do."

"I couldn't have your job. You must have to do some unmentionable things."

"I just love older people. The older they are, the more interesting they are, and I'm happy to do anything for them."

"I suppose no one can live that long without doing a few things worth talking about. But most of them probably can't even remember what they've done!"

"You'd be surprised. If you spend time with them, they relax and remember the most amazing anecdotes."

"And Charlie obviously told you she's coming carol singing. Can you imagine!"

"It will be lovely."

"They'd like the parents to attend. I soon put paid to that idea!"

"Oh, Belle, you should try to come along. It will only be a few carols. "Silent Night," and "Once in Royal David's City", I expect."

She started laughing. "And "We Wish You a Merry Christmas" to end with," she said.

She'd started me giggling, and soon we were both singing.

*"We wish you a merry Christmas,*
*We wish you a merry Christmas,*
*We wish you a merry Christmas*
*And a Happy New Year!"*

"There, I knew you could do it!" I said.

She eventually left. I put my party invitation on display on the mantelpiece in the front room. Belle had been a good deal more friendly than I would have expected. My general impression of her was that she tolerated me because I was helpful but otherwise pretty much ignored me. It was surprising to find she was prepared to go out in the dark and cold to deliver an invitation to me and then come in and spend some time with me, even though I'd tried to bash her over the head with a tree branch. At the same time, I didn't want her, or anyone else, to like me too much because I knew I'd let them down. I realized that a friendship was like a contract. You gave A; they gave B. You asked for C; they asked for D. It worked as long as everyone was happy with that; what they'd given was fair exchange for what they received in return. To me, the whole of life was that way, and I had to keep giving because soon I was going to take so much. I should pull back with some people. Perhaps I could share myself around more. It was fine with work. I could always put in extra effort there because I was paid and no one felt obliged to reciprocate. I could do a lot of additional giving at work. Somehow it was also fine when it came to a child because children weren't expected to give back, even though, as I was beginning to learn, they gave all the time, in a different way, often without knowing.

\*\*\*\*

I had to take a trip into Melstow, and on a whim, I went into Lows, the upmarket hair salon. As I opened the door, I was met by an overwhelming scented air that billowed out warmly. A young man, with bleached, spiky hair and various nuts and bolts in his face, rushed to usher me in and welcome me. How could he help me, he asked. I walked to the counter, very much out of my comfort zone, and spotted the rate cards. I said I just wanted to take one of them, but it was, it seemed, a quiet day, and he was determined to snare me. What was I thinking of having done, a new look, some color perhaps? He'd immediately fetch Darius, a senior stylist who came highly recommended. He'd previously worked in Paris. I could sit down right away and have a consultation with him. I anticipated an exotic Middle Eastern accent, but Darius turned out to be an Australian. He had almost no hair, having pretty much shaved it all off. I wasn't sure that was a good sign. He had tattoos everywhere, some of them patterns, some of them gothic-type hieroglyphics. I began trying to decipher them via the mirror, which made it quite tricky.

"What were you thinking of having done? A whole new look for you?" He ran his fingers through my hair, pulling it this way and that. He was behind me, addressing my reflection as he performed.

"I'm not sure, really."

"You have beautiful hair. Very strong. Very healthy."

"Thank you."

"I would suggest some color. We could lift the tones."

"I've never had color before."

"I would suggest lo-lights. We would bring out the natural shades, make your hair even more glossy." He tugged at it forcefully.

"And if I wanted a cut?"

"A bob, I think. Not too short, sculptured, sophisticated. Ready for all those social occasions, that special Christmas event."

I wondered what he would think if I told him so far, I'd been invited to a ninth birthday party and carol singing at a retirement home. His next appointment arrived, and he graciously handed me back to the first young man, Marcus, who was to book me in. He took my name and number.

"How about tomorrow? Or Thursday?"

"Thursday is better for me."

"Thursday. Let me check Darius's availability. He could do the color at midday, yes, and then the cut straight afterward at two p.m."

"That's a long time, isn't it?"

"I could have you out by three-thirty."

"That's three and a half hours. It seems like a very long time, and I have a dog. I don't think it's going to be possible, sorry." I had made my excuse and was about to charge out of the salon.

"We love dogs. A lot of customers bring them along. We'll make a fuss of him."

"She's a girl, actually."

"Here, I've written it all down for you. See you on Thursday."

I left feeling as though I'd been blindfolded and spun round a number of times. I could always phone and cancel, I told myself.

\*\*\*\*

Night shifts seemed dull with Moonstones decorated and knowing the festivities were in full swing during the daytime hours. I would have preferred to have been working mornings and afternoons, but it wasn't all bad. I kept up my routines with the notebook, the exercises, and the magazine research. I didn't need to fill in the personal achievement pages so regularly; my new standards had become second nature to me. I reduced my entries, deciding to update them weekly rather than daily.

In terms of my village notes, I was at a standstill.

I'd seen nothing of Fergus and little of Amber. There'd been the strange incident at the house with the intruder; I couldn't make sense of that. Nothing seemed to be progressing.

Chapter 14
Hairdo

Charlie's party was the day before my appointment at Lows, which was a shame, but I imagined I didn't really need to impress the nine year olds with my coiffure. I'd managed to get a Steely Green FC football shirt in Charlie's size as a present for her. It had a stitched-on SGFC motif on the front and a large number nine on the back. The team played in purple and white striped shirts. I thought the strip quite attractive. Belle was unlikely to agree, but after all, it was Charlie who was having the birthday.

As soon as I arrived at the house, I developed new respect for Belle. She appeared to have a building full of children, both boys and girls, running, shouting, and pulling at things. Wherever you looked, there was a child. Belle had particularly wanted to have a makeup session for the females, but of course, her daughter was in no way interested in that. She'd gone ahead with it, painting nails with sparkly varnish, putting glitter onto cheeks, applying lip gloss, and plaiting colored twine into hair. Some of the boys wanted to join in. Charlie, and at least two other girls, had chosen to play football in the garden instead. David, Charlie's dad, had organized the latter activity, making use of one of Charlie's birthday presents, a small set of goal posts which he'd erected on the lawn.

"That's a great shirt you've given Charlie," he said. It was the first time I'd seen him with her, and I realized he adored the fact that his little girl was a skateboarding footballer who dressed like a lumberjack. "She's told me over and over how much she loved going to watch Steely Green play. I'd like to come with you next time I'm home. I want to meet George and the dogs too."

Later we were offered all sorts of party food, and I stayed long enough to enjoy a slice of the overdecorated cake Belle had slaved over before saying my goodbyes and heading back to the cottage to get ready for work. The children were hopefully going to settle down and watch a film together. Belle was relieved that holding the party on Charlie's actual birthday, a weekday, meant she'd got away without having to accommodate a sleepover.

****

Going to Lows was a quite ridiculous experience. I tried to imagine how people did this on a regular basis. On arrival, the pirouetting Marcus ushered me in before another extremely young-looking assistant proceeded to undress me and help me into a large gown, fussing over Morsel all the while. He took me to a seat to await the grand entrance of Darius. I sat considering my reflection and thought that, in fact, I didn't look too awful. I had lost weight. My face had changed; it was somehow more animated, the features were stronger, and I was getting better at putting on makeup. The daily walks had improved my complexion. I suddenly felt quite confident. Darius greeted me, checked if I'd had any after thoughts about style or if I wished to continue as discussed. He went off to mix up his concoctions, and soon he was wrapping me up in tin foil, the young assistant constantly asking if he could bring me drinks or reading matter. A few other customers came in during the process. I observed them via the various mirrors and listened in to their conversations about work, holidays, and a pop-up shop that had opened nearby. It was fascinating.

At the stage where the color had to be given time to do its work, I felt sure there was a moment to bring Morsel onto my lap and allow her to view herself in the mirror, but another assistant materialized. I wasn't ever left to sit. The latest assistant, a girl, who had a particularly intriguing hairstyle even for Lows, asked if I would like a shoulder massage, then a manicure. I went along with everything. The appointment continued. Some hours later, after coffee, herbal tea, magazines, the manicure, the massage, lo-lights, hi-lights, and various hair enhancing treatments, to name but some of my experiences, I was finally set free again. I'd spent pretty much a week's wages but had emerged a different woman, the type who wouldn't be seen out unless they'd recently attended a high-end hair salon. I had to admit, my new style looked impressive. I hoped I could stay in touch with my earlier confidence and manage to carry it off.

During the coming days, the makeover encouraged me to experiment a little more with my wardrobe. I received a good number of compliments and thought I noticed people I didn't know looking at me in an admiring manner. It wasn't what I was used to. People were giving me more respect than I normally received. How strange! Could a hairstyle really be so powerful?

Sunday brought plenty of positive comments. Miss

Pickering told me I looked as though I could be in a film.

"Do you remember when the film stars came to the manor?" she asked me. "I was telling Nathan about it the other day. He rang to see how we were."

"I remember hearing about it. I'm not sure I can remember it, though."

Candy joined in. "I remember! They had an open-top car, and they drove around the village. They went into the shops and chatted away to quite a few of the locals."

"It was an American actor and his Canadian co-star," said Miss Pickering. "I was working at the manor at the time. We had to order in extra cases of wine, and Reg hired a chef for the weekend. He thought the staff might be put out, but we weren't; we were glad of the help. The chef brought along several assistants, and they cooked huge roasts and special sea food dishes. The co-star hardly ate at all, of course," Miss Pickering looked at me and nodded. "She was watching her figure."

I wasn't sure if Miss Pickering was implying she thought that was what I was doing.

"I couldn't be bothered with that," I said, not wanting people to think I was purposely dieting. A gradual, inconspicuous transformation was what I was after. "I'd rather wear a bigger skirt."

Candy laughed. "Yes, me too, especially if I had my own special chef."

"There was an enormous party, a lot of drinking…and I mean a lot," Miss Pickering continued. "Someone woke up in one of the flower borders the next morning. I can't quite remember who."

Mr. Pickering had been dozing. He came round at this point and could make neither head nor tail of the conversation.

"Was that at Moonstones?" he asked.

"No, Bob," Pru said. "Now, that really would be a story, wouldn't it?"

"We'd better make sure Bert doesn't overdo it with his sherry," Candy said.

\*\*\*\*

George turned up on my doorstep in the evening. Helen had gone to Ange's, and I could tell he needed company. He'd brought a shopping bag full of drinks, crisps, nuts, and chocolate.

"I thought I'd come and make sure you'd not had any more strangers in your garden," he said. "And to be honest, I was hoping you might invite me in."

"It's nice to see you. Come in, come in."

"I've brought some plonk."

"Lovely. I'll find some glasses. Is Wotnot all right?"

"Daniel's in the house for a change. He has a stack of homework to do, but he'll keep an eye on the canine one. Your hair looks very nice indeed."

"Thank you. It took forever to achieve, I can tell you."

"It suits you. You look rather glamorous, might I say?"

I dug out a cork screw and a couple of glasses. George poured wine generously into them. He took two large gulps from his and topped it up before sitting down in my armchair. I looked through the snacks and transferred them into a selection of bowls. I sat on one of the hard chairs and tucked into some coated peanuts.

"I just wanted some company. These days Helen is either at work or at Ange's. She never spends any time with me. I just wanted to sit with someone. I thought you might enjoy that sort of an evening too?"

"Yes, I think I would."

"I can't get over your hair. It's sort of transformed you. Tell me more about yourself, Lucy. I sometimes feel I don't know much about you at all."

"Nothing to tell, George. My life has been very uneventful."

"That I find hard to believe."

I tried to think of something interesting I could tell George about my life. He finished his wine and poured more for himself. I told him my dad had been a painter and decorator. George started telling me about his ancestry and the area where he'd grown up. I put the television on in the background. A black and white film we'd both seen many times was on, and now and then, one of us commented on the scene, or the actor, or the costume. We both seemed to be enjoying the wine. We opened a second bottle. George had brought four.

George said Helen remembered me being quiet at school. She'd told him I was good at drawing.

"I was a quiet child, I suppose. I had one close friend."

"Is she still living here?"

"No. My family left the village, and my friend's family also moved away."

"I was of the impression that no one ever left Steely!"

I think I was drinking too freely. I knew I was saying more than I should. It was only George I was talking to, but I still needed to be careful. Tonight I'd spoken about Rosamund, though I'd not named her. I'd always promised myself I would never speak about her, not to anyone.

Rosamund was the most delightful person there ever had been. She was a slightly plump, freckled, red-headed girl. She and I soon found each other at school. We had many things in common. We didn't belong to the popular group of children, or the clever group, or the group who were good at sport. Both Rosamund and I were made fun of by the others; we were ignored by the teachers; we immediately became friends. We liked to paint and draw. We enjoyed making things. Soon we began spending time together outside of school as well. Like me, she was an only child. She lived with her parents in an old house on the edge of the village. They had a sort of small holding. I loved going there. The family kept pigs and chickens, and they had a collie dog and a cat that frequently gave birth to kittens. Unlike our house, where everything had a place, and things were cleaned before they were ever dirty, Rosamund's house was a ramshackle place; the rooms were untidy and cluttered but homely. Rosamund's mum would always have something baking in her old range oven, and we were regularly offered items that emerged, slices of warm buttered bread or piping hot scones.

George was pressing me with more and more questions. Did I keep in touch with my friend? Was I not tempted to look her up on the internet, visit her, arrange to meet her for a drink? I told him it was many years since I'd seen her.

"I don't remember this scene," George said. He was squinting at the television.

"I think this is a different film. The other one

finished a while back."

"Am I outstaying my welcome? Do you need to get to bed?"

"No, it's fine. I don't have to work again until tomorrow night."

"Shall I pop out for fish and chips?" he said.

"I am a little hungry, come to think of it. Will they still be open? We could both go."

We somehow wobbled to the chip shop. Not long after, we embarked upon the last bottle of wine. We'd managed to eat all the food even though we'd been alarmed by how much we'd ordered.

"It's a long time since I've enjoyed an evening as much as this," George told me when he finally decided he should be getting home.

The following day, I wondered if he had been hoping to arrive home later than Helen and that she might have been questioning where he'd been all evening.

\*\*\*\*

During the week, I kept thinking about Fergus and Amber. Was there anything I was missing? Was I wrong about them? Was I wrong about the whole situation? I had to be patient, but I didn't want to wait forever; I wanted something to happen.

\*\*\*\*

Rosamund and I weren't like the other children. We were aware of that, but it didn't bother us. We had a string of pastimes we shared a love of. We enjoyed doing jigsaw puzzles, often having one on the go at my house. We liked larger puzzles most of all, ones that had a lot of pieces and were hard to complete. Whenever there was a school sale or a church fete, we'd use our pocket money to buy any second-hand jigsaws which had been donated. There always seemed to be a few, although sometimes several pieces could be missing. That didn't bother Rosamund, who simply made new pieces to fill the gaps. We both liked to knit. We each knitted a jumper when we were at quite a young age, mine a plain color and in a thick yarn, but Rosamund's with a pattern, in different color wools and incorporating various stitches. We liked to sew and taught ourselves to crochet. We loved to make things, and we adored drawing and painting. Rosamund was especially talented when it came to painting. I marveled at some of the pictures she produced. However, for some reason, at school, she could never paint or draw or show off any of her talents so well and was generally labeled as a complete non achiever right from the start.

\*\*\*\*

Christmas was getting closer. I bought a few items as presents in case I was suddenly expected to provide somebody with a gift. I chose some nicely packaged bath foams, some small tins of expensive biscuits, and a number of packs of novelty socks. I bought something for Ethel, who was to be the recipient of my Secret Santa present.

I'd tried to forget about Rosamund, but George had brought her back into my thoughts. I kept seeing her angelic smile. She was a girl with no bad bone in her body or bad thought in her head. She was kind to everyone, adored all animals, and loved the countryside. She was concerned for every being she encountered. She would be fastidious in freeing any wasp or fly that came into the house; she mused over the spiders that she found in the garden and rescued snails that strayed onto the path. She was the sort of person who felt pain for hours if she came across a sick animal or, heaven forbid, one that had been killed, perhaps run over.

"Lucy, Lucy!" Miss Pickering shouted to me, but in a voice I knew meant she wanted to tell me something in confidence.

I'd popped into Moonstones to leave my Christmas cards. The Pickerings were in the lounge. Apart from the two of them, only Agnes and Lolly were in the room, and they were engrossed in a drama on the television. They had the volume turned right up and were oblivious to any other goings-on.

"Hello, Miss Pickering. How are you, Mr. Pickering?" I said.

Miss Pickering could hardly contain herself. She beckoned me closer. "I've heard a rumor about the will. You'll never believe it!"

"About the will," Mr. Pickering repeated, nodding his head.

"Really? Is it something very unlikely?" I asked.

"I'd say so. I'm taking it with a pinch of salt."

I thought I might be wrong, but I hoped I knew what the rumor was going to be. "Who did you hear it from?" I asked.

"Can't tell you," she said. I didn't know if she was being serious or if she was teasing, but that information would be equally as interesting from my point of view. "Well, do you want to hear it?"

"Yes, I can't wait," I said.

"You mustn't pass it on."

"I won't tell a soul, I promise." I did wonder if, by the end of the afternoon, she would have told everyone she came into contact with.

"They say someone from the village is mentioned in the will."

I crouched down beside her. "What does that mean, do you think?"

"They'll get something, perhaps money."

"But you don't know who, or what?"

"No, I keep trying to think."

"Well, it is a rumor, as you say, and you also said you were taking it with a pinch of salt."

"It might not be true, but I have a feeling there's something in it. I heard it from a reliable source." Miss Pickering sounded convinced.

I tried a different angle with my question. "Was it someone here who told you? Someone at Moonstones?"

"Heavens no! No one here would know about something like this."

"Miss Pickering, you'll have me thinking about that all evening now!" I said.

"Isn't it exciting?" she said.

"I suppose in one way it is," I agreed.

"Are you going again, Lucy?" Mr. Pickering asked.

"Yes, I'm on the night shift later. I won't see you properly until the weekend. Don't forget, on Saturday, the school children are coming to sing carols."

"How lovely," said Mr. Pickering. Miss Pickering wasn't listening; she was far away in her thoughts.

Chapter 15
Carols

Forty-eight hours later, I still had the headache that followed my drinking session with George. I didn't feel too guilty about it. He'd instigated it; I'd just gone along with him. It could be seen as a good deed in a way; he'd needed someone to help him let his hair down, and I'd happened to be the best bet to join in with him that night. When I thought about it, although George was clever, kind, and very good company, he didn't seem to have many friends. At the same time, I imagined that was how he liked things. It had also occurred to me that he probably preferred the company of women. George should have a daughter, I thought. Though he got on with Daniel, I was sure he would have loved to have had a girl in the family. Then again, Belle would have liked to have had a girly daughter. It demonstrated that you really couldn't choose, and though you could nurture, children did seem to have an uncanny knack of becoming exactly what you hadn't anticipated.

That day I made a sort of breakthrough. We were walking beside the river, Morsel and I, when I spotted a woman coming toward us. She was wrapped up in a warm-looking jacket, her face partly covered by a scarf. I spoke as we passed, just a polite 'good morning.' Her eyes darted in my direction, but she didn't respond. She strode on, her hands pushed deep into her pockets, her stylish walking boots appearing large on the ends of her slim legs.

As we continued along the track, it suddenly came to me who it was that we'd just encountered. It was Vicky Lester. We'd walked on several hundred yards, but I turned in time to see her disappearing into the copse. She was headed for the village. I called Morsel, and we made our way briskly to the bridge and crossed over so that we could take the path that wound round and led to the far end of Broad Street. I was determined to find out where Vicky was going and who she might be meeting, but I couldn't follow her too obviously. I took the route and stepped into the village, reminding myself I was out with my dog as usual, that I must keep calm and behave naturally. I doubted Vicky would recognize me, and even if she did, there was nothing wrong with my being seen out walking Morsel.

There was a conveniently situated antique shop on the corner of Broad Street and South Street. I stood as if looking at the items displayed in the windows. From there, I could see right along the main street in both directions. I felt sure I would see Vicky again.

"Hello, Lucy." Helen emerged out of nowhere.

"Oh, hello, Helen."

"I didn't know you were interested in antiques?"

"Um, I'm not, really. Well, I do like antique items, but I don't know much about them."

"You've been leading George astray, I hear."

I think I blushed. "No. We had a glass of wine or two, that's all."

"I'm joking, Lucy. You're so serious sometimes! I think it did him good. He's never been able to relax, you know."

"Oh, I see, sorry. I rarely drink much, and George doesn't overdo it, does he? I don't know what got into us that night."

"Letting off steam, maybe. He's seemed stressed lately, not himself. I must go. I have work. Call round any time."

"Thank you. Goodbye then."

Helen had taken me by surprise, and I felt I'd missed my chance of another sighting of Vicky Lester. I started toward home. I thought about popping in to see Linda. She liked a chat, and lately, she always gave the impression she was pleased to see me. I was about to cross the road. Almost without thinking, I glanced over to the café. She was in there, Vicky Lester. And I was sure she was talking to Amber. At that moment, I spotted Jenny entering the café. This could all work in my favor.

I weighed things up and made a swift decision. I crossed the road and calmly walked past the newsagent's and on along in the direction of the cottage. My behavior was completely normal. What was pleasing me was that I felt I would be able to follow up on this situation, and it might provide valuable information; I would find Jenny in the next day or so and interrogate her.

****

We gathered in the lounge on Saturday afternoon. I'd finished my shift but was more than happy to stay for the carols. The children were arriving at three p.m. We arranged the furniture accordingly, making sure there was room for the choir to stand beside the piano, facing the residents and visitors. The Christmas tree lights were turned on, and the whole room looked fittingly festive. Two teachers, who were accompanying the group, arrived nice and early. As the children came in, they were helped out of their coats, and we could see that each was wearing a special Christmas jumper. I caught Charlie's eye and gave her a wave. A few mums and one dad had come along; I helped show them to seats. The newly arrived adults were in good spirits and greeted the residents with friendly smiles. Soon, one teacher sat down at the piano, and the other, a tall man with fashionable glasses, stood out in front of the children. Joe gave him the signal, which meant the afternoon could get underway, and the teacher took over.

"Good afternoon, Moonstones," he said. "My name is Mr. Harrison."

"Good afternoon, Mr. Harrison," we said rhythmically, as if we had all returned to education. He then turned to face the choir, and there was some final shuffling. Mrs. Baker played an introduction on the keys, and Mr. Harrison started to conduct with flamboyance.

"God rest ye Merry Gentlemen..." the children began. It wasn't a carol I was expecting; I thought it seemed quite an ambitious choice. The children, however, were well-practiced and sang beautifully. After the last verse, Mrs. Baker went round the room with some song sheets and invited everyone to join in. We had "Silent Night" next, and then "Away in a Manger," which we were warned would include a verse performed by a soloist so that we didn't ruin it.

I was sitting between Molly and Mrs. Roberts. It pleased me that Molly was able to hum to the tunes and was definitely getting some satisfaction from the afternoon's arrangements. She even knew one or two words, though was late with her timing on occasion. She moved both arms up and down as Mrs. Baker played. Every resident was in the lounge. Barbara and Mariana were on duty and had managed to persuade Mrs. Cook to come in at the last minute. It looked as though she was thoroughly enjoying herself.

Being so engrossed in the occasion, I didn't see the person who'd arrived behind me and was squeezing my shoulder. It was Belle.

"Belle, it's so good to see you here!" She sat down behind me.

"I've come especially for "We Wish You a Merry Christmas," " she whispered.

She wasn't disappointed, and we glanced at each other and tried not to laugh when Mr. Harrison announced it and Mrs. Baker began to play.

Afterward, there was time to mingle. John had laid on some drinks and snacks for the children: chocolate brownies, cheese straws, and jugs of bright-colored squash, which clinked with sparkling ice cubes as he carried them in. He proclaimed that singing was a hot business. Barbara circuited the room, offering tea and biscuits to everyone else.

Charlie came to find Belle and me. "Hello, Lucy. Hello, Mum. I didn't think you were coming!"

"You were brilliant. I really enjoyed that," I said.

I could tell Belle was proud of her daughter.

"Would you like to meet some of the residents?" I asked Charlie. I took her over to Mr. Pickering, who was with his sister unsurprisingly, and also Bert.

"This is Charlie," I told them. They melted. She

asked them if they'd liked the singing.

"Very much, very much," said Mr. Pickering.

"Could you come every day?" asked Bert.

Charlie laughed. Miss Pickering asked how long they'd been practicing and if they were going to perform anywhere else. Belle looked on as, with ease, Charlie charmed anyone who crossed her path.

We left together, Belle and I walking quickly in the chill afternoon air, Charlie skipping along between us, the daylight already dimming. Belle was dressed in long white boots with mock fur tops, close-fitting black trousers, and a mid-length white coat with a wispy mock fur collar. Her long hair had been wrapped up in a white hat with side flaps and more wispy fur.

"Your hair looks fabulous," she told me.

"Thank you. Are you sure?"

"Yes. It's very you. Did you go to Lows?"

"Yes."

"The best we have in the area. Darius?"

"Yes. How did you know?"

"He's very good."

Charlie looked at me. "Lucy's always had nice hair," she said.

"I know Charlie, but it's even nicer now." Belle suddenly turned her head. She looked back over her shoulder, and I sensed something in the way she moved.

"What is it?" I asked.

She didn't answer but grasped my arm above the elbow and increased the walking pace. Charlie was a few steps in front of us. The light had all but gone.

"Come to the house for a drink," she said.

"I have to get back to Morsel. I left her at home

today."

"We'll collect her on the way."

"All right. Thank you."

\*\*\*\*

Belle sent Charlie to the fridge to decide what she'd like for her tea. Morsel went with her.

"I had the feeling someone was behind us on the way down the hill," she said. "I didn't want to say in front of Charlie."

"How do you mean?" I asked.

"Following us," she said more loudly.

"What made you think that? Perhaps it was another parent…or one of the teachers?"

"I could feel a presence."

"You didn't see anything?"

"Not exactly. I turned quickly…you noticed me turn. It was as if someone slipped into the shadows."

I immediately thought of the intruder, but I didn't want Belle to be alarmed, so I said, "Why would someone follow us?"

"I'm not sure. No reason I can think of. Maybe it was just my imagination." She poured out two glasses of wine.

I felt uneasy going home, but Morsel would sense if anything was wrong. I could tell that evening she was nothing more than hungry. She couldn't wait to get inside. There was no sign of anything out of the ordinary, but I still made doubly sure both doors were locked. I put on all the lights, pulled the blind, and drew the curtains.

I realized I was becoming a person who liked to talk to others, who no longer wanted a completely solitary existence. I very much wanted to share what was on my mind, but I didn't feel I could. For a while, I sat in my chair, a magazine open on my lap but my mind exploring what it might be like to tell somebody everything. I imagined telling Belle or George, or perhaps Candy or Jenny, even Miss Pickering. Was there anyone I could confide in? What about Lianne? She'd always been extremely nice to me. Momentarily, I felt comfort, but then I imagined the reaction I would get. Whoever I told, if ever I found the courage, their reaction would destroy me. They would find out the truth about me, and then they would be bound to intensely dislike me. They would realize why I lived alone, that there was a reason why I tried to give the impression of being a nice person, and they'd see it was all an act. However long I lived and however many good things I did, I would never be exonerated. Everyone I'd encountered would turn their back on me, and any friendships I thought I'd built up would straight away vanish.

So who was it that had been informing Miss Pickering, and did they really know anything at all? I found my notebook. Recently I had made very few entries. I thought and thought about who Miss Pickering could know that may have connections with the Lesters. Of course, she knew the Lesters themselves, but I was sure they wouldn't be idly chatting to her about Reg's will. She must know people who'd worked at the manor, possibly even still worked at the manor. As far as I knew, the Cranes still did all the gardening, but apart from that, nowadays I understood, the rest of the staff were not from the village. If Vicky had a housekeeper, or a cook, or a cleaner, she must have employed them from elsewhere.

Algie must have nurses or carers, but again I'd not heard of anybody local to the area who was employed to carry out those duties. In terms of Miss Pickering's informer, I felt sure it had to be a local person. Therefore, I concluded, it must be a Crane. Then it struck me that a Crane could be informing someone else who in turn had informed Miss Pickering. If that was the case, it could be anyone. Putting down my pen, I started thinking about Belle's stalker. Had someone been following us that evening? If so, who? Was it me they were following? Who was my intruder? Was it one and the same person? Belle didn't come across as the nervous type. I felt sure nothing would have made her think there was someone on our tail unless there was indeed a person pursuing us.

Chapter 16
The Rumor Grows

I had it in mind to find Fergus. I'd walked past the B&B a few times but was fairly sure there were no guests staying. The *No Vacancies* sign was up, and the whole place looked particularly quiet. There was only one car parked on the driveway in front of the house, and I recognized it to be the one that belonged to the owners. I'd asked Linda about possible projects going on locally: construction work, forestry work, road improvements. She couldn't think of anything.

Sunday at Moonstones had been even better than usual. Lianne had summoned me and asked if I'd go back to working day shifts throughout Christmas and New Year. She'd like me to swap back to daytime hours straight away. She said she wanted to make sure to maintain a caring, warm atmosphere and that I had the skills required for this; all the residents loved me, she said. It was more evidence that I was achieving my goals. Lianne would make sure I still had Thursdays and Fridays off because she thought it only fair, and I may already have made plans. Joe would cover some of the nights. Jackie was happy to do additional shifts, and agency staff would be brought in where necessary.

I had treated myself to a few new items for my wardrobe and decided I would make an effort to look my very best over the festive period. Back on day shifts, I rose early to walk Morsel. I was soon in the copse, and there was Fergus. I supposed it had been on my early walks that I used to bump into him. It could be why I'd not come across him for some time.

"Hello, Lucy."

"Hello, Fergus. Are you well?"

"Yes, I am, thank you. I've not seen you recently. Have you done something with your hair?"

"I've been working all sorts of shifts." I analyzed his physique and height. Could he possibly have been my intruder?

"The village is looking well, with the Christmas lights and all," he said.

"Yes, they make an effort. The councilors…and the church committee do a lot." I concluded that he was the wrong shape. I was convinced the intruder was slimmer.

"I didn't need that accommodation in the end. I managed to work something out."

"That's good. I'm pleased to hear it."

"I better let you get on." He turned to follow Bones, who was snuffling amongst the leaves farther into the copse. Then an afterthought came to him, it seemed. "Who's the young lady who works in the café, Lucy?"

Why did he want to know about her? "You mean Amber, I think."

"Amber," he repeated as if fitting her dreamy name to her image.

"Yes." I deduced it was simply that he found her attractive. He walked away without another comment.

Next thing, Jenny appeared. "Good morning, stranger," she said.

"Yes, stranger indeed. We've been missing each other recently or avoiding each other!"

"It's been work, work, work for me lately, but the holidays are coming. I can't wait."

"I think I saw you going into the café a couple of days back," I said. "I was too far off to speak. Vicky Lester was in there."

"You're right. I was in there at the same time as her. She doesn't venture into the village very often, does she? Caused a bit of a stir…the way a Lester in the village tends to do."

"I've never seen her on Broad Street before. I was out with Morsel and found myself walking behind her. She was coming along the riverbank." Wesley was anxious for his ball. He moved it closer and closer to Jenny with his nose so she could throw it. She bent to pick it up. "Was she just buying cakes?"

"Yes, I think so. She was in front of me. She was buying something, bread or cakes, I suppose." She threw the ball.

"That seems odd, doesn't it?" I said.

"I'm not sure, does it?"

"Was she talking to Amber?"

"Not that I noticed. I mean, Amber was serving her, I think."

"I wondered if they were friends," I said. I was probably pushing the conversation further than I should, but Jenny didn't appear to think I was saying anything out of the ordinary.

"It didn't come across that way to me." Wesley was back with the ball already.

"Did you see Fergus just then? He was asking after Amber."

"Fergus?" She looked at me. "Who's Fergus?"

"Fergus. You know. Fergus…with Bones."

"I don't think I do."

"You must. He's often here with Bones. Bones is the white bull dog."

"No, I don't remember meeting them." She threw the ball again. "You've heard the rumor, I imagine?"

"About…?" I started to query, but Jenny was already telling me.

"About the manor. About the will."

"People at Moonstones were talking about some rumor at the weekend."

"Well, I've heard part of Reg's estate is left to someone from the village."

"Where did this rumor come from? Do you know?"

"I didn't think about that. It was Malcolm who heard it—at school, I suppose."

"I'd love to know where it started. The contesting of the will has been going on for some time, it seems to me?"

"It's probably wishful thinking. I like the idea, though, and I wouldn't put something like that past him, old Reg." I didn't speak, but Jenny had a few more thoughts to share. "I wonder if the rumor's actually come from the solicitor. Perhaps they've said something, and it's been overheard? They might have been talking on a mobile phone?" I nodded. "Perhaps one of the Cranes heard something. They're up at the manor a good deal, aren't they, handyman, gardener, etcetera. All those jobs are done by one Crane or another."

"Perhaps," I said.

Poor Wesley was waiting patiently for his ball

again. I picked it up and threw it a good distance.

"I expect if there's any truth in it, if anyone from the village were to be in the will, it would be a Crane," said Jenny, sounding disappointed.

"I expect so," I said

She looked as though she were about to leave. "You must come to our drinks, Lucy. We usually have people round for drinks just before Christmas. On the twenty-third this year. Starting early afternoon. Come any time."

"I think I'll be working, Jenny. I'd love to have come."

"Come after work? We'll still be there, I'm sure…and later on, we'll probably be in need of an injection of fresh conversation!"

"In that case, I will come. Thank you."

"You don't need to bring anything, just yourself. See you anon."

She strode off. I bent to tickle Morsel and decided to take her on across the common and mull everything over.

Things had begun to happen. It was what I'd wished for, but I could make neither head nor tail of any of it. I thought hard about the rumor. Where had it come from? Was someone leaking it into the village for a purpose, and if so, who…and why? Was there truth in the rumor? Of course, I thought the answer to that was yes. The last thing I'd written in my notebook was a sudden thought I'd had about Amber. Things had been churning round in my head, and I began wondering if Amber could actually be a Lester. It might sound unlikely, but she was staying in one of the cottages at Hedge End, and I was sure they were still owned by the family. I couldn't help wondering if she had some connection. She might be Reg's secret love child or a stepdaughter, the offspring of one of Reg's various lesser-known partners. That's why Vicky was in the café. She and Amber were acquainted. Amber was to inherit something from the will, and Vicky was angry about it...or Vicky was pleased about it and wanted to support Amber at the expense of some other family member. On the other hand, I still thought Amber might be a plant set up in the village with the task of monitoring me.

I mustn't forget about my other suspect, Fergus. I still couldn't make him out. Was he, like Martin, nothing to do with anything? Had he been brought to Steely for some specific, justifiable reason connected with his work, whatever that work might be? If that was the case, why hadn't anyone else come across him? It seemed to me he must be making an effort not to encounter them. I couldn't imagine how you could go to the copse and the common on a regular basis and not meet anyone unless you were purposely keeping out of sight. If that was the case, the next logical question became, why had I seen him? Was the answer that he was looking out for me?

If a rumor was purposely being passed around, more people would be bound to have heard it. I decided to see how many villagers would tell me about it in the coming days. I would put myself in a position receptive to rumors. Could I somehow find out where this one had originated?

****

Every day at Moonstones brought another event. There was such a cheerful atmosphere, and everyone was picking up on it. The residents were all smiles, the staff was bubbly and talkative, and Joe and Lianne expertly steered the ship, encouraging us all and putting in a good amount of extra effort themselves. On the weekend before Christmas, Joe planned to take those who wanted to go along to the local carol service. I volunteered to attend and provide help where required. Lianne was busy online shopping for residents who wished to purchase gifts for family and friends. She'd bought rolls and rolls of wrapping paper and a collection of padded envelopes. Joe was on call to take packages to the post office on a daily basis. Lianne had arranged for charity Christmas card sellers to come in and set up in the lounge on a couple of occasions. We'd had the school choir, and a nativity play was to be put on by the Melstow Cub Scouts. On top of all that, there were the usual exercise sessions, the regular weekly afternoon sing-alongs, and a bridge afternoon was starting up, a new venture which could become a regular thing if it took off. Moonstones seemed more like a holiday camp than a retirement home.

"Hello, Bert. Hello, Lionel, Ethel, Marcia. How are you all?" I'd gone to chat with the residents I'd found in the lounge. "Who's turn was it to open the advent calendar today?"

"It was mine," Ethel told me. "A shepherd with a darling lamb."

"Ah, how lovely."

"My turn tomorrow," said Lionel.

"You look very nice today, Lucy," said Bert.

"Leave her alone, Bert." Marcia gave him a shove. "She's not interested in you!"

Everyone laughed.

"We'll have a dance at Christmas, won't we, Lucy?" Bert said. He winked mischievously.

"Yes, Bert, and I'll look forward to it."

Molly was in the corridor, just popping to the shops. I greeted her, and she offered me a toothless grin. I went to find Lianne, who was in the office surrounded by paperwork.

"Can I help with something?" I asked. "The residents are happy at the moment."

"No, I'm fine. It may look untidy in here, but I have my own way of doing things!"

"Shall I bring you a cup of tea?" I sat down opposite Lianne and watched her going through documents, entering things onto the computer.

"I'd love one, but don't make one especially. I'll have a cup when you're making one for the residents."

"I'll leave you to it then." I was hoping Lianne would drink tea with me, and we'd chat. If she'd heard the rumor, she'd tell me about it. Surely she or Joe would have heard it by now.

John was on duty.

"What are you wearing to the party?" he asked me.

"Moonstones party?"

"Of course! It's the only one that matters!"

"Well, I'll have to make an effort because Bert and I are going to dance."

"Wonderful, and I hope to also have the pleasure."

"I'm not sure my wardrobe is going to be adequate."

The party was to be in the afternoon on Christmas Eve. Then, on Christmas Day, I was told, everyone, as far as was possible, would spend the day in the lounge. There would be the exchanging of presents followed by

Christmas lunch, the Queen's speech, games, and then Christmas tea.

I arrived back in the office with tea and biscuits for Lianne. I brought mine with me too and sat down.

"I had something to tell you," said Lianne. "What was it now?" She was still grappling with disorderly piles of paperwork. I was convinced she wanted to tell me about the rumor, but what she said pleased me very much. "I was thinking about poor Morsel," she said. "She must be lonely now that you're working all these day shifts. I had a word with Joe, and we think you could bring her in with you over Christmas. She can stay in the office here, can't she, like she does at night?"

"Oh, Lianne, thank you! She's so good. She never complains, but it would be lovely if she were here and I could keep an eye on her."

"Don't think I don't notice how you get carried away and frequently forget to go home on time." She wagged a finger at me. "I'm not expecting you to cover any extra hours, but at least you won't be worried about her, and you won't have to dash home in the cold for the Morsel breaks."

"Thank you, Lianne."

I returned to the kitchen. I'd heard no rumor from Lianne and no rumor from John. I was certain if either had heard it, they'd have passed it on. Mariana was on the shift with me. She was one member of staff I didn't know that well. She was somewhat reserved, and probably not the type to be gossiping. I enjoyed working alongside her, though. She was diligent in her duties. Every time I went to do something, she seemed to have beaten me to it.

The afternoon rolled on, and it being a weekday, few visitors showed up. There was no sight of Miss Pickering. A friend of Lolly's was with her in her room, and someone dropped by briefly to see Mrs. Cook. Otherwise, all was quiet.

I checked on each resident, asked if they would like their tea and sandwiches in the lounge. Mr. Pickering was a little low and wanted his brought to his room.

"Is everything all right, Mr. P?" I asked.

"I can't complain. But the day always seems rather long when Pru doesn't come."

"Bert's in the lounge with a few others. You could join them for a chat."

"I don't think I will today, Lucy."

"I'm sure your sister will come tomorrow?"

"I think she's been busy."

"Everyone has extra chores at this time of year. She'll have all the more to tell you when she sees you."

"Yes." He smiled bravely, but he wasn't himself.

"Is there anything I can get you, Mr. P? Would you like to look at the newspaper or the TV listings? The Christmas magazine has arrived."

"No, Lucy. I'll just look forward to the sandwiches."

Mariana informed me, that unlike Mr. Pickering, the residents in the lounge were buoyant. Agnes and Mrs. Roberts had joined the others. They'd put the television on loudly and were shouting to each other over the top of it.

\*\*\*\*

Belle called me in the evening. She asked if I'd come round for a cuppa. She was bound to be going to tell me the rumor. I dashed round straight away.

"I have a favor to ask," she said. "I was wondering if you're working on Friday?"

"No. I'm off."

"It's a real imposition, but I wanted to ask if you'd have Charlie? Only if you have nothing planned. It would just be for the morning?"

"I'd love to have her."

"Oh, thank you, Lucy. She'll be so pleased. I need to meet my mum, you see, do a bit of shopping and pick up a few gifts. It would be so much easier if Charlie didn't come along. School will have broken up, and David won't be home until Christmas Eve."

"If there's anything I can do, just ask, Belle, anytime."

"Thank you. I can't tell you how helpful it will be."

I went home and made cheese on toast before getting out my magazines and looking through them for ideas on party attire. Really, I thought, I should have a little black number.

"Listen to me, Morsel! Imagine, even a year ago, a thought like that would never have crossed my mind." I admired the elegance of the models in their black dresses, simple yet stylish, perhaps worn with a single stunning piece of jewelry to complete the look. "Can I afford another dress, Morsel?" I picked her up and carried her round the house with me as I checked the doors and drew the curtains, pulled the blind, and turned up the heating. "We will have to get something for you as well," I told her. "We'll bathe you, and brush you, and buy you a new coat. You'll be the best-looking dog in the whole of Steely Green!"

****

Sometimes as I walked through the village, Rosamund's angelic smile haunted me. At this time of year, when the afternoons became shorter and the dark evenings longer, we would have been doing our puzzles, reading poetry, drawing and painting, or thinking of something to make. We would have created our own Christmas cards, not that we had many friends to give them to. We'd make them for our parents and for each other.

\*\*\*\*

Miss Pickering was soon visiting again.

"Pru went to the disco in Melstow," Bob told me proudly.

"The bistro, Bob. There's a new restaurant in Melstow, a bistro. Very good it is."

"I've heard about it," I said. It must have been the one Helen had gone to.

"Very dashing, the owner."

"Is he? It will definitely be popular, so."

"A Christmas party," said Mr. P.

"It was with the other ladies from the church. We do the flower arrangements and things like that. We decided to treat ourselves."

"It sounds wonderful and well deserved," I said.

\*\*\*\*

Charlie arrived early on Friday morning, and we went for a long walk. It was a lovely bright day, and people were in a Christmassy mood. The dogs all seemed to be out, Banjo, Smudge, Wesley, Mimi, and Polo. We kept meeting more. Then, hurtling toward us came Wotnot and Moose. George followed.

"Hello, you two," he said.

"Walk with us," I suggested as the two bigger dogs

vied for my attention.

"Yes, I'd like that," he said. "How is Charlie?"

"I'm very well," she said. "I'm on holiday now."

"And have you put up plenty of decorations?" George asked her.

"Yes, all over the house. Mum likes decorations. She bought a new Christmas tree as well. It's gold. It's not a real one."

"And you have lights in your garden," I reminded her.

"Yes. We put lights on the outside tree. They go on and off."

"Flashing lights!" said George.

"It looks really pretty," I said.

"Have you got a present for Mum and Dad?" George wanted to know.

"I've made some presents for Mum. I made a calendar at school, and I've made her some sweets. Gran helped me. Mum is buying me a present to give to Dad."

"It sounds as though you've got it all sorted," he said.

Moose and Wotnot were running on ahead of us, disappearing into the trees to chase other dogs and re-emerging. Charlie walked with Morsel, throwing her ball for her. George managed to find a few moments to ask some quick non-child-friendly questions.

"No more intruders?"

"No, all's been quiet," I said. "I'm working day shifts again. I feel more comfortable, not having to be out after dark every night."

"I haven't heard of any other incidents in the village."

"Neither have I." Moose and Wotnot, followed by Wesley and Banjo, ran across in front of us and charged on without stopping. "All okay with Helen?"

"Seems to be. We're still not seeing much of each other. She's been out late on a good few occasions, but she's always had some explanation."

"She's busy with her work?"

"Yes, she is busy."

"And Christmas? What will you do?"

"Ah, we're doing what we always do. We have a no-fuss one. Just the three of us…and Wotnot…and most of the contents of the supermarket. Christmas Day and Boxing Day, we don't go out at all as a rule, apart from walking Wotnot."

"I'm working, but I think I'll enjoy it."

"You'll have as good a time as me, I'm sure."

"I think I'll get a good dinner from what I've heard."

"Lucy, what I think is, if anything is going on with Helen, it will come out over Christmas. If there's someone else, she won't be able to resist a few calls to him."

"I really don't think there's anyone else, George."

"If Ange is seeing someone, I'll get to the bottom of that too. We're due to see her a couple of times, with Will. Their relationship's a bit rocky, but there might be other things going on. I'll be able to tell if something's up."

Jenny appeared with Wesley, now on his lead.

"He's full of running today, but I have to get home!" She hurried off.

Wotnot came back momentarily, but Charlie called him, and he went off to join in the ball game. George hadn't volunteered anything about my burning question. I decided to put it to him.

"You obviously haven't heard the rumor, George?"

"About…"

"Not about Helen or Ange. Nothing like that. It's about the village."

"No, I don't think so. I did hear something about the statue they want to erect, but people have been talking about the statue for years. You don't mean that?"

"No. It's about the Lesters."

He stopped walking. "Tell me," he said.

"Something about someone in the village inheriting something in the will."

"I didn't hear that. Is that why it's being contested?"

"Probably. Does that sound likely?"

"It's interesting, isn't it? I'll have to ask Helen. Who is it supposed to be?"

"I've not heard any more than that, only what I've told you."

"Maybe he left something as a prize for the treasure hunt?"

It was a thought. "That might be the sort of thing Reg would do," I said.

George was a good thinker. He pondered some more. "It could be anything, couldn't it? He was an extremely wealthy man, wasn't he, so they say?"

"So they say."

"So he could have left a lot of money…or he could have left a set of crockery or a single old vase, something like that."

"Or there could be no truth in the rumor at all."

"Well, it will make the Christmas gatherings all the more intriguing! We can all speculate together."

Charlie had realized we'd stopped walking and was on her way back with Moose, Wotnot, and Morsel beside her.

"Shall we go to the café?" I suggested.

George agreed. "Yes. Let's take the dogs to mine and go from there."

"Daniel could come," Charlie said.

"I'm fairly sure he's at football practice," said George.

In the space of a few months, I'd come a long way in terms of my attire. I supposed I might now be described as well-dressed. I'd thrown out a sackful of old frumpy garments and replaced them sparingly and carefully with a selection of more stylish items. They weren't necessarily showy, though I'd bought a few items to wear to the upcoming parties and gatherings. My aim was that my new look should be considered and make a statement.

As we walked into the café, we were met by a steamy atmosphere and delicious smells. The tables were almost all taken, and there was a nice buzz about the place. Mrs. Wise was at the counter. Her daughter, presumably on her school holiday, was making drinks and waitressing. Amber was in her glory, taking orders and generally winning over the customers. She came to greet us.

"Good morning! Let me find you a table! We're just clearing this one near the counter. We'll give it a wipe, and you can sit here."

"Thank you, Amber," said George, falling for her sugary, well-practiced charms.

"There! It's all ready. We'll come back for your order momentarily."

I spoke to Candy and Paul on my way through, and then to Mrs. Partridge, who I only really knew from the garage sale, but who greeted me like an old friend. Charlie's 'mate' Lee was there with some of his relatives, and she said hello to him.

"What have you got, Lee?"

"Cream bun."

"Looks nice. But I'm having a meringue."

We ordered the meringue, two mince pies, and various drinks. I imagined we may have to wait a while with the number of orders that were being taken.

The vicar came in. He went round to each table. He came over to us and asked if we would be attending the carol service. I was able to say I was coming with some of the Moonstones' residents, and George said he would certainly be there. Charlie looked up at him and stated that she would ask her mum if they could go along. I informed him Charlie was in the school choir and knew the words to any number of carols. The vicar moved on to the next table, which I realized was taken by two of Lolly's friends. I mouthed a hello and gave them a wave, which they both acknowledged.

The mince pies arrived, warm and accompanied by little jugs of cream. We sat and ate, enjoying the experience and the atmosphere that could not have been created at any other time of the year.

"I can't stand her; I know I shouldn't say it." I overheard Mrs. Wise make the statement to Amber as they were busy serving behind the counter.

Amber caught my eye. She must have known I'd heard the comment. "You don't mean it," she said, for my ears.

A little later, Amber, who had never before spoken to me, except in a way I believed to be purposefully belittling, stopped at the table and bent toward me.

"She was talking about Vicky Lester," she whispered, and then she carried on to another table to deliver two large plates of toasted sandwiches.

George and Charlie were oblivious, enveloped in the moments of pleasure the Christmassy morning was providing.

\*\*\*\*

Mr. Pickering, Ethel, Lolly, and Bert all wished to attend the church carol service. We helped them button up their coats and wrapped their scarves around their necks. Lolly wore a purple hat, Ethel a green one, and Mr. Pickering and Bert had both found their caps. Candy and I guided everyone onto the mini bus. Joe climbed into the driver's seat, and we set off. The vicar was going to be pleased with the turnout.

I'd never seen the church so full. The organ played softly as we greeted other villagers and chose our pews in the candlelight. We were early, and Lolly had time to find her friends. She would sit with them. Miss Pickering was seated with the ladies who decorated the church, and on that winter's evening, they'd made it look truly magnificent. At the entrance, there was a charmingly decorated tree hung with silver baubles and with a shining silver star on the top. The windowsills were decked with garlands, made from holly and fine branches of pine, entwined with red and gold ribbon, and studded with fir cones. We headed to the front, near the lectern, to sit where our residents would be able to hear the lessons. Mr. Pickering managed to tear himself away from his sister and her friends and came to sit beside me.

"I shall say a prayer for Joan," he told me.

Soon Jenny and Malcolm were sitting in the pew behind us. Belle and Charlie came swiftly down the aisle and also sat in the row behind. Charlie and Belle began chatting with Bert, Mr. Pickering, and Ethel. I looked round and spotted George sitting near the back with Helen, Daniel, Ange, and Will. I hoped all was going smoothly for them. As the vicar came along the aisle, there was a clamor; some latecomers could be heard entering. The heavy door opened, and the thick curtain was pulled aside to let them in. The door clunked closed again, and the newcomers noisily found seats.

Jenny leaned across. "Lesters," she whispered loudly.

Vicky was there with two other women and a young man. The older woman was Vicky's mother, Cristabel. I realized the others must be the half-brother and sister I'd not previously come across, Leo and Beatrice. The whole congregation had turned to look at them, and muttering could be heard as comments were made before everyone reluctantly turned back to face the altar and the vicar as the service began. We all sang heartily. The choir was in good form, and several choristers read a lesson, as did Doctor Stevens and also Jenny's Malcolm, both of whom were church wardens. The village had come together, and we all felt we had a part to play. We were pleased to have come through another year. We'd come to the church to rejoice, though we also remembered those who weren't able to be with us. The vicar added a cautionary tone during his sermon when he reminded us that although it was nice to receive gifts at Christmas time, giving was the more important thing. The spoils of the material world were far less rewarding than the simple things we were all able to offer, love, support, and friendship.

On the way out, you could have imagined almost the whole village had been in attendance. I noticed Martin, and some other members of the football team, several of Charlie's friends with their parents, the Wises, the Partridges. Wine and a mince pie were on offer at the vicarage for those who could stay, but our party was happy to leave and head back to Moonstones.

\*\*\*\*

The festive season was in full swing. I set off to the Browns' for the drinks do. Malcolm let me in and took my coat, looking round for Morsel.

"You didn't bring her, Morsel?"

"No, she'll be fine at home. She's had a good walk."

He ushered me into the open-plan downstairs area. The lighting was dim, with strings of tiny decorative lights in abundance. Christmassy classical music played in the background. I moved to the kitchen-diner where the bifold doors were slightly open. A few people were outside, gathered around a fire pit which blazed a welcome and also, as I was soon to find, gave off good warmth. I went out to explore and sat down on one of the outdoor seats. Malcolm had been taken away by some loud, laughing women, and at first, I couldn't see anyone else I knew. I imagined there were fellow teachers in attendance and perhaps some of the parents of the children whom Jenny and Malcolm taught. Next thing, Jenny was sitting beside me.

"Lucy, I'm pleased you could make it. You don't have a drink."

"I'll find one in a minute, Jenny."

"Some guests have left already, and you may find some of those still here are quite merry."

"I don't mind. I've been on my feet all day. It's nice just to sit."

Jenny called to one of her teacher friends to bring over a couple of glasses of mulled wine. The drinks duly arrived, and we sat by the fire sipping them.

"So the Lesters are here for the holidays," she said.

"I've never seen those other two children before," I remarked.

"Beatrice and Leo. They don't come often."

"I didn't think they got on with Vicky and her mother."

"No. You wouldn't have thought they'd be spending Christmas together. It's surely to do with the will. They're probably here to look after their interests."

"It all seems so complicated," I said.

"All the talk here tonight was of the Lesters."

"Did anyone know anything more?"

"People were speculating. John Crane was here. He says nothing has changed at the manor as far as he knows. He's still getting paid, he said, which is probably all he cares about."

"Did he say anything about the rumor?"

"He laughed about it. He said no Crane would be likely to inherit anything." She sipped at her glass again. "He said it was true though, that Reg cared about the villagers, that he genuinely did. But the rest of them just look out for themselves."

"Sounds like most people."

"If anything substantial was left to a villager, the family will be contesting it. They'll pay for the best lawyers, and they'll probably win."

"Do you think so?"

"I'm sure George is still here," Jenny said. "I'd better go and speak to that bunch over there but find George. He's inside somewhere."

I sat longer, then moved inside. George was nattering away with a group of people in a corner of the lounge area. Amber was amongst them. I went back to the kitchen, replenished my glass, and returned outside. A drunken geography teacher came and sat beside me. He chatted to me in a nonsensical manner for a while. It was much later that George appeared at the door and came over.

"I didn't see you arrive," he said.

"I was a latecomer," I told him.

"Aren't you cold?"

"No."

"Look at you in your little dress. You must be chilly out here. Let's go in?"

We found a comfortable sofa in the lounge. George said he had a bit of information about the Lesters to pass on.

"I may be a little drunk now," he said. "But I've been working on getting to the bottom of this rumor."

"Oh?"

"I won't tell you now. Too many people to overhear us."

I looked around me and could see that, in fact, there was only a handful of people left, and wouldn't they all know about it anyway. I wanted to know what George had found out.

"You could whisper."

"No. It's not all that exciting, to be honest. I'll tell you tomorrow."

"Will I see you tomorrow?"

"I'll drop round. I was planning to pop by. I have something for you."

We took that as agreed. I was tired, and George was at a stage of drinking where he just wanted to sit and smile out into the room without having to bother thinking up the sentences required to make conversation. We sat for a good while longer before we said goodnight to the hosts and tottered off home.

Chapter 17
Christmas

Thankfully I'd managed not to drink too many glasses of wine at Jenny's house. I had to put on festive clothing again the next day and be the life and soul of the party at Moonstones. To be fair, I would be one life and soul amongst many.

A good deal of preparation had gone into making Christmas Eve a day to remember. Joe had the music playing in the lounge from early afternoon, and we cleared an area for dancing. I went to Molly's room.

"Are you ready for the party, Molly?"

She was sitting on her bed with her walking frame at the ready.

"Do I need a comb?"

"I'll brush your hair for you. Aren't you going to wear your new cardigan? Come on, I think you should put it on." I spent some time with her.

"I haven't had a bath," she told me.

"You had one yesterday, Molly. You'll be fine."

She smiled at me, and I felt a huge pang of love for her. It was a privilege to help to look after people who had become unable to do it for themselves. It would have been nice to spend all my time with just one resident and give them the one-to-one care they deserved. If only we lived in that sort of a world.

We went to the lounge, and it soon began to fill up.

## The Ultimate Village Game

Lianne handed out crackers to pull, and in no time, we were all in party hats. Joe was distributing sparkling drinks, the nearest nonalcoholic beverage to champagne he'd been able to find. John and Larry were both on duty and in the kitchen preparing food for the Christmas dinner the following day, as well as the party tea. They took turns to come to the lounge and spend time with the residents. Our ladies, Ethel, Lolly, Agnes, Mrs. Roberts, and Molly, of course, had all dressed up. They looked lovely, sitting together in paper crowns of various colors. I was pleased to see Molly joining in with the others; they helped her on with her bright yellow headwear. Joe took a photo, and at that moment Bert and Mr. Pickering made their entrance, Lionel following behind, doing a few dance steps on the way.

"I'm a little rusty, I'm afraid," he said to the group of ladies.

"I'm sure Joe can find some oil," Lolly said.

The men took a table and received their crackers and sparkling drinks. Sadly, Marcia and Mrs. Cook were going to miss out on the occasion; neither felt well. We would make sure to look in on them frequently.

"Any chance of a real drink?" asked Bert.

Joe conjured up a few tiny glasses and gave out some measures of sweet sherry. Molly preferred a large glass of orange squash, and Agnes wanted ginger wine. She sent me to her room to find the bottle, a Christmas present she'd received. She offered it around.

Soon the dancing began. Ethel and Lionel were up straight away. Not long passed before Joe was dancing with Lolly; her leg had obviously improved. Bert summoned me over, his sticks were abandoned, and we managed a few steps. Molly made use of her walking frame. She was to be seen making shapes with John, the frame complementing the imaginative moves. Mr. Pickering said he couldn't dance, but Agnes wouldn't listen to that and soon had him out on the floor. We swapped partners and danced some more. Then we all needed a sit-down.

Joe and Lianne had thought up some games that everyone would be able to take part in. We started with pass the parcel. At the same time, Lianne began to throw balloons to us, which we batted around the room. It didn't feel like being at work. Mariana was on duty with me and happy to maintain a low profile, keep an eye on things, and make sure Mrs. Cook and Marcia were looked after. Candy and Jackie dropped in just to attend the party. We ate sausage rolls, sandwiches, mince pies, and trifle, not to mention drinking the usual copious amounts of tea.

"I'll stay and help get everyone off to bed," said Candy. She and I would both be working the following day, Christmas Day. We didn't mind at all. "Paul has tomorrow off. He's going to make dinner, and we'll eat in the evening when I get home," she said.

"Lucky you!"

"He's quite happy to spend the whole morning asleep."

Eventually, I collected Morsel from the office and strode down the hill with her. I had things to do when I arrived home. George was popping in to see me, and that had inspired me to bring in some wood. I'd get a fire going in the lounge and wrap a few small presents for him and the family. These things were on my mind as we approached the cottage.

I hesitated, noticing the gate was open. It might be nothing, but after the recent happening, I was cautious. Picking Morsel up so that she wouldn't begin to bark, I crept slowly along the last few yards toward home. I could see that it wasn't Belle, it wasn't George, it wasn't Charlie, but somebody was standing in my garden. I stayed on the pavement where I could spy through a thin part of the hedge. It was dark, but as usual, I'd left a light on upstairs…and the person in the garden had a torch. It seemed to be my same intruder, a slender figure, light on their feet. I didn't attempt to interrupt, simply watched as they worked their way along the front wall of the house, shining the torch in through the windows. The figure bent down at the front door, lifted the flap of the letterbox, and peered in, pointing the torch beam into the hallway.

I kept still, with Morsel in my arms; she seemed to understand we had to stay quiet. Looking on, it struck me that when this unwanted visitor came to leave, they would surely see me. I took a few steps back to where the hedge ended and a fence bordered the neighboring land. I clambered over it and crouched down, still able to see the figure through gaps between the wooden slats. The shadowy person finally started to move back to the gate. I strained to see more. The figure stopped again, eying the upper floor. Dressed in dark garments and with a black woolen hat pulled low, it was hard to make anything out, but just for a moment, the torchlight crossed over the intruder's face. I caught a glimpse of their profile, and although I couldn't bring the person to mind, I was almost certain this was someone I'd seen before. A moment later, the torch was switched off, the figure was out through the gate, closing it without a sound, and on their way off along the road, away from me, in the direction of the village.

I waited two or three minutes before standing up and climbing back over the fence. At the cottage, I unlocked the door and entered. Somehow, I couldn't say why, but I didn't feel anxious. I set about getting ready to welcome George. He soon arrived.

"Did you have much of a hangover after Jenny's do?" he asked me.

"No, but I didn't drink that much. I arrived quite late, if you remember?"

"I'm still suffering," he said.

"Come into the lounge. I've got the fire going," I told him.

"Ooh, lovely," he said

We sat in the warmth. George preferred coffee that evening. I cut him a slice of Christmas cake and told him about the party at Moonstones. Soon we moved on to the subject I'd been waiting for.

"Right," he said, "let me tell you what I heard about the rumor."

"Yes. I'm dying to know."

"Everything is left to Nic. That's what I understand."

It was what Nic had told me would happen years before, but I didn't believe it at first. How could that be? The family had become more extensive, and Nic didn't even live in England; no one had set eyes on him for years.

"But who's told you that?" I said.

"Elaine French told Helen."

I knew Dr. French had a connection with the Lesters. She'd been involved with Algie from time to time and was one of the doctors the family called on if they needed to consult someone in the local area. She was also quite a good friend of Helen's.

"It doesn't make sense," I said.

"Well, perhaps it's not right. No one seems to know what's true and what's not. But Elaine would hardly say it if she didn't believe it to be the case."

"What about Algie? What about the other children…and Cristabel?"

"Ah yes, there's some sort of trust fund for Algie. That's always been in place. Algie will always be looked after. But apparently, everything else is left to Nic. He can do what he wants with the estate."

"Nic's in America, I think." I pulled a piece of icing from my cake and bit into it.

"Yes, that's what people say."

"You'd think he'd have come back to sort it all out."

"Perhaps he's come to London? There's a house there too, I think."

"The other children all seem to be at the manor at the moment. That was Beatrice and Leo at the carol service, with Vicky."

"Perhaps Nic is joining them for Christmas," George suggested. He went quiet, staring into the flames that leaped in the hearth. My mind puzzled over the rumor. Had it just been imagined by the highly inventive minds of the villagers of Steely Green?

George couldn't stay for long. He handed me a bag of presents. I gave him my offerings, and we wished each other a Happy Christmas. We promised to phone each other in a few days if we hadn't happened to meet beforehand while walking the dogs.

I put my presents with the others, one from Belle and one from Charlie, and sat enjoying my fire. I thought about my progress. A year ago, I hadn't even begun my job at Moonstones. I was still something of a hermit, a misfit, a person who no one really spoke to or took notice of. Now, I had a good job; people relied on me. I had friends who bought me gifts; a friend who'd asked me to a party. I received compliments on the way I looked and the way I dressed. I was a changed person and suddenly felt overcome by a new understanding. It could have been partly because I knew something was stirring…but maybe nothing else mattered anymore. I'd come back to Steely for a reason, but had I, in fact, been drawn back by fate? Was my new way of life the way I should have been living all along? Was I beginning to fulfill my destiny? I'd found meaning in my life, begun to feel real emotions, could empathize with others. I was honestly looking forward to another year in Steely: taking part in village life; building on what I'd achieved and my new friendships.

"Aaaaaaaargh!" I shouted. Morsel ran to hide. I charged upstairs to the bedroom and found my notebook, rushed back down, threw myself to my knees in front of the fire, and started to tear at the book. I tore it apart in some sort of frenzy, pulling and ripping, my nails breaking and fingers bleeding.

"That's the end of it! It has to stop!" I was shaking and crying as one after another, I screwed up the pages, covered in my silly notes and crazy thoughts, and tossed them into the flames. "The end!" I laughed hysterically. Leaning back, I folded my arms and watched. It was more than satisfying to observe as the fire took hold and devoured the browning paper.

\*\*\*\*

Christmas day was to be the first day of my new life, though no one else would notice a difference. Candy and I carried out the chores, imparting, as best we could, an atmosphere of warmth and joyfulness, togetherness, and belonging. We welcomed the visitors who came to see the residents and worked harder still to make the day perfect for those who had no one. We gave and received gifts and shared the experience of the gorgeous Christmas meal. I knew now that what I was doing was what I was cut out to do, and just for a day, Candy and I felt we could take on the world; there was no challenge too big for us to conquer.

Chapter 18
A New Life

I had set out my new resolve and was determined to stick to it. However, things began to happen that would immediately test me. The first was that Miss Pickering asked me into her cottage. She spotted me walking past, appeared at the gate, and asked me in for sherry. It was early afternoon on a day between Christmas and New Year. She directed me into the lounge, Morsel too, and quickly produced two small glasses containing sweet, dark liquid. The room was furnished with Victorian items, save for the three-piece suite, which I could tell was newer but in period style. There were mahogany bookcases and display cabinets containing porcelain ornaments. A leather-topped desk stood against the far window. There were a couple of decorative inlaid side tables, and an elegant chiming clock was positioned centrally on the mantelpiece. We sat down.

"Have you enjoyed your Christmas?" Miss Pickering asked.

"Yes, my first since coming back to the village."

"I've very much enjoyed mine. All went well with the church services, and not having to worry about Bob meant I could relax in a way that has not been possible for some time."

"Yes, you must have been freed from a raft of

chores."

"I do feel guilty sometimes, being here and Bob elsewhere. I miss his company also."

"I don't think you should feel guilt." I said. "He needs professional care now, you know that, and I think Mr. Pickering had a thoroughly good Christmas."

"He certainly did. He loved all the parties and the gorgeous food. And he takes pleasure in the friendship of the others. He sees far more people at Moonstones than came to visit here at The Flower Pot."

We chatted easily, and the manor didn't even cross my mind until Miss Pickering brought up a new line of conversation.

"You noticed Leo and Beatrice," she said, "at church?"

"Yes, they caused quite a commotion."

"They must be here about the will."

I didn't feel I could say anything about Nic and the fact that he was supposed to be the beneficiary. I thought I might get George into trouble if I started passing on the things he'd told me.

"Perhaps," I said. Miss Pickering also had the son I had known on her mind.

"Who can tell what will go on now? I do wish I could hear from Nic."

"Do you think he will come to the village?" I said.

"No, no. He won't be able to."

"But why wouldn't he come?"

I could see she was now a little uneasy. She shifted around in her chair and took another sip of sherry.

"He can't, Lucy. I'm not sure I should say this, but you'll keep it to yourself?"

I nodded.

She paused and looked down. "He's not well, you see."

"Oh, dear. And he's still in America?"

"Yes, in America and not at all well."

I knew I wouldn't get anywhere by asking her where she'd heard this. I thought I would just brush the information aside and continue a more general conversation. She'd confided in me several times now, and as usual, I felt she'd be more likely to share any further facts if I didn't show too much interest. It seemed she trusted me, and I had not to forget I had my new focus; I was no longer interested in the Lesters or Reg's estate.

"The Lesters will always be a talking point, it seems," I said. Miss Pickering smiled but didn't expand on the conversation. I'd finished my drink. I had the feeling I was expected to leave.

"Do you need anything, Miss P? I was on my way to get a few grocery items from the store. I could pick something up for you?"

"No, thank you, Lucy. They delivered my usual, plus a few extras I ordered for the holidays. I still have plenty in stock."

"I'd better get going. Thank you for inviting me in."

As I went, I noticed the heavy framed oil paintings on the walls in the hallway, portraits, and landscapes, original works I felt sure.

The second thing that happened was to do with Agnes. I came into Agnes's room one morning to collect her breakfast tray. By that point, I'd not had much of a chance to get to know her. She wasn't a resident who needed a great deal of looking after. That meant, unless she demanded it, she wouldn't be overloaded with attention. She'd finished with her cup and plate, and I put them on the tray. I pushed the curtain back for her. We were probably chatting about the weather or what might be for lunch, but then she said something that stopped me in my tracks.

"Lucy, you wouldn't remember me, but I remember you, you know."

"You do?"

"I remember you as a child."

"Do you?"

"Think back. Do you recall a teacher by the name of Miss Morris?"

"Miss Morris, let me think. Yes, I'm sure I do. Miss Morris was at the school for just a term or two. She was a nice lady, I remember that."

"Well, I married. It's a long time now since I was a Morris…but that young teacher was me. I'm glad you remember me as being nice!"

"I recall Miss Morris well now, when I think about it. I remember you well. We were sorry when you left because you were kind to us, the pupils. That wasn't the way with all the teachers."

"It was my first job, a temporary position."

"I didn't stay at the school for much longer. We moved away. My family moved to Morley Brook."

The last thing I wanted was to talk to anyone about being a child in the village. Since I'd returned to Steely, no one had started that sort of conversation. Helen talked about school once in a while, but she was older than me, and we'd had little to do with each other back then. I wasn't expecting my past to come up in any detail. The present had taken over. I wanted to think about what came next, not what had gone before.

"You must have missed the village?"

"I was young. Dad found work in Morley Brook." I wouldn't acknowledge any feelings of sadness or regret, any feelings at all. "Can I fetch you another cup of tea?" I asked her.

"Yes, please, Lucy. That would go down very well."

Agnes was talkative. I hoped she wouldn't speak about this anymore, to me or to anyone else. Back in the kitchen, Candy offered to go up with the tea, and I accepted.

\*\*\*\*

Algie was always somewhat wayward. You never knew quite what he would do, and he didn't ever seem to care about consequences. It was true that his father had money, but Reg was strict with his children. He believed discipline was good for them. Reg owned a number of cars: the black car we were used to seeing in the village; also, over the years, sports cars; large American cars; various vehicles that all had in common the ability to take your breath away. Even if you knew nothing about cars, when you set eyes on one that belonged to Reg Lester, you knew it was special and generally very expensive. The boys of the village, the men too, would be awestruck. Algie, when he wasn't much more than a child, began to ask his father if he could drive the vehicles on the grounds of the estate. Once in a while, his father would consent. But Algie didn't drive carefully; he had no respect for the vehicles. I'd heard about one going out of control. He'd driven it right across the lawn in front of the house, making deep furrows in the grass, before crashing it into the trunk of a tall conifer. Presumably, he wasn't allowed near the cars for some time after that, but soon we heard he'd become keen on other people's cars. He repeatedly stole vehicles and drove them at speed through the local country lanes until, in general, he crashed them. Fortunately, no other drivers or vehicles had been involved. His father would pay for the damage. Algie would be reprimanded and made to apologize, but not long after, another car would go missing.

I remember being told that Algie, again when he was far too young, had been known to go into the village inn and demand to be served. He would tell the bar staff he was allowed to drink and threatened that if they didn't serve him, he would tell his father. No one wanted to fall out with Reg. I understood that there were occasions when he was sold drinks. Other times, he seemed to acquire his own alcohol, and could be seen wandering around the village drinking from a bottle, perhaps offering swigs to other children. Parents would disapprove, but they'd be torn because they enjoyed the thought of their offspring being in the company of a Lester. They would stick up for Algie; there was no real harm in him, they'd say. As children, we also looked up to the Lesters; everyone wanted to spend time with them.

Algie was suspended from school more than once. People said Reg had pretty much bribed the headmaster to take him back. The police had, at times, had reason to call to the manor, and not only because of stolen cars. Algie wasn't just a handful, he wasn't simply a headstrong youth; he had a streak of wildness about him over and beyond that. I'd come across it. It came from his mother, they said. Nic was different, a thinker. He could be described as considered. Nic was clever; he was also a kind person and had a lightheartedness about him. The two boys looked much alike but were dissimilar in character. If Algie was north, Nic was south. If Algie was rock, Nic was sand. If you tried to separate them, however, tried to side with one or other, they would pull back, draw close together mentally and physically. Being apart caused them anguish, it seemed.

****

After Miss Pickering's latest news, I found myself thinking about Nic and Algie all the more. Just when I'd found something real in my life to live for, it seemed the past might get in the way. I'd planned and waited and hoped for so long, but when I'd finally returned to Steely, I'd learned I hadn't needed any of it. I'd be better off without it. I was Lucy, I'd always been Lucy, and nobody minded anymore. I'd started enjoying my life in a way I could never have envisaged. I'd found that what I really wanted was all the normal things, and what's more, they were available to me: friendship, mutual understanding, appreciation.

****

I met Ange in the copse.

"Hello, Ange," I called to her. "Hello, Moose." Moose had run up to see me.

"How are you, Lucy? Good Christmas?"

"Yes. Busy, but good fun. Yours?"

"Same as usual. Don't you ever get bored, Lucy? I get so bored."

"Things are different for me. Coming back to Steely has given me a new beginning."

"I suppose so. You see, I should leave the village, I

know I should…but I don't think I'm brave enough."

I took a step closer to her. "How do you mean?"

"You know what I mean. When you have something that makes you feel safe, it's hard to give it up. You can keep doing it forever and never have to worry. If you were brave, though, you could break the pattern, change everything, but you'd also be walking into the unknown."

It was quite a deep conversation to be having with Ange. I'd only spoken to her a handful of times. I felt she thought what she was saying would make sense to me.

"It sounds like you're looking for an adventure, but perhaps you're better off where you are?" I said. "I can assure you that's not what I did. I didn't give up a safe life. I sort of had to do what I did. No choice."

"I think you've been courageous. You made a big change. You moved your whole life, on your own, and started over."

Moose stood while I scratched him behind the ears. "What I think, Ange, is that the boring, tried and tested, is the best way. I wish I'd realized that a long time ago," I said.

"Really?"

"Really."

We sat on the bench and watched the dogs snuffling the pungent ground beneath the trees. Maybe we had some sort of understanding about each other's experiences, and the coming year might see us become friends.

Jenny was walking in our direction. She was with Malcolm and Wesley. Ange stood up and made her way toward them, briefly speaking with them before carrying on out of the copse. Jenny and her husband sat down beside me on the bench. Morsel and Wesley went off to explore.

"What a beautiful day," said Jenny.

"Did you have a good Christmas?" I asked.

"We had a lovely Christmas," said Malcolm. "We ate. Not much else happened."

"That sounds perfect."

Jenny looked at Malcolm in a contented way. I thought, seeing them together that day and recently at their house party, that Jenny was different in Malcolm's company. She seemed calmer somehow. I'd taken her usual energetic personality to be her character through and through, but when Malcolm was with her, she was quiet and composed. She took his arm and leaned into him. I could tell she wished for no more. We sat for a few minutes and exchanged a few comments, nothing dramatic, nothing out of the ordinary. Malcolm had seen a bird he couldn't identify in the garden; Jenny had received a card from an old friend she'd not heard from in a long time.

I walked on and out across the common. I noticed some of the Cranes coming in my direction, John and his wife, Michelle, and Crinkle. They had a fox terrier with them.

"Hello, Lucy," they chimed.

"Hello."

John bent to pat Morsel, and I called the terrier to me.

"What a sweet dog," said Michelle.

"Oh, so is yours! What's his name" I said.

"He's called Bruce," said Crinkle. "I don't usually bring him into the village, but I should. There are some good walks around here, aren't there?"

"Yes, and quite a few dogs, and they all enjoy meeting each other. This is Morsel."

We exchanged a few pleasantries before Morsel and I walked on.

I came to the back of the village and made my way along Broad Street. The shops were closed, but the Christmas displays and festive lights meant the street looked enchanting. The storekeepers had put in a great deal of effort, I thought.

I carried on home, and as I walked past Belle's house, I hoped the family was enjoying their time together. Somehow, I knew they would be. Morsel and I came to the cottage, our own home. Inside I sat in my armchair, and Morsel jumped onto my lap. I gently stroked her until she slept.

I began to think of all the people I'd seen that day and also about the villagers I hadn't come across. I'd not seen George and Helen or Daniel. I hoped and hoped they'd enjoyed Christmas and their time together, made the moments count, and communicated their true feelings to one another. Their lovely homely house and all the effort they'd put into it over the years, their so established friendship, I felt strongly about it. They needed to recognize what they had and look after it.

I thought about Miss Pickering, alone in her cottage, but I knew, given a new lease of life. She had her friends in the village. Bob was just a short walk away, and she didn't need to worry about him any longer. She could finally do a few things for herself in the knowledge that he would come to no harm. She could spend time with him doing only the nice things, chatting and sharing memories, rather than coping with chores. I thought about Candy and Paul. I particularly liked those two. They were a solid couple, great friends, and the sort of people who made the world a better place. They worked hard and had strong values. They didn't have an easy life, they didn't have a lot of money, but they would always try to help and offer support. They gave whatever they could to help others. I thought about John, Larry, Jackie, Mariana, and Barbara. They were all good people that I now counted as friends. I thought about Joe and Lianne. They ran a business, they were entrepreneurs, but for them, it wasn't all about profit; it was a business that provided a five-star service with impeccable standards at its core. They couldn't run their business with any more energy or warmth. Even so, each and every day at Moonstones, they would strive to improve things for the residents and staff.

Morsel was sleeping. Listening to her breathing was soothing. She'd taught me about priorities, companionship, and mutual support. I'd lost my bitterness, my need to prove myself, my urge for material things. I'd known those things were wrong, and I was wrong to pursue them, but I'd still done it. I'd tried to trick myself, told myself that if I gave enough, it would be all right to strive for those things. It wasn't right. I was finally back in touch with the values I'd been brought up with, simple values like goodness and honesty, giving for the sake of giving. Could this little scrap of a dog be partly responsible for my newfound understanding of the world? I'd sleep well that night. I'd finally learned how to deal with my own strengths and my own failings, and I felt that whatever was thrown at me, I could meet all of it head-on and survive.

A week or so later, Lianne asked me if I would be interested in assisting in managing Moonstones. I found it hard to believe.

"Me?"

"Yes, you Lucy," Lianne said, with a bemused expression. "Is there any reason why not?"

"I've never done anything like that before."

"I think you are almost doing the job already. Of course, there are some additional tasks I would like you to take on. I'd show you the ropes, and obviously, Joe and I would be here to support you while you came to grips with the new role."

"I can't think straight, Lianne. I wasn't expecting this at all."

"Why don't you let it sink in? Think of any questions you'd like to ask, and then we'll have a proper chat about it all later in the week?"

"Yes. Yes," I said. I was stunned. "Would I still be able to do my usual work?"

"You could perhaps work some regular shifts as well as carrying out additional duties."

"Ooh."

"Are you all right, Lucy?"

"Yes," I said, trying to come up with a more meaningful response. "I just can't think of what to say."

That evening, back at home, I literally shrieked with pleasure. I had been offered a promotion I wasn't expecting, a job I didn't even know I wanted or that it existed, and I was so excited about it I couldn't contain myself. I went up to the bedroom and looked in the mirror. There was Lucy Short, a well-dressed, healthy-looking woman with a good haircut. She was well thought of in the village, and she was soon to be a manager. She was an independent woman with a career that she'd carved out for herself.

I bumped into Amber. She was out walking, wrapped up in a long coat in a tweed fabric and long leather boots. She greeted me.

"Good afternoon, Lucy."

"Hello, Amber." With all the good feelings flowing through me, I still couldn't bring myself to like her.

"Have you had a nice Christmas. Did you manage to get a few days off?"

"I've been working, but that's the way I like it."

"I understand that. The café is closed for a few days, and I miss going in."

"All will be back to normal in no time."

"Yes, and then I'll long for a holiday!"

"Nice to see you," I said before walking on. It had pained me to say it.

Chapter 19
The Past and Promotion

It was strange to think back and wonder about how Rosamund and I, at least for a time, came to be friends with Algie and Nic. We had nothing, and they had everything.

We were playing by the river one summer afternoon, and we heard a shout from the opposite bank.

"Don't fall in, girls."

It was Algie. He had a mischievous grin and was waiting for us to offer some sort of response. Rosamund hadn't previously met the Lesters, but I'd come across them a few times by then. She looked down, consumed by her shyness. Her reticence made me a little braver; I would have to come up with an answer.

"We can swim if we fall in. We'll swim to the bridge and climb out," I shouted.

Nic looked at Algie and laughed. I think he approved of my response.

"Come up to the bridge now!" Algie shouted.

Rosamund seemed unsure, but I told her I'd spoken to them once or twice, and they weren't so bad. In the early days, Algie seemed cheeky and funny. He was naughty but not unruly. We walked along on our side of the river, and they walked along on theirs until we all came to the footbridge. We met in the middle. Algie had picked up some sticks; he threw them, one at a time, into the water, and we watched them make their way downstream.

"Were you just playing?" asked Nic.

"We were counting butterflies," I said. "This is my friend Rosamund. We come to the river sometimes to see how many different butterflies we can spot."

"How many did you find?" he asked.

"Red Admirals, Peacocks, Large Whites, and a Brown, but nothing unusual today," I said.

"Does she speak?" said Algie, nodding toward Rosamund.

My friend, who I knew had just been gaining confidence with all the talk about butterflies, looked down abruptly and was again struck dumb.

"Rosamund doesn't want to speak to you, Algie," said Nic, smiling at me to include me. "She obviously has some sense!"

"Argh, I've no time for quiet little girls," Algie declared. "Come on, Nic. Let's get back to the boat." He crossed the bridge to the bank and continued walking.

"Ignore Algie, Rosamund," said Nic. "Lucy knows what he's like. I'm sorry if he was rude." He looked us both in the eye. "See you," he said, and he ran off after his elder brother.

Rosamund and I were left standing on the bridge. I imagined she'd been horrified by Nic and Algie, but in fact, it was more that she was curious.

"Have you met them at the manor?" she asked.

"Yes, when Dad's been working there."

"I've seen them in the back of the car," she said. "Mr. Lester has them with him sometimes."

"They seem okay. They go to boarding school."

"Where's their mum?" my friend asked.

"I've never seen a mum." Strangely I'd not thought about that before, but it was true. Their mum didn't seem to feature in their lives, at least not in terms of the part that went on in Steely Green. Over the next days, we met the boys a few more times.

"What have you found today?"

"A tortoiseshell."

"Show us?"

"It was back toward the copse."

The boys accompanied us to see if we could find the tortoiseshell butterfly again. It seemed they could become engrossed in such a thing in the same way that we could. They had an interest in wildlife and were fascinated by the river. We didn't say it to each other, but Rosamund and I began to seek out the brothers. Our own visits to the river became more frequent, and though in a lot of ways, we had nothing in common with them, we had more to share with them than with the other children of the village. We'd never been included by the locals, and they didn't consider Nic and Algie as boys they could get to know. What was pleasing for us was the Lesters didn't make assumptions about us; they'd not ruled us out before giving us a chance. They seemed to accept us, and we were captivated by their difference and charm.

The boys had a rowing boat that they took up and down the river. Upstream, the river flowed through the grounds of the manor, and they would often row right along, almost as far as the bridge. At that point, they would tie the craft up. Beyond, the river became wider and more shallow so that it couldn't be taken any farther. We spent time sitting on board, where it was tied, or rowing upstream and drifting back down. Rosamund and I could never have imagined being welcome in the company of other children, let alone other children who had a boat. Everything looked different from the craft. The reeds at the bank made a border between the water and the land. They grew tall, lining a tranquil, private place we'd lived beside all our lives but never seen. The boys were vigilant when it came to the river, Nic in particular. There were rules in terms of the boat. We were told where to sit, and he and Algie took their rowing duties seriously. They tied and untied the vessel carefully. It gave pleasure, but it wasn't a toy; both boat and river were to be treated with respect.

Rosamund soon found her courage and joined in with things.

"A painted lady," she called to the brothers one morning as they came along the bank. "We've seen a painted lady today."

We'd watch the water boatmen and the tiny mice, which could sometimes be seen scurrying amongst the foliage.

\*\*\*\*

"I'm going to miss sharing my shifts with you," Candy said.

"I'm still going to be working here."

"It won't be the same, though."

"I'll still be covering some shifts, just as normal."

Candy looked saddened. I'd told her the news that I was to train to be assistant manager at Moonstones.

"I'm really pleased for you," she added. She had such a kind heart. She wouldn't dwell on her own disappointment for more than a moment. I knew what she meant. I had always looked forward to my shifts so much more when Candy was going to be on with me. The hours would fly by because we'd have some fun, gossip a little, give mutual support, and not least because we trusted each other in terms of the workload. Candy wouldn't see my name beside hers so frequently on the rota, but I had to take this opportunity. Opportunities in my life had been few and far between.

On my way home, I met Belle and Charlie. They were out shopping, and we made a spontaneous decision to go to the café. We bumped into Daniel on the way and persuaded him to come with us. We ordered mugs of hot chocolate, and I filled everyone in on my promotion before Daniel brought us up to date with SGFC's league position and the team's recent away win. Every time I saw him, he looked less boy and more man, and spending time with the older players gave him a mature attitude. Not only that, he was becoming increasingly handsome, I noted. He swept his floppy blond fringe off his forehead with his hand and sat back in his chair.

"It's nice to be in the company of three ladies for a change," he remarked.

\*\*\*\*

Common Blue, Fritillary, Orange Tip, we found more and more varieties out on the marshland and along the river. Rosamund became entranced by the boat. She loved to be on board, but even just to sit on the bank beside it pleased her.

"I would love to have a boat when I'm older," she told Algie.

"And you shall," he declared. He turned the

statement into a chant and ran along on the path repeating it. "Rosamund shall have a boat! Rosamund shall have a boat!" he shouted, and she laughed and laughed, loving every moment.

Nic sat on the grass laughing too. "My brother is as nutty as a fruitcake," he said.

We found so much to do with Nic and Algie. The boat took up much of our time, but on a windy day, Nic would bring a kite, and we'd fly it for hours, taking turns to hold the cord. Algie could always find something to get up to, and as time went on he seemed to become wilder. He was an expert at climbing trees and would climb so high it would make us feel anxious. He would sit on a branch admiring the view and yelling down to tell us what he was able to see. I remember him wading from the riverbank through the rushes on several occasions, sending birds scattering. He didn't think twice about his footwear or his clothing. He would emerge covered in runny blue-gray mud, appearing delighted with himself.

****

Lianne was to give me lessons so that I would become capable of the new tasks which were to be part of my managerial role. She didn't actually call them lessons, but we had earmarked two mornings a week when I would spend time with her. She'd go through various procedures, such as making out the rota, ordering the multitude of items that were regularly delivered to the home, answering telephone enquiries, dealing with tradesmen, and so on. I was to shadow her, then gradually take on tasks under supervision until I had the confidence to carry them out on my own. I would work two days each week in my managerial role and also cover three shifts on a flexible basis, day or night. Lianne hoped to find a couple of new staff for the shift work as well; I was to help her with sorting through the applications and even with the interview process.

"I'm so grateful to you for this opportunity, Lianne," I told her.

"I'm very pleased that you've accepted the role," she said. "I've been thinking of offering it to you for some time now. You've proved yourself over and over. You're an asset to the business, Lucy."

I was often taken aback by Lianne's praise. I could hardly believe it was me she was speaking about.

On the days when I was working as assistant manager, I made a point of reaching out to the residents. I felt they should know me as someone they could speak to about the home or anything else they might have on their minds. I felt this was even more important now that I had more responsibility. I resolved to find each of them and spend time with them individually every week, even if it meant doing this in my own time.

"I don't mind if I go over my hours sometimes," I told Lianne. "I like chatting to the residents. I might visit them even if I wasn't at work because I've come to know them now. I want them all to be happy."

"You are so conscientious," Lianne said. "You may be learning a new role, but I'm also learning from you, you know. You mustn't work too hard, though. We don't want you to burn yourself out."

****

George came to the cottage. He said he'd dropped by because he felt it was a long time since we'd seen each other. He'd been having to go into the university more frequently and had been walking Wotnot early morning and late evening; he'd often had to walk him in the dark. He said Christmas and New Year had gone without a hitch. He'd finally come to the conclusion that I must be right. Helen was busy, a little worn out, covering for Ange, and not after all, in the throes of a huge and scandalous affair.

"I think I was told that too, in so many words," I told him.

"Really?"

"Yes, by Ange. She didn't say it outright, but she gave me a good hint on the matter. I'd say she intentionally communicated something to me."

"So, you think she was having an affair?"

"I'm not sure about having an affair. Maybe just toying with the idea of it."

"She was on the lookout for one?"

"Or she had an offer. She considered it but didn't follow up on it."

"You really think that?" George had become animated. I could tell he liked the idea of this. He wanted to think nothing had really happened; temptation had been resisted.

"Look, I don't know for sure, but with something like that, it's not wise to ask too many questions."

George's eyes looked brighter, his expression more relaxed. It was as if the explanation was helping to give him his old life back.

"I think you're right, Lucy, now I think about it. Somehow that all fits. It makes sense."

"Well, perhaps one day, someone might offer more information, but at the moment, feelings are probably heightened. There may be soreness and even a certain amount of longing."

"Longing for what might have been."

"Yes…or longing for something that could never exist."

"A dream world." He sat down in my armchair with a sigh. A weight had been lifted.

\*\*\*\*

Rosamund painted two small pebbles, each with a picture of a butterfly. She brought them with her to the river. She produced them, one in each hand, and offered them to Nic and Algie.

"I painted these for you. The red admiral is for you, Nic, and the blue is for you, Algie."

The boys took the pebbles, and to my surprise, both seemed grateful.

"This is very well painted, Rosamund. Thank you very much," said Nic.

"Mine's good too," said Algie. "Why are you giving them to us?"

"You're nice to us. You take us on the boat. I wanted to give you something, and this is all I could think of."

"You have a sweet-natured friend, Lucy," Nic said. "You are lucky to have her." He studied his pebble. He turned it over, and I noticed that Rosamund had painted all of our names onto the back of it, *Algie & Nic, Lucy & Rosamund*. He slipped it into his top pocket. "It'll be safe in there," he said. "I'll look at it often."

Algie carried on rolling his stone over in his fingers for some time. I could tell he really liked it. There was plenty of detail on his, some reeds and flowers, and again, it had our four names painted carefully on the back.

"This is one of the best presents I've ever had," he said. "I'm going to call it my lucky stone. My lucky stone from lucky Rosamund." He took out his handkerchief and wrapped the stone up inside it. He plunged it deep into the pocket of his shorts.

The boys were away at school for long periods, and at those times, we looked forward to their return to the village. We'd look out for the black car, and when Dad was working for Reg, I'd ask him who was staying at the manor and when the family was next expected. We didn't talk to the local children about our friendship. We might have been able to impress them, but we didn't care about things like that. Rosamund and I preferred to keep the fact that we knew the brothers a secret in case the others wanted to join in and spoil things. We sometimes laughed at the fact that no one had a notion and wondered if they'd believe us, even if we told them. When they made fun of us at break time and goaded us in the games lessons, we looked at each other and smiled. They thought they were better than us, but we had something special.

I told Mum and Dad when we played with Algie and Nic; Rosamund told her parents as well. They didn't seem to find anything wrong with it or unusual. Mum told me to be careful on the boat, but Dad said it was good for me to learn about the river. Rosamund's dad thought the same. He thought it something of an opportunity for us and loved it when we said we'd been allowed to have a go at rowing. Her mother had a similar demeanor to Rosamund. She took an interest in everything we did, no matter what, and was always keen to hear about our new pastime.

## The Ultimate Village Game

\*\*\*\*

Lolly and Agnes had become keen on the bridge games. Lionel and Bob were also happy to play. The games hardly needed organizing, but I made sure to list every other Wednesday as 'Bridge Afternoon.' We set a table aside in the lounge and checked the television wasn't on too loudly. John or Larry would provide refreshments. I was pleased Bob was becoming more independent. He was joining in with the other residents more and more and becoming less reliant on his sister. Of course, when Miss Pickering visited, they were still to be seen huddled together, deep in conversation.

Most of the residents had managed to keep well during the winter, but Mrs. Cook, who was the frailest, was prone to becoming wheezy, and Ethel had suffered from a persistent cough. She'd found it impossible to shake it off. It tired her, she'd lost her appetite, and she'd taken to staying in her room all day. I went in to see her.

"Hello, Ethel."

"Hello, Lucy. How nice to see you." She was up, sitting in her chair, but looked pale.

"How are you feeling?"

"Oh, a little low, you know. I wish I could stop coughing."

"What did the doctor give you? Lianne said you have a new prescription."

"I'm not sure, but it tastes horrible!" She managed a smile.

"I could make you a hot lemon drink with some honey. Would you like that?"

"I don't feel like eating or drinking a thing."

"Shall I make it anyway? You might fancy it if it

was in front of you."

"Yes, all right, if it's not a bother. Perhaps when the others have their tea."

"Is there anything else you'd like? I could get you something from the village. I need to do some shopping in my lunch hour."

"I can't think of anything."

During my break I went to the chemist's and bought some menthol sweets, then I went to the newsagent's.

"Hello, Linda, how are you?"

"Well, thank you. I've not seen much of you lately."

"I have a new job. It's keeping me busy."

"You've left Moonstones?"

"No. I've become assistant manager at Moonstones, or I should say, I am training to become assistant manager."

"That's wonderful news. Well done, Lucy. I love to hear a success story, especially when it's a female one!"

"Thank you. I'm trying to learn new tasks and new skills. I hope I'll be able to master the role. I don't want to let everyone down."

"I'm sure you won't do that, Lucy. You wouldn't let anyone down."

"Now, what can I buy for someone with a cough?" I scrutinized the large jars of sweets that sat high up on the shelves and scanned the various packets which abundantly crowded the counter.

"Cough candy? ...or I have these blackcurrant sweets." Linda used her expert eye.

I decided to buy a few of each. Even if Ethel didn't consume them, I hoped she'd be cheered by being brought the items.

Linda weighed the sweets carefully and put them into separate paper bags. "Any magazines today?"

"I don't seem to have a spare minute to read them lately. I should get one for Ethel, though." I selected a magazine full of stories, recipes, and gossipy articles. "I'll take this one, Linda, please."

"Don't be a stranger," she called as I left.

It would give me such pleasure to hand Ethel my selection of offerings. I wanted her to feel better and be able to return to the lounge.

I'd found a blackboard in the store cupboard, and on it, I listed the activities for the coming fortnight. I would find a place for it somewhere in the lounge and update it on a regular basis. Apart from bridge, we were to have Monica, who would run the exercise afternoon, Rita, running the music club, and the vicar was coming to pay a visit. As part of my new role, I decided I should be on the lookout for more visitors and provide additional activities. Events like those did the residents a lot of good, I thought. They loved to chat about them afterward too. It wasn't necessary to have activities every day, but one or two a week made for something to look forward to, take part in, and then discuss.

Chapter 20
Another Visit to Miss Pickering's

I was immersed in my new role and enjoying my social life so much that I had almost forgotten my original reason for returning to the village. I was convinced I had found the life that was meant for me. I'd stumbled upon it, but it was as if something had brought me to it. I was determined to put every effort I could muster into fulfilling this new destiny. Free from the pain and negative emotion I'd been accustomed to, I'd become someone who had something to offer and to people who appreciated me. Please, please, I told myself, don't make a mess of this. Morsel was my soulmate. I discussed everything with her. She was my sounding board, my sounding hound. She was also my constant companion. Lianne and Joe expected Morsel to be with me, and the residents, Bert in particular, had taken a liking to her. She often spent time in his room, and he'd asked if come the spring, he could take her for walks in the garden. Life could be no better, I thought.

"Someone was asking after you," Candy said.

We were on a weekend shift together, and it was just like old times.

"Do tell," I said.

"I didn't realize you knew him."

"Who was it?"

"I'll give you a guess."

"I've no idea. Where were you?"

"At the inn. Paul was playing darts."

"I can't think. You're going to have to tell me."

"Crinkle Crane!" She smiled at me in a way that seemed to suggest an attraction. "He appeared very interested to find out how you were."

"Really? I've only spoken to him once. I met him out dog walking."

"Well, I think you made an impression."

A Crane asking after me was not what I wanted to hear because my new life was precarious and not yet established. Any Crane had a link to the manor in some way or another, and all I could think was that my old life was going to rear up again and get in the way.

Miss Pickering was visiting. I noticed her in the lounge.

"Bob says this was your idea, the blackboard," she said.

"The events were already planned. I thought it would be nice to have them on the board. Then the residents can see what's coming up."

"Yes, I agree…and you've written it all so beautifully, hasn't she, Bob?"

"She has, Pru."

"Mr. Pickering is enjoying the bridge games. Aren't you, Mr. P?" I said.

"I like the bridge afternoon," he said to his sister. I don't think he'd heard the question, but the answer made sense.

"When did you learn to play bridge?" she asked him.

"I don't know. I've always played, haven't I?"

"I can't remember you playing before. It's quite a

complicated game, isn't it, Lucy?"

"I think it is, yes."

"Lionel cheats, of course," said Mr. Pickering, and then he and his sister went off into a fit of giggles.

Back in the kitchen I started preparing for a tea round. We were back to plain cake for January, it seemed. I found the items John had left: Madeira cake, fruit loaf, and various everyday biscuits. I arranged them on plates according to appetite. Along with the Pickerings, four other residents were seated in the lounge. Bert, Mrs. Cook, and Lolly were in their rooms. I'd been told Lolly had two friends with her. She'd need extra slices of cake, but in general, visitors seemed thin on the ground that day.

After Candy and I had drunk tea and nibbled a couple of the more interesting looking of the biscuits, I set off with the trolley.

"Can you pop in and see me, Lucy?" Miss Pickering said.

"To your house?" Mr. Pickering had gone to spend a penny, and his sister had grasped the moment; no one would overhear.

"Yes, come to The Flower Pot. I have something I'd like to discuss with you." She looked round to make doubly sure no one was listening in, "About the Lesters," she said.

"I can come, of course. Tomorrow?"

"Are you off tomorrow?"

"Yes."

"Come at this sort of time. And I'll make you a cup of tea for a change."

Bob was on his way back. He'd taken to using his stick, and with it, he seemed quite speedy. He sat down.

## The Ultimate Village Game

Miss P produced a letter she'd received from Nathan, put on her glasses, and began to read it to her brother.

\*\*\*\*

Playing with the Lester boys made us happy. When they were away, thinking about them cheered us up. At school, we continued to suffer the bullying and name-calling the other children put us through. Rosamund's treatment was worse than mine. Michael Wilson was the meanest. We were in the school hall for assembly, and he was late. The teacher told him to sit next to Rosamund. It was the only seat left. Even in front of the teacher, he didn't hold back.

"I'll catch fleas if I sit there," he retorted. The whole school laughed, and I remember the pain I felt for my friend. I heard her breathe in sharply, but that was her only reaction.

"Sit down and be quiet," the teacher said. There was no further admonishment.

I spoke to him in the classroom afterward. "Don't be nasty, Michael Wilson!"

"Shut up! You smell!" he said.

"I'd rather smell. I'd rather have fleas than have anything to do with you!"

He laughed, but I felt better for saying it, even if it did get me into trouble.

"Lucy Short, do you want a detention?" The teacher scowled at me.

Later Rosamund told me not to listen to the others, and I reminded her that soon Nic and Algie would be back, and we'd have better fun with them on one day than we could have in a whole term with any one of the horrid village children.

We were never invited to the manor, and the

brothers didn't come to our homes. That didn't matter. Our friendship was nurtured by the river, in the copse, and on the common. Those were the places we met and played. On one occasion when we were out with them, I remember seeing Michael Wilson not far off. He was with some of his mates from school.

"Those boys don't like us," I told Nic and Algie.

"Those boys are silly and daft," said Nic

"Those boys are stupid," said Algie, and then he and Nic thought up a catalog of other names to call them.

"Those boys are ghastly."

"Those boys are frightful."

"Those boys are ugly."

"Those boys make me feel sick." Algie added a realistic sound to go with this declaration.

Rosamund and I laughed so much. The more descriptions they came up with, the more we laughed, and I can still remember the feeling I had that day. I felt a real love for the brothers and believed we'd become true and proper friends, the four of us. Rosamund and I were inseparable, and we'd somehow forged a powerful bond with Algie and Nic.

****

Miss Pickering brought me into her lounge and told me to sit on the sofa. There was a low table in front of me, and on it, she served a dainty tea. She laid out two platters of tiny sandwiches: egg and cress and salmon paste with cucumber. There was a tiered cake stand with iced fancies, butterfly cakes, and flapjacks, the corners dipped in chocolate.

"It looks almost too good to eat, Miss P," I told her.

## The Ultimate Village Game

"Don't be silly. Tuck in."

Tea was strained into bone china cups. I was given a small plate with a tasteful floral design and a delicate blue handled knife. This was to be afternoon tea like something from the past, or perhaps from a grand contemporary hotel.

"Is this the sort of thing you might have served at the manor?"

"On occasion. It's more the sort of tea I might serve to the church group, and sometimes when I'm just having an afternoon here on my own! I enjoy having a nice tea at four o'clock. I like the tradition, and why not?"

It was easy to enjoy small talk with Miss Pickering. She was an accomplished practitioner. I supposed it was a necessary skill for a housekeeper, but it was a gift, something one couldn't entirely learn. Of course, I knew she had something specific to tell me because she'd let me know that when she invited me, but she didn't rush into it. We chatted about all sorts before the subject was approached.

"I wanted to tell you about Algie," she said finally.

"Algie Lester?"

"Yes."

It was a long time since I'd heard anything about Algie. I knew he was at the manor and had been for many years, but not much more than that.

"He's deteriorating, and I think it has to do with Nic," said Miss Pickering.

Algie had become disabled. He used a wheelchair, and I understood he also had other health issues. By now, he required full-time care, and this was in place for him at the manor. No one seemed to encounter him.

He didn't appear to be taken out, and no news of him ever reached the village.

"Nic is unwell and in America?" I checked.

"Nic is unwell, and although I don't believe they've seen each other since Nic left the county, I think Algie is suffering from the knowledge of his brother's ill health."

I couldn't understand why Miss P wanted to tell me this. It also struck me that she wasn't really saying it in a gossipy way. It was almost as if she felt I needed to know. I'd never told Miss Pickering I once had a friendship with Nic and Algie. That was in the distant past, and I couldn't think she'd have any knowledge of it. Perhaps she just wanted someone to talk it over with.

"Have you seen Algie?" I asked her.

"No, I've just heard about the situation. You know how it is."

"Do you feel something should be done?"

More tea was poured. A few more things were said, and then the subject was changed. A little while later, I left. I went over the conversation again and again in my head but couldn't fathom it out. I just couldn't work out why Miss Pickering had brought me round to tell me this. Not much information had been imparted. I was given the basic information about Algie, just as I was previously given the information about Nic. Of course, I didn't know if what she told me was true. In both the case of what she'd said about Nic not long back and the new information about his brother, I'd anticipated additional facts or explanation, but no more was forthcoming. Miss P was elderly but in no way muddled. She clearly wanted to tell me these things, but why? I had to assume it was purely because I'd taken an interest on previous occasions. Then again, as far as I knew, she could be having endless similar tea parties with all sorts of other people and giving them the same news. All I could do was listen, take in the information, and see what happened next.

\*\*\*\*

At Moonstones, we were having an afternoon of singing around the piano. Our workshop leader, Rita, was a good musician and extremely popular with the residents. When she first came, she brought recordings and gave out instruments for them to play and join in with. She soon started asking what sort of music they enjoyed and worked out how she could incorporate their choices into the workshops. Each session was different and continued from the one before. This time Rita was playing piano, and the residents were singing along, mostly to songs selected by one of the group. There was a chance for solos and also time to discuss why the resident liked the song and if it brought back memories. Rita made sure everyone made a contribution. Molly was able to hum along to a good few of the tunes and had a look of pleasure the whole time. Bert was a bit of a star and had been given a number of verses to sing. He knew the words off by heart. Marcia, we discovered, was herself something of a pianist. She'd had to miss out on most of the Christmas activities, so it was particularly pleasing to see her back in good health and showing off her talents.

I made sure to properly thank Rita as I helped her gather her things and load her car at the end of the afternoon. I made sure she knew I was aware of the effort she was putting in and that I thought she was managing to get the most she possibly could out of the sessions.

I had recently decided to organize some slide shows. There would be endless subject matters that could be covered. I planned to try to rope George in on this in the first instance. He took a lot of photographs of the local area, and I thought showing them would surely make for an interesting afternoon. There was a local bird-watching club, and I thought it would be a good idea to contact the group and see if they too could offer a slide show. Jenny and Malcolm were avid garden visitors. I felt sure they'd have a good collection of photos ready and waiting to be exhibited at Moonstones. They went all over the country visiting places of horticultural interest.

\*\*\*\*

It went without saying. Everyone in Steely had sympathy for Algie. After the terrible accident, a quietness had come over the village. People said it would never be the same again. I think they expected Reg to leave the manor and take his sons with him, also his cars, his glamorous way of life, the village game, and everything the Lesters had come to represent; even the most down-to-earth of the villagers would speak about the magic Reg had brought with him. It wasn't the case; Reg employed a team of doctors, nurses, and caregivers and adapted a section of the manor so that Algie could be taken care of. No expense was spared. Reg was the type of man who wouldn't give in. He was determined he would bring Algie back to full health. I was told he held on to the belief, right up until his own death. He continued to insist that somewhere out there in the world was a means to cure Algie, and if it didn't exist right at that moment, it would exist in the future.

## The Ultimate Village Game

A breakthrough was just around the corner. His son was going to walk again, regain his full mental capacity, be a picture of health, and be ready to take his right and proper place in the world.

\*\*\*\*

"George!" I called out. George was walking along Broad Street, and I was out giving Morsel a quick once around the block before going home for a restful evening.

"Lucy, I didn't expect to see you. I thought you'd be at work."

"I'm done for the day."

"I've heard all about your promotion. I wasn't surprised. It's only what you deserve."

I let George know that in my new role, I wanted to do all I could to improve the lives of the residents. "And that's where you come in," I told him.

"Me?"

"Yes, I have you down to present our first slide show."

George looked bemused, but once I'd employed my best persuasive skills, he began to warm to the idea. He said he had arranged some presentations at the university, austere, educational, factual affairs, but that he thought it could be fun to put some photos together to show off the local beauty spots. He soon became quite enthusiastic. He had a collection of shots of the surrounding hills and farmland and stacks of images of the river. He would have a good look through them and see if he could make an event out of them. He'd have a think about the best way to exhibit them.

"Is everything still all right at home?"

"Do you know, Lucy, everything seems to be going

well at home at the moment. I'm so glad I listened to you. I didn't make accusations. I gave the situation time and space. That was exactly the right course to follow. You are very talented when it comes to understanding human nature. You can read a situation like no one else I've ever come across."

I let George speak. His compliments were always hugely overblown, but I'd become almost used to them by now. I'd learned to smile, accept them, and not to get too embarrassed.

"I suppose that means you won't be popping round for drinks anymore," I said. "You'll be enjoying cozy family nights at home again."

"On the contrary. I think getting out and about is good for all of us."

"I'm pleased to hear that."

"So what nights are you in this week? My workload has lightened, and I'm in the mood to spend a gossipy evening with you," he said.

"The day after tomorrow would be best for me."

"I'll be there…armed with a good bottle of red."

I was more self-assured these days. Socializing was no longer out of the ordinary, but when we parted company, I continued my short walk with an extra spring in my step.

"My life has turned a corner, Morsel," I told the little black dog who was enthusiastically scurrying along beside me. "And I wouldn't even have met George if it wasn't for you."

At home, I made supper and watched bits and pieces on the television. I didn't pore over magazines, agonize over my wardrobe, or exercise obsessively. It wasn't as if I'd gone back to my old ways; I'd incorporated the new ways more comfortably into my life. I'd become a new me, and was enjoying every minute of it.

I spent the next evening with Belle and Charlie. They'd invited me round. Belle said she was fed up with the long, dark evenings and wanted some company. I brought a selection of drinks with me: a bottle of wine, some cherry fizz, and an interesting elderflower-flavored cordial. I'd also selected a luscious-looking box of chocolates. David was away, and we were going to have a proper girls' night in.

Belle and I were soon enjoying the wine. Morsel had come along at Charlie's request, and the two of them had gone off to play upstairs.

"So, how is your new job?" Belle asked.

"I'm enjoying it. It seems to be giving me more energy. It's challenging, but I think it's good for me to do something that stretches my capabilities."

"I do wish I were more like you, Lucy."

"I suppose it wouldn't be everyone's choice of job, but I love it. I get pleasure from learning the new tasks. The managing side is less hands-on, but I'm still helping people, and I still cover some regular duties as well."

"It's a career you have now, not just a job."

"I suppose so. Imagine that, me with a career!"

"Do you think I'm wasting my life away? I sometimes think that, Lucy."

I was surprised to hear Belle say that. She came across as a super confident woman of the world. She was elegant, with a perfect figure and an envy-inducing wardrobe. She was one of my role models.

"No, I don't," I said. "I've always thought of you

as someone who knows exactly what she wants and goes on and achieves it."

"I'd like to achieve something outside the home."

"You have the blog," I said.

"Yes, but that's all a bit false."

"Do you mean you want to go out to work? I suppose Charlie is old enough now."

"I think it would be good for Charlie to see her mum earning her own income."

"What sort of job would you choose?"

"Do you know, Lucy, I have no idea. I was rubbish at school."

"Well, that makes two of us!"

Belle poured more wine. I suggested she make a list of things she enjoyed doing, then try to work out what job might require her to do those sorts of things. We talked about Charlie and David and the new clothes shop that had opened in Melstow. We had a thoroughly good evening, and I went home thinking how nice it was to spend some time with Belle that was not arranged entirely around Charlie. Belle and I would meet more often. She was keen for me to help her work out what sort of a job would suit her and assist her in finding a position. She needed someone to give her a bit of a shove, she said. She thought I was just the person for that.

By Thursday, George had done so much thinking about the slide show he was pretty much ready to come and present it. He brought his laptop with him, and we sat at my table while he showed me some of the stills he'd selected. He showed me a program that allowed him to add a soundtrack, the images changing in time with the music.

"Do you think this sort of thing would work in terms of the residents?" he said. "I can project it."

"I think so. Perhaps we don't need any explanation at all?"

"No, just a series of photographs accompanied by a few pieces of music."

"I think they would love this. You can always talk to them at the end. They might want to ask you about where the photos were taken and so on."

"I'm sure I'm going to enjoy this, Lucy. I want to get out and take some additional pictures. There are a few places I have in mind that I'd like to include. Then I'll spend a bit of time polishing it all, picking the order, getting the timings right."

"As soon as you're done, let me know, and we'll book you in."

"Let's drink to that!"

We didn't drink quite as much as we had on previous evenings we'd spent together. It was plain to see George was now a much happier man.

"I have high hopes for this year, Lucy," he said. "Things seem to have got off to a good start for me, and for you, I think?"

"Yes, I can't remember when I last felt as optimistic about the future. In my case, it's been a long, long time."

George was full of ideas for other slide show events and also said he'd be happy to help present them if required. He told me there was a local history archive and that he thought the images available there would make for an interesting evening for the elderly residents. The residents might even have something to offer the archivist in terms of their memories of the area, he suggested. He liked the idea of a quiz too. I wasn't so sure about that, but he said we could show pictures and ask questions about them. We could design it, especially for an older person, with questions relating to past times. He would consider it further and talk to me about it again.

"I think this is something I've needed for a while, Lucy," he said.

"How do you mean?"

"Something I can do to help the community. I don't think I've been pulling my weight in that way."

"You've always supported local causes…the church sales and so on."

"It's not the same, though. That's just turning up and donating money at the end of the day. This way, I get to put a bit of myself into it."

"Well, you will be appreciated; you wait and see. It will be very rewarding."

Morsel came and sat at George's feet. She gave a little whimper. He reached down and brought her up onto his knee. He rubbed her back, and she gazed into his eyes, enraptured. George and I smiled at each other, enjoying the understanding we had. We had something of an unlikely friendship, but a better one I couldn't possibly imagine.

Chapter 21
The Fire

I settled into my new role at Moonstones. In due course, Lianne announced I was no longer a trainee; I was the fully-fledged assistant manager. That didn't mean I had no more to learn. As she pointed out, we would always have to carry on learning, not only me; she included Joe and herself in this. Nevertheless, she assured me she was happy I had acquired the necessary skills and demonstrated I had the right attitude to help to look after the business and to take it to new levels.

Fortunately, I was still popular with the rest of the staff. Candy I counted as a close friend, John also. John told me he preferred to deal with me on managerial matters because I actually listened to him. He said he trusted my judgment, and that if I told him there was a problem with something, he took it seriously because he knew I wouldn't say it unless it were true. I wasn't one to make a fuss, he said.

The slide shows were a big success. We also had a regular quiz. There was bridge and music, and there were exercise sessions. Bert and Lionel started taking Morsel for walks in the garden. Everything was going well.

George arrived on Thursday, as arranged, for our show on local history. He'd contacted the local society but ended up putting the exhibition together himself. He was becoming quite a regular at Moonstones. I decided to sit down at the back of the lounge and enjoy this show, just like any other member of the audience. We began with views of the older streets of Steely and images of other villages in the area, then Melstow, which had been an important market town since the seventeenth century. Some pictures showed cobbled streets with horse-drawn carriages and horse-drawn carts carrying produce. George had compiled photos of some of the important buildings, the churches and meeting halls, the old inns, and hotels. There were images of housing built long ago, some of which was no longer standing. He showed a series of photos with local dignitaries from the area's past history, cricket and football teams, the home guard. We came to a picture of the upper school in Melstow, then various shots of the pupils from the junior school in Steely, including a relatively recent photograph. A few comments were made by the residents. They remarked on people they recognized, told stories that related to certain scenes, and when the school image came up, Agnes cried out with pleasure.

"That's me. I'm in the photo." She laughed while the others tried to work out which was she. "Lucy," Agnes continued. "Is that you too…in the front row?"

I was there in the picture, second from the left, trying my best to smile.

"Yes, you're right, Agnes. That's me."

Everyone studied the image on the big presentation screen: me at the front of the group and Agnes standing at the back. But I was looking elsewhere, at the little girl sitting beside me in the picture, a mild, kind-looking child. It was Rosamund.

Bert piped up, "You must have a shot of me somewhere, George. I was in the Boys' Brigade…and I went to school in the village, back in the thirties."

"Do you know," George said, "I think I'm going to have another look into the archives and put together a second show about the area. It's fascinating, and most of you have local connections, don't you? I wonder if I can find pictures of more of you. I'll take a look."

"Steely Green Part Two!" announced Lionel. He banged his walking stick down on the floor.

"Yes, indeed," George said, "…and surroundings."

The slide shows brought people together. John had slipped in at the back of the room near me, and become engrossed. After the show, I noticed him deep in conversation with George. I spent a good deal of time in the kitchen with John, whether on a regular shift or as assistant manager. It was comforting to have a hot drink and pass the time of day while he carried on industriously with the preparation of the food, the cooking, the serving, the cleaning of equipment. John was a contented person, happy in his work and satisfied with his lot. In the kitchen, things always seemed better, problems seemed manageable, long hours seemed to quickly dwindle.

"You're not a local, John, are you?" I asked him the following morning.

"No, not at all. I came here six years ago. I knew nothing about the area." He was watching the ingredients of his recipe being slowly churned around by the electric mixer. "I applied for a job at the inn. I was successful. I worked there for a year or so, and then I saw this job advertised. At the inn, I wasn't in charge of the kitchen. Here, I am. It's what I wanted. The

Peters were really nice about it. They knew I had more to offer and encouraged me with the application."

"And you never looked back!"

"Never." John switched off the machine and turned to face me. He wore his long white apron, his face spattered with spots of the floury mixture.

"I'd better get on. I forget the time when I come in here!" I rushed off back to the office.

"Something I was going to put to you," said Lianne. She looked up. She looked down again. She was reading a document. I waited for her to speak again. "Joe and…" She carried on reading. Finally, she stopped and properly focused on me. "Joe and I were thinking of booking a weekend away."

I swallowed hard, immediately realizing the implication. "You mean…" I began.

Lianne beamed. She could see the fright in my expression.

"I can see you've had exactly the right reaction!"

"I have?"

"Yes, you're thinking about what that involves, and you're not too sure you can deal with it. You feel a little challenged."

"I feel very challenged, Lianne. Are you suggesting you'd leave me here, in charge of Moonstones, for a whole weekend?"

"That's exactly it."

"I'm not sure I'm ready."

"Well, I think you are, and what's more, so does Joe." With that, she picked up her keys and walked to the door. "We'll speak about it later," she said, and went off back to her own house. She had a way of doing this. She'd leave me to think things through. I believed it was part of the way she assessed me.

Back in the kitchen, Mariana had joined John, and they were performing a sixties number in accompaniment to the radio. Barbara was even getting involved, attempting to join in with the chorus. I'm not sure she knew the words, but she was having a go. Mariana did a few dance steps with a tea towel partner. I crossed my arms and leaned against the doorframe marveling at them.

*"Why must I be…"* they sang.

A bell went. It was Mrs. Cook's, and straight away, Barbara was gone.

"Quick! The potatoes!" John had to dash to turn down the gas.

"Whoo, I'm quite out of breath," said Mariana.

"How do you find Mrs. Cook, Mariana?" I asked her.

"Not so good. She's terribly frail," she said.

I nodded. "She's sleeping more and more."

"There's nothing else we can do to help her, is there?" Mariana asked.

"I don't think so. I wish there were," I said.

"She eats relatively well," John put in.

"That's true," Mariana agreed. "She always looks forward to her lunch. She's a savory girl, like me. I often joke with her about it."

I was pleased to hear Mariana say this. It confirmed to me she knew Mrs. Cook as an individual and not just another resident. Mrs. Cook wasn't the easiest to look after. She could be sharp tongued. Conversation didn't always flow, but I knew it was important to try harder in the case of such a resident, and Mariana had obviously made an effort with her.

Barbara returned.

"The singing is over?" she said.

"We were rudely interrupted by the potatoes," John told her.

"Mrs. Cook is fine. She asked what we were having for lunch."

Mariana laughed. "I told you so!"

I left them and went to retrieve Morsel from Bert's room.

"Shall I take her, Bert?"

"Yes, better had. I'm having a bath this morning."

"What's this?"

Bert had made one of his socks into a ball.

"A game we play, watch." He tossed the sock up into the air in front of him, and Morsel jumped expertly to catch it. She dropped it at his feet. "Thank you, Morsel." Bert looked over at me with satisfaction. "Once more." He threw it right across the room, and Morsel carefully retrieved it from under the curtain. She didn't tear across the carpet or disturb the furnishings. She brought it back and dropped it again, this time receiving a rub behind the ears.

"Very good, Bert, though you might need your socks for other purposes."

"I never liked that pair much." Barbara arrived with a look of purpose. She stood with her hands on her hips. "Have you come for me?"

"Afraid so, Bert."

"Let's get it over with then."

I went back to the office and sat, deciding that for the rest of the day, I'd imagine Joe and Lianne were far away on a sandy beach, and I was in charge of everything. You never know, I thought, I could even get to like it.

I was often taken over by thoughts about Moonstones, my head working away at the challenges it threw up. I generally had at least one of the residents on my mind, wondering if there was more we could be doing for them. On days like this, I could quite easily neglect my own needs. It happened often, not that I cared. I'd not considered anything apart from Moonstones that day, and when I finally left the building in the evening, I remembered I didn't have a thing to eat at the cottage. I walked along Broad Street to the grocery store and picked up a few basics. It would be cheese on toast for tea, though I did indulge in some of the chocolate they had stacked up enticingly by the till. I walked back through the village. It was dark by then and raining. I was juggling my shopping bags and Morsel's lead, plus my umbrella, which was determined, at intervals, to catch gusts of wind and try to escape across the road. As I stopped to rearrange my grip, I noticed someone coming out through Miss Pickering's gate. He was a good way off, but I recognized him. He slipped out, glanced in my direction for an instant, almost as if checking to see if anyone had noticed him, then walked quickly off the other way. He couldn't have seen me. He didn't have the bulldog with him, but I was sure it was Fergus. What could he be doing, I wondered. I walked toward The Flower Pot. The curtains were open, and I could clearly see Miss Pickering in the lounge. Had she just had a visit from Fergus? It was so long since I'd seen him he'd started to slip my mind. I wanted to go to the door and ask Miss P what he'd been doing there. I thought I could knock and ask if she was all right. I could say I'd seen a man in her garden and wanted to make sure she was safe. After all, I'd had a stranger in my garden not that long before.

I didn't do it. I went on home, changed out of my wet clothes, and dried Morsel off with her towel. I gave her food, put on the grill, and absentmindedly grated a too large pile of cheese. One minute my thoughts had been absorbed in the wonderful world of Moonstones, and the next, it was plunged back to Fergus, Miss Pickering, the manor, and the Lesters. I didn't want to go back to that. I wanted to move on. Moonstones was the future; it had to be. The manor and everything about it should be forgotten, left forever in the past.

"What will I do, Morsel? What will I do?" The past was such a burden. I wished there was someone I could talk it over with. It was a long time ago, but in some ways, it didn't seem that way. I could remember everything so clearly, though I tried to fight the thoughts and expel them from every corner of my mind. Rosamund's face came to me again, her kind and sensitive demeanor, then the look on Nic's face, and the memory of being told about Algie.

We'd gone to play by the river. The boys were there, and they weren't happy. Their father had invited a friend to come with them to the manor, a lady friend. Algie and Nic were close to their mother, but they understood their parents no longer got along. They'd coped with that, they'd even managed to accept some other female friends Reg had entertained from time to time, but he'd never before brought anyone with him to the manor. Nic was subdued, but Algie was angry and animated. He kicked out at things. He sporadically gave out frighteningly loud yells to demonstrate his discomfort.

"She's stupid and ugly," he shouted.

"We'll make her unwelcome," Nic told us. "We'll make sure she has a horrible time."

"I can't stand it. I don't want to be at the manor at all if she has to come." There was another blood-curdling yell from Algie.

Rosamund and I didn't know what to say. We didn't have any experience of this kind of thing.

"We could go on the boat?" Rosamund suggested.

"What good will that do?" Algie said, kicking out again.

"It might cheer you up."

"It won't."

"How could it?" said Nic.

We spent several hours with them, and we met up again the following day, but their mood hadn't lifted. We wandered around together, in the copse and on the common. It was getting quite late as we walked farther and farther along the riverbank. We reached the old mill and the string of little cottages that stood beside it. Algie seemed to have some sort of idea. He wanted to stop there. He wanted to sit on the bank looking over toward the properties. It was evening, and I was supposed to get back, Rosamund too, but we stayed with them for a while. It was a pretty spot, and the sun was still warm. In a nearby field, horses grazed. We lay back and watched the birds flying over us, across the wispy cloud-streaked sky.

"I'll have to go now," I announced eventually.

"Stay a bit longer," said Nic. "We don't want to go home."

"Come and look at the cottages," Algie said. There

was a footbridge near the mill, and he started to walk over to it.

"They belong to Dad," Nic told us.

Rosamund and I tagged along. We reached the row of houses. We weren't sure why we were there. We knew the cottages and were aware of the people who lived in them. The door of one property was open. Algie went in.

"Why's he going in?" I said to Nic.

"Well, the door is open."

"But does he know the lady?"

"I don't think so."

Algie re-emerged with a grin on his face. "Come on. Let's all go in."

"I'm not," I said.

Rosamund stood back, but Nic stepped over to the cottage.

"I don't like this," I said to Rosamund as the brothers both disappeared through the front door. We watched for a few minutes, but they didn't come back out.

"I'm going home," I said.

"I'll go too," said Rosamund. She lived nearby, whereas our house was more of a distance. I left her and went on my way. I was already going to be late, and Mum would surely tell me off.

I thought no more about the situation. Mum was unusually forgiving. She realized it was a lovely evening to be out of doors. By bedtime, I was very tired, and that was something which always seemed to please her.

Noises disturbed me that night. I woke a few times but fell quickly back to sleep on each occasion. It was unusual to hear anything during the hours of darkness, except for the wind in the trees or the call of a fox. In the morning, I found out what had happened. Mum and Dad were talking about it, and the neighbor had come to discuss it with them. There'd been a fire. What I'd heard was the sound of fire engines: two from Melstow and one from farther away; also the ambulance's siren.

"Where was the fire?" I asked.

"At the mill," Mum said.

"The mill cottages," Dad added. I felt a wave of anxiety roll up through my body. "I'm going to see if I can do anything to help," Dad told me. Ned, the neighbor, hopped into the truck with him, and they set off.

As the hours passed, bits and pieces of information reached us at the house. Mum and I were keen to hear them. We found out the fire had swept through three of the four cottages. Someone, we weren't sure who, had been rescued from the bedroom of one property and was in hospital in a serious condition; another person, perhaps one of the fire crew, had been forced to jump from an upper window to save their own life after taking part in the rescue. During the day, I heard more details, and the more I heard, the more worried I became. Gradually the news seeped through that the fire was thought to have been started deliberately. It had started at the Bensons', the house Algie and Nic had gone into, and had spread to two adjoining cottages.

I tried to keep my head down, but I asked my dad one question. "How did the fire start, Dad?"

"They don't know at the moment," he said. "But I'm sure they'll get to the bottom of it."

\*\*\*\*

So I was looking after Moonstones. I'd had to move into Joe and Lianne's house for three nights. I'd not even thought about nights until they told me I'd need to be on the premises at all times; I had to be on call. At least Lianne had booked the best workers for the shifts and some additional day cover so that I could concentrate wholly on overseeing things. She'd made a special bed up for Morsel.

Mr. Pickering was in a mischievous mood.

"I might complain," he said.

"Please don't do that, Mr. P. Lianne will definitely sack me!"

"It was a joke," said Barbara. "But not a very good one, Bob," she told him. She was quite strict with him, but he was having a good laugh about it anyway.

"You were teasing me?" I said. "I think I must have lost touch with my sense of humor. It's all this responsibility." I stuck my tongue out at him.

I followed Barbara along the corridor.

"At least it's not gone to your head," she said.

"Oh, no, it won't do that."

"It's good you're not over confident. It will keep you on your toes."

"That's what Lianne says. I hope you're right."

"Listen to me trying to advise you, and you being my manager!"

"I don't mind."

"I covered a few times in the last place I worked."

"Do you mean you were managing there?"

"Once or twice, but it was a different sort of business, more about rehabilitation."

"Well, I'm pleased you're on shifts each day while the real managers are away. You are a safe pair of hands, Barbara. I appreciate that."

"I enjoy Moonstones. It's more friendly than the other place." With that, she swept into Lionel's room and began what I could tell was some regular banter with him.

Miss Pickering didn't visit that day, Friday, and didn't appear on Saturday either. I mentioned this to Candy.

"I think she said she wasn't able to come for a couple of days. I can't quite remember what she said to be honest." Whatever it was, Bob had forgotten as well, and he asked me more than once if I'd seen her in the village.

"There's flu in the village," said John. "We're bound to be low on visitors. They're advised not to come if they're feeling unwell themselves."

"Of course. That's probably it."

We spent the weekend with the stir-crazy residents, deprived of their trips out and their sources of news from the outside world. I tried not to fuss, imagining I was sitting up in the clouds looking down on Moonstones and tweaking anything that needed attention with a long pair of eyebrow tweezers. Shifts started and finished. I went through the invoices, updated the bookkeeping spreadsheets, ordered the cleaning products, dealt with the laundry van. The doctor visited Mrs. Cook.

"The flu outbreak is taking hold," he told me.

"We've had very few visitors," I stated.

"Good thing," he said.

Sunday still flew by as it did every week: the morning routines, the roast lunch, the gathering together of most of the residents in the lounge for the hymn singing. Candy and Barbara were on together. I told them I was slipping out for twenty minutes. They were busy with their chores. I walked as fast as I could. There was a light on at Miss Pickering's cottage, and I could see into the lounge. I knocked. She wouldn't be at church at this hour, but it didn't seem as though she was at home. Everything in the lounge was tidy. There were no cups on the table, no Sunday newspapers. I knocked again, waited for a few minutes. No sound came from inside. I left and set off back to work. No one had missed me. In the lounge, Candy brought me tea and a slice of carrot cake. I sat with Molly and sang along to a number of hymns.

"Did you ever meet Fergus?" I said to Candy when she found a minute to sit.

"I'm not sure. Was he a resident?"

"No, I see him in the village sometimes. I think he knows Miss Pickering."

"Fergus? Is he Scottish?"

"Yes." For a moment, I thought she knew him.

"No, I've not met any Scots round here."

"He has a dog."

"You know I don't know any of your dog walking friends," she said, then added, "only Crinkle." She winked and gave me a nudge.

"He's not interested in me."

"I wouldn't say that. I have a little feeling."

"I've only spoken to him once!"

"It's a shame Valentine's Day is over."

She smirked, gathered some of the used plates, and went back across the room in the direction of the kitchen.

By the time Monday morning came, I was more

than ready for Lianne and Joe's return.

"We've had a lovely time. How were things here?" Lianne threw her heavy holdall from her shoulder onto the floor.

"I think I need a fortnight off," I joked. I was proud of myself and had enjoyed the time in a way, though I'd been more than tested. I began to tell them about everything that had happened and about the flu outbreak. "And to top it all, last night there was a call from the agency. The night shift worker had canceled at the last minute due to illness. They were ringing round, but they were struggling to find anyone who could replace him."

Joe spoke. "You obviously found a solution?"

"I thought about trying Jackie, but in the end, I covered it."

"You've not slept?" Lianne said.

"No, but I'm fine. And nothing happened. It was a quiet night."

"I think we should send you off home," Joe said.

"Yes," Lianne agreed. "You go off, and we'll chat about it some more on Wednesday when you're back in."

"You had a good time?" I checked.

"We had a wonderful break," said Joe. He came over and embraced me. "Thank you so much for looking after Moonstones."

"We weren't sure how we'd feel," Lianne said, taking her turn to give me a hug. "But we soon realized, knowing you were here, we could relax."

****

By Wednesday, Miss P still hadn't turned up.

"She's away," said Lianne. "Didn't I say?"

"Candy said something about it," I told her.

Lianne looked up. "Poor Bob. Was he worried?"

"Where is she? Gone up to town with her friends from the church?" I asked.

"No," Joe said. "She's gone to America."

Chapter 22
Blame

Algie was badly injured. He was taken to a specialist hospital; updates on his condition were hard to come by. News about the fire and how it started came through more quickly. I was completely dumbfounded when I began to hear the suggestion being bandied about in the village. To me, it was impossible and unimaginable. A few days later, I spotted Nic. I think he was looking for me. He was out walking on his own near our house.

I went straight up to him. "What happened at the cottages? You were in there. What did you see?"

"You haven't heard what happened?"

"No. Only silly stuff. Mum calls it tittle-tattle."

He was calm and purposeful as he continued. "She did it. She came in after us. There was a paraffin heater in the room with the old lady. She knocked it over. The curtains caught fire."

"That's not what happened."

"Algie tried to put it out. He managed to drag one of the curtains from the rail and started stamping on it. He told us to go. I ran outside; she did too. Algie stayed in there. The fire was spreading. He was trying to stop it, trying to help the lady."

"She wouldn't have gone inside."

"I banged on the doors of the other cottages. Told

them to get out. One of the neighbors tried to get in to assist Algie. The flames were huge by then. Algie got stuck upstairs."

"She was just about to leave. She was going home, like me."

"He had no option. He had to jump."

"She went home!"

"No."

Rosamund was getting the blame for starting the fire. I turned my back on Nic and went indoors, stunned by disbelief and anger. Trying to think, I set off to Rosamund's house but stopped and went back home. I didn't know what to do. Over the coming days, the accusations were repeated, and Rosamund was taken away. I'd not even been able to speak to her.

It wasn't until several days later that I saw Nic again. By this time, I'd worked out what I wanted to say to him, and I confronted him.

"I know Rosamund. I know her better than anyone. She wouldn't start any fire. I saw your brother that day. He was mad about everything. He was cross the whole day. He went into that cottage to do something bad. That's why I left. Rosamund left too."

"No. She came in."

"The only reason she'd have gone in was to get you and your brother to come out!"

"She knocked over the heater."

"How?"

"She pushed it. She was trying to impress Algie."

"She wouldn't have done that."

"She did. I wish she hadn't, but she did."

I was finding it hard not to cry, but Nic was fully in control of himself.

"Is Algie getting better?" I asked.

"He's going to be in hospital for a long time."

I couldn't help caring about Algie, but I didn't believe Nic's story. "What did your dad say?"

"He thinks Algie was very brave."

I almost didn't like Nic anymore. He was lying. I made my mind up. I would talk to my own dad and explain to him what had really happened.

\*\*\*\*

George met me in the copse, and I told him all about being in charge at Moonstones. By now, I could see the funny side of my experience and all the problems I'd had to deal with, especially since nothing had actually gone wrong. I made him laugh, recounting the various incidents.

"You're well and truly capable of management now, I'd say."

"I suppose so. But I could have done with a more gentle introduction!"

"You've learned so much in such a short space of time. It's good."

"I think the main thing I've learned is how important it is to have a good team…work together and get on with everyone."

"That's hard, I think, to pull all that off and still be in charge."

"Maybe, but I think I can do it."

"Good for you, Lucy. Good for you."

\*\*\*\*

I talked to Dad. He listened and nodded. He said to leave it to him, he'd speak to Reg. I saw Nic once more before his holiday came to an end and he went back to school.

"I told Dad what really happened. He'll tell your dad."

"I know what happened. I was there, Lucy."

I glared at him. I knew he was lying. "You can't just blame someone else. They'll find out, and then you'll get into big trouble."

His expression didn't change. "I understand you. Rosamund was your best friend, and you're sticking up for her. That's to be expected."

"Rosamund *is* my best friend," I corrected him. "And I'm going to keep telling everyone she wouldn't have done something like that. She's never done a thing wrong in all her life, not anything at all!"

"It was out of character. That's true."

"She didn't do it!"

****

It was mid-week, the afternoon, and I was out for a long walk. I was in my own world, tossing Morsel's ball ahead of me, her curly coat blowing in the wind as she chased after it.

"Lucy! Lucy!" I heard. It was Crinkle Crane. He was striding in my direction. "Can I speak to you for a minute?"

"Um, yes." We were on the wildest part of the common with our dogs, and no one else was in sight. There was nothing I could do but listen. He was an attractive man, tall with well-cut dark hair and strong features. I tried to prepare for what he was going to say.

He seemed tentative. He looked down at his shoes as if he were preparing his sentence. He lifted his head and said, "Do you know anything about Reg Lester's will?"

It wasn't what I'd expected. "No."

"It's just that we're getting a bit worried about our jobs." Bruce was beside him, panting. "We don't know what we'll do if we lose the work at the manor. We look after a few other gardens, but most of our hours are spent there. We're a hard-working family, but it won't be that easy to find new clients."

"You're good workers. Everyone says so. But I don't know anything about the will." He looked disappointed. He plunged his hands into his pockets. "Why would I?" I wasn't sure if I should have asked that question.

"Oh, you know. Perhaps hearsay." His piercing eyes were now locked, looking into mine.

"About me?" I'd asked another now. For a few more heartbeats, he continued to look at me. Then he relaxed and sighed. He stared over my head, out across the countryside.

"I don't really know," he said.

\*\*\*\*

I'd not been able to talk to Rosamund. Dad said he'd find an appropriate moment to speak with Reg, but nothing seemed to change. The village carried on with the tittle-tattle, and over the weeks, it appeared that the story Nic told became accepted by everyone, except for me. I stopped voicing my opinion, but I didn't change my mind. I continued to tell myself that I was right, and come the next holiday, I saw Nic again.

"I haven't forgotten about what you've done," I said. "I'll never forget. One day when I'm older, they'll believe me."

"Come on, Lucy. You're still my friend. What's more, I told Dad what a good friend you are, and I told him I admired you for sticking up for Rosamund."

"You're trying to fool me."

"I'm not. I like you. And Lucy, you know, one day, I'll be in a position to look after you."

"How do you mean?"

"I'll help you out."

Not long after, Dad found work in Morley Brook. In no time, we were moving.

"What about the treasure hunt?" Mum said. "We won't be able to take part if we're not living in Steely."

"We wouldn't be likely to win anyway, now would we? It's better to go where the work is." Dad's mind was made up. "I'll have a guaranteed income for some time."

I had to change schools. I'd be going to Morley Brook Comprehensive. At least I wouldn't have to face Michael Wilson anymore.

Several school terms went by. I heard almost nothing about Rosamund. I understood she'd been put in some sort of detention center, a place where she could be monitored and assessed. There wasn't anything I could do. I carried on, but on the inside, I was sore. I was furious about Algie and felt wounded by Nic. Gradually, as time passed, I became angry with myself too. What sort of a friend was I? I had done nothing to help poor Rosamund. Whatever had I left her to face that night? She wouldn't have been equipped to deal with what she'd been put through. It was my fault as much as anyone's. I'd abandoned her. My life would always be tainted by betrayal.

****

Back at Moonstones, my days off spent, I was on a regular shift with Candy. I came back down to earth, changing bedding and helping to bathe the residents.

The flu virus was on the way out, and there was a scattering of visitors to let in and bring tea for. Miss P was in the lounge with Bob. I spotted her on my way to Bert's room and stopped in the doorway to give her a wave. Bob was beaming with pleasure.

"Is it the singing today?" asked Ethel, up and about and lively having fully recovered from her bad cough.

"No, tomorrow, Ethel."

"Oh, pity." She hurried on into the lounge.

"The singing," said Molly, who was loitering in the corridor. She gave me a strange look, which was hard to decipher.

"Yes, Rita will be here tomorrow afternoon," I told her.

"The singing," she said again.

Candy and I saw little of each other as we carried out the chores and responded to residents' bells. We finally made it to the kitchen for a break. Larry fussed about, getting drinks and opening a new box of biscuits especially for us.

"Miss Pickering's been in America," he said.

"I heard that," said Candy. "I've never been. I don't suppose I ever will go either."

"I went to Las Vegas once," said Larry.

"Really?" Candy chose a chocolate digestive.

"Yes, a few years back, with a few mates."

"Were you gambling?" she asked.

"Yes, but only in a very safe way! We just went for a bit of fun."

I didn't join in with the conversation. I was consumed by my own thoughts, wondering if what I couldn't help thinking Miss Pickering might have been doing in the States would prove to be correct. I didn't want to rush to ask her; I'd wait for her, hopefully, to offer up the information.

\*\*\*\*

Time passed. Steely people no longer talked about the fire. They didn't like to hear about it or think about it. It ruined the fairytale image of the village they had become accustomed to being a part of. They would have been happy to allow that one dreadful night to be airbrushed out of its history. Reg spent a large sum of money repairing the cottages. By the time he'd finished, they were of a much higher standard than they'd ever previously been. The surrounding area was tastefully landscaped, and the track via which they were accessed was vastly improved. I'd heard that he hadn't increased the rent. For the inhabitants, the renovated abodes were of a kind they never could have imagined they'd be able to afford. Reg made a fuss of the Bensons. Old Mrs. Benson survived and returned to her home, having been "rescued" by Algie and the fire brigade. Algie eventually left the hospital and was brought to the manor to recuperate. His father continually insisted he was improving, progressing. Things were back to normal. At least, that was what everyone wanted to believe; it was in everyone's best interests to stick to that interpretation.

\*\*\*\*

I went to the lounge with the large teapot loaded onto the trolley, hoping to catch up with Miss P and find out all about her visit to America. I greeted her on my way to the far side of the room, planning to distribute drinks to the others first and buy some time to spend with her. I served Lionel and Ethel, bantered with Bert and Agnes, and helped Molly settle into a chair.

Then I turned and made a beeline for the Pickerings.

"Here's your tea, Mr. Pickering. Where has your sister gone?"

"Gone."

"Gone to the ladies?"

"She had to leave. I can't remember why."

"I was hoping to hear all about her holiday."

"It wasn't a holiday, you know."

"It wasn't?"

"No, no."

"Was it to do with the church?"

"No. Business. A business trip."

"I see." I didn't see, unless my hunch was correct, because whatever business did Miss P have anything to do with, except for the one possibility that was on my mind.

"I'm pleased she's back," Mr. Pickering said.

"I know. I am too, Mr. P."

\*\*\*\*

George was to present another slide show. I wrote it beside the date on the blackboard, *Steely Green Archive Show—Part Two*, and everyone began to look forward to it.

\*\*\*\*

I came across Nic a few years later. We were in our mid-teens by then. There was a rowing event on the river near Morley Brook. I'd become a nondescript teenager, plain and a little overweight. I had no idea about clothes and possessed a broad rural accent. He was even more elegant than I remembered: a good-looking, well-dressed, and well-spoken young man. I recognized him straight away and went up to him.

"Hello, Nic Lester."

He turned, and after a moment, a smile spread across his face. "Lucy Short!" I didn't smile back. He wasn't perturbed. "Good to see you. How are you? It seems an age since I last had the pleasure."

"How's Algie?" I asked. The question was bigger than the words that shaped it. Nic's expression changed a little.

"Ah. He's not that bad at the moment, I suppose."

"Are you staying at the manor?"

"Yes. Is this where you've moved to?"

"Yes, Morley Brook."

"It's rather nice here."

Some friends of Nic's butted in. "Come on, Nic. Let's get down to the finish line. The next race is starting."

He had the same calm demeanor, unrushed, fully in control. "I'll catch up with you later, Lucy," he said before accompanying the sophisticated group of young companions he fitted so comfortably into.

I was with Mum and Dad. They'd gone to buy ice creams, and we found a bench seat and sat to eat them. We looked at the stalls, set up beside the river, and walked along the path studying the longboats, which the rowers were skillfully propelling through the water. Mum had brought a rug along, and we found a place to spread it out on the grass, higher up on the bank, from where we could watch the various events.

Come the late afternoon, Mum and Dad began to talk about leaving. I told them I'd stay for a while. There was still a throng of people, crowds spilling out of the beer tents, large groups gathering to eat at the little tables where you could order food served by a waiter or a waitress in smart black and white attire.

Some people were picnicking on the riverbanks. I moved the rug closer to the path and sat waiting.

\*\*\*\*

I seemed to keep missing Miss Pickering, to the point where I began to wonder if she was avoiding me. I enquired after her, via my colleagues, to see if I could glean any news. I tried Joe.

"Miss P was in America, I hear."

"Yes, I was surprised, but apparently, it's not the first time she's been over there," he said.

"A long way for her to travel."

"Yes, I think she must have gone to visit friends…or family perhaps."

Joe didn't seem to know much. I tried John and Candy, and then Barbara.

"Did Miss P tell you anything about her travels?" I asked. "I've hardly seen her since she came back."

"She was busy, I think she said. A whirlwind trip."

"Oh, she must have had some reason for going then."

"I don't know. Perhaps she just meant busy sightseeing?"

"Possibly. She must have friends there."

"She stayed in a hotel, I believe."

I didn't get much out of any of them.

\*\*\*\*

I had more to say to Nic that day by the river. I thought he'd come back along the path, and I'd get my chance to state my case. I sat on the rug and waited, and my patience was rewarded. I saw him walking in my direction and jumped down in front of him.

"I knew I'd see you again one day," I said.

"I hoped we'd meet up, I have to say." He seemed

at ease.

"You need to listen to me," I told him.

"Would you like a beer or a glass of wine?" he asked.

We weren't old enough to drink, but that didn't seem to be a boundary for Nic. He walked over to one of the bars and was served with a bottle of beer and some fizzy white wine in a see-through plastic beaker. He came back over to the bank and sat down beside me.

"What a lovely day it's been," he commented.

I'd not mastered small talk, whereas Nic was already in possession of a toolbox full of social skills. He was in the midst of being processed through his private education, acquiring the talents of diplomacy, learning etiquette, developing a winning smile, an engaging look. I blundered out short-worded sentences.

"I know Rosamund didn't start the fire."

"Lucy, do we have to go over that again?"

"I won't ever forget, you know. She got the blame. They put her in some special school. I wasn't allowed to see her."

"I don't think she really meant harm."

When he said that, an anger rose in my blood. "It was Algie! We both know that!" I shouted.

"Shhh... Look, I've told you everything I know. Lucy, can't we just have a drink together and enjoy the evening?"

"You made me a promise too. You said you'd look after me," I yelled.

"I remember saying that." I could feel tears welling, and though I was fighting them back, I felt sure he was aware. "I meant it," he said. He looked into my eyes with a gentle expression, then threw an arm around my shoulders. I began to sob. "You're too nice, Lucy."

"You tried to blackmail me."

"Come on now. It's not good for you to get so upset. You're unhappy, but there's no need to be."

"I believe you saw Algie do it. Between you, you made up the story about Rosamund…and then you stuck to it. Algie threw himself out of the window to save his own life, but the fire brigade rescued Mrs. Benson. Rosamund wasn't even there! Of course, everyone listened to you rather than her."

"Algie and I were downstairs. Rosamund came in. She said she heard something in the bedroom and went up there. The was a *bang*. There was a smell of paraffin, then burning. We heard Rosamund laughing. Algie ran up. He shouted down to me that the stove had been pushed over and the curtains were on fire, that there was an old lady in the bed. He told me to get Rosamund away and then to get help. I went to the other cottages, knocking on the doors. Mr. Jackson called 999, then he came to assist us. We told the other residents to evacuate. It was a horrible night for me…and for Algie."

"I don't believe you."

"You were great friends with Rosamund. We liked her too."

I sobbed some more. I knew I must look a mess and was finding it increasingly hard to express myself, with my bad grasp of language and my inability to stay calm.

"Why try to bribe me?" I said.

"I didn't."

"So why say you'd help me?"

"I felt sorry for you. What I mean is, I understood

your feelings. I cared about you."

"Well, I'm going to bring it all up again. I'm going to go to the manor one of these days and find your dad and let him know that what you told him was all a pack of lies."

I could see my comment didn't cause Nic any concern. "I meant I could look after you," he repeated. "Look, I don't like talking about this, but since Algie was hurt, my father relies on me more and more. He sees me as the person who will look after Algie once he gets too old to do it. Dad's leaving everything to me when he dies. He's told me that. I'll make sure my brother is taken care of. I have a half-brother now as well and a half-sister, but Dad sees me as his heir. One day I'll be head of the family. I'll have to look out for everyone."

Nic was again making me some sort of promise. I still thought he was weaving an intricate deception. He'd reiterated his version of the story of the fire, and he wanted me onside. However much I wanted to oppose him, I felt helpless. I had no power in the situation. I knew I wouldn't get anywhere with my argument. Imagine trying to get Reg Lester to believe me rather than Nic, after all this time, with my cheap clothes, broken sentences, and bad grammar.

"So you'll look after me?" I said after a long silence.

"Yes, I'll look after you."

"Like you'll give me some rotten job at the manor or something."

"No, I'll give you something meaningful. We have other property you know, London, the South of France, and Paris, a place in the Scottish Highlands…we have assets." He wasn't showing off. He was opening my eyes to the world he belonged to, trying to explain it to someone whose life experience was limited. He wanted to give me an insight into his world, and I had the feeling he was trying to make me feel safe. I still wanted to fight against it.

"You're making fun of me again."

He took a slip of paper from his pocket and wrote something on it. He pushed it into my hand.

"My phone number," he said. I pushed it away. He stuffed it into the little canvas shoulder bag I had beside me on the rug. "I plan to give you something that will make a difference to your life, something you really want. Don't tell anyone else in case they try to stop me." He met my eyes. "I'm serious about that," he added. For a moment, I was won over, corrupted by the thought of riches. "All you have to do in return is keep being Lucy, the lovely person I remember."

I glowered at him. "There's only one thing I want." He stood up, preparing to leave, but I knew he was listening. "I want the manor," I said.

Chapter 23
Everything Comes To a Head

Belle, Charlie, and I were at the café. We'd planned a long walk, but it had begun to rain heavily, and we were all feeling glum. The café was always the answer at such times. Charlie ordered a meringue, as usual, along with a cola; Belle and I ordered Florentines and tea.

"Charlie, that's too much sugar to have all at once," Belle informed her. "You should have a cup of tea." Her daughter gave her a look that needed no explanation. I tried not to get involved. Fortunately, Belle didn't pursue her line of argument with much conviction. "I've always disliked cola," she stated.

Charlie seemed to have suddenly grown about a foot in height; she was beginning to have the same willowy figure as her mother. She looked more like Belle with her long hair, and there was more of a likeness in her features, the changing shape of her face bringing out the similarities.

"Charlie has started taking dance lessons, haven't you, Charlie?"

"Yes, Mum. But I'm sure Lucy doesn't want to hear about them."

"She loves her music. She's still singing with the choir, and we're looking into piano lessons."

Charlie rolled her eyes.

"I think it's good, Charlie," I said. "It's good to do all these things if you get the chance, and music and dancing will benefit you in all sorts of ways."

"I'm still playing football, and Dad says he'll buy me a mountain bike so I can go on long rides with him when he's home."

Charlie hadn't forgotten that I'd supported her in her football and skateboarding while her mum hadn't been over-enthusiastic. I could tell she wanted to reassure me that she hadn't sold out to convention.

"I think all those things are of benefit," I said, trying hard not to take sides.

"I don't mind you having a bicycle," said Belle.

"There's plenty of exploring to be done along beside the river if you have a bike," I told them.

"Yes, I really want to ride along that track. It goes on for miles, doesn't it?"

The late winter days were cold but would soon give way to the warm spring months and the opportunity to spend more time outside, enjoying our local landscape.

"How's everything at the home?" Belle asked.

"Good. Everything is fairly quiet at the moment. No dramas to report. The villagers are over the flu, Miss P's no longer on the missing list. Things are almost boring."

"I've done more thinking about what I could do."

"Excellent! Have you come up with anything in particular?"

"You'll think I'm daft." I could tell Belle was feeling self-conscious, and she seemed anxious about how I would respond. I found it difficult to imagine my reaction could be so important to her.

"Tell her, Mum," Charlie pressed her. "This cola is

lovely, by the way, mmmmm."

"I wondered about teaching some yoga."

"Are you interested in yoga? I hadn't realized."

"I used to be obsessed!" Belle laughed.

"I remember that," said Charlie.

"And you still enjoy it?" I asked.

"I do some most days…just on my own in the house! I find it relaxing, and I like to think it keeps me fit."

"It sounds like a great idea," I said.

"You'd need a big room, though," Charlie advised wisely.

"I'm sure we can think of somewhere," I said.

"I don't know how to teach. That's the other problem," Belle said.

"There must be a course you can take?"

"I suppose so."

"Let's look into it."

"You'll help me?"

"Yes. Not that you'll need my assistance."

"You'll keep me motivated?"

"I can certainly do that. That's one of my strong points."

As we left the café, I noticed Amber staring after us. She always managed to unnerve me. I tried to put her out of my thoughts.

****

George rang and asked if I could come round. He was missing me, he said. He had most of the next archive show ready, so we started off in his study, looking through some of the latest images he'd uncovered. He had a good few photos of the old blacksmiths that no longer existed and the bakery that did, although in a different incarnation. There were pictures of the workers, customers, and various passers-by.

"Did you find anything for Bert?"

"Not so far, but I'm working on it."

"I hope you're successful. It would mean so much to him."

"If it's there to be found, I'll find it!"

I marveled at some of the clothing people wore. "It must have been so hard back then to dress well…even just to keep your clothes clean. Imagine all the hard work it took."

"It was time consuming, I'm sure, but I think people enjoyed the process. The same with cooking, gardening, all sorts."

"Yes, we have nothing to do these days. We buy everything ready-made or grown."

"And we all think we're so busy!"

George showed me some early shots of Broad Street. It was thronging with people walking up and down, horse-drawn transport, a barrow being wheeled.

"The residents are going to love all this," I said.

Helen was working. She had paperwork distributed all over the dining table, piles of various heights sporting colored sticky notes that stated the content which lay beneath.

"It's my filing," she explained. "I get it all into piles here where there's space, then it's easy to put it into the right drawers back at the office. I've left it a bit long this time. It's the most tedious task!"

"I'll get you a glass of wine," George said comfortingly.

"That will certainly help," Helen agreed.

We adjourned to the sofa and drank large glasses of red from a bottle George said he'd been dying to open for days.

"Is Daniel at training?" I asked.

"Yes, and then going to a friend's with some of the others," Helen replied. "We've hardly seen him this week."

"At least he's not under our feet," said George. "Some kids never leave home nowadays, do they? Daniel was pretty much gone by the age of thirteen!"

"He does still sleep here," Helen confirmed.

"Most of the time." George put his feet up on the footstool. I could tell from his expression there was a whole other story behind that comment.

"He looks so grown up now," I said. "Every time I see him, I think that…and he's confident."

"He's one of those kids who grow up easily," Helen said. "He's not timid, that's for sure. He's always been ready to take on the world, and he's accepted into most company."

"He'll go to University?" I asked.

"We expect so," said George. "But we're not sure what he'll study."

"He has a good grasp of most subjects," Helen added.

"Jenny says the main thing is to find something you like doing," I told them. "She says a teacher's job is to make sure you learn how to enjoy your life."

"That's a wise statement." George nodded his head.

Fortunately, George had a second bottle of the wine he'd been looking forward to. We decided to have another glass.

"Anything more on the rumor?" George asked. He was looking to Helen to answer.

"The manor? The will?" she checked.

"Yes, yes. Did you hear any more?" said George.

"No, just that it's Nic who gets it all. He gets everything," she said, "…whatever everything amounts to."

We digested the thought.

"Perhaps there's a lot of debt? Who knows?" George said.

"Yes, I'm not sure any of them had much of a career, or a job of any sort, apart from Reg himself," I said.

Helen agreed. "That's true. Reg always seemed to be the provider."

"The fortune might have been squandered years ago!" George said, pleased with the idea that had come to him. He and Helen laughed loudly together.

****

It was another couple of days before I saw Miss P. I was hurriedly walking home from an excursion with Morsel. I'd soon need to set off for work. I was on Broad Street, about to cross, when I saw her waving to me from farther along the pavement. It wasn't just a greeting. She was trying to attract my attention.

"Hello, Lucy, I'm glad I've caught you."

"Hello, Miss Pickering. Is everything all right?"

"Yes. Nothing to worry about."

"Mr. Pickering's all right?"

"Bob's fine."

"You're sure?"

"Yes. I just wanted to tell you that I'll need to set up a meeting with you."

"Will you?"

"Yes, we'll have to have a meeting."

"Oh?"

"I'm not quite ready yet, just gathering the last few bits of paperwork and things. You know how it is."

"I suppose so."

"Well, mustn't keep you."

"No. I'll be late for Moonstones if I don't get off."

We went our separate ways, Miss P obviously unaware she'd said anything out of the ordinary, and me feeling part perplexed, part anxious, and part elated. Though I saw Miss P again, only two hours later at the home, no further words were spoken on the matter.

All my life, I'd been pulled this way and that. I couldn't stop craving for the material assets that might be about to come in my direction or avoid the truth of the betrayal that constantly ate away inside me. A pain came into my stomach and punished me for having greedy thoughts. Nevertheless, in the evening, unable to resist, I indulged in them once more. This was the closest I'd come to achieving my dreams. Nic had made a promise. I remembered it clearly, and I'd stuck to the rules. What if Miss P did know something about the manor, about Reg's will, and what if, however ridiculous and unlikely it might seem, the manor had been left to me?

My brain went into overdrive. I was living at the manor. I was lady of the manor, dressed beautifully, looking every bit the part. I considered how I'd make use of the building, adapting part of the space so that it was the perfect place for Morsel and me to live. I would start a business as well, become an entrepreneur. Perhaps I could open a residential home and compete with Moonstones, or have a wedding venue, or perhaps a retreat for wealthy people who were depressed or suffering from stress. I could employ Belle to run yoga classes. My mind wouldn't stop. I had skills; I was good at solving people's problems; I could venture into marriage guidance or life coaching. It came to me that I'd be in charge of the treasure hunt too. That tradition would have to be continued. In my new world, everyone would look up to me and envy me. Everyone would want to please me and praise me.

Morsel observed with her expressive eyes. She'd sensed a change in me. I'm not sure she liked that type of Lucy. She brought me back down to earth.

"Oh, Morsel, I'll probably just be left an old jug if he's left me anything at all. But what else could Miss P want to set up a meeting about?"

I made a drink, refreshed Morsel's water, and opened the back door so she could run in and out. I sat in my chair. It was hard to settle my mind. But then, I had a thought that brought me back down to earth. Miss P was part of the flower arranging group. They were hugely interested in the church buildings, the congregation, and the associated history. What if Miss P wanted to put on a slide show about St Michael's? I'd put a notice on my board about the slide shows. The upcoming subjects were listed, but I'd also stated that ideas for further shows were welcome. I'd seen Miss P reading the board on several occasions.

"That's it, Morsel! I'll bet that's what this meeting is for. She wants to present a show." I paced around the room. "Then again, why on earth did Miss P go to America? She went to America, on her own, purportedly on a business trip."

My head carried on in the same way for a number of days. One minute I was Lady of the Manor; I was a fairly nasty piece of work, making a show of myself, highly demanding, a flashy no-nonsense type with little time for the locals. Then I would be a philanthropist, setting up charity events and allowing everyone to share the manor and use the numerous grand rooms and the gardens. Next, I would be in self-punishment mode, with stomach pains and headaches, giving myself duties to perform to recompense the world for my evils. I could easily believe I was mistaken about the entire situation too. I was to remain a poor villager, like everyone else. The worst thought of all was the one I'd always had to manage the whole of my life, since one night, as a child, I'd walked away and left my best friend in a situation she wasn't able to deal with. I'd allowed the truth to remain undiscovered, untold, left her to lead who knows what sort of life as a young offender, a criminal. I'd accepted the bribe. I'd kept quiet to pursue material wealth.

Chapter 24
Fergus

The doctor's car was outside Moonstones. I felt my heart beat faster, knowing it wasn't a routine visit. I went to the back entrance so I could hear what was happening from management rather than the shift workers or the kitchen staff.

"It's Mrs. Cook," Joe told me.

"What's happened?"

"The doctor's with her. She seems feverish, and she's quite incoherent."

"She wasn't too bad yesterday."

"No, but she wasn't too good either."

A solemnity could be felt in the atmosphere. I stayed in the office with Joe for a time, neither of us speaking. Eventually, I broke the silence.

"I can't bear this. I feel so helpless. What can I do?"

Joe was trying to busy himself on the computer. He looked up. "Nothing."

"I wish I were a doctor or a nurse."

"You can't be everything. You do a great deal for Mrs. Cook, Lucy, for all the residents."

Lianne came in. She looked as though she hadn't slept in a long time. Her skin was gray, her eyes puffed.

"Hello, Lucy." She attempted a smile.

"Were you up all night?"

"Yes. No matter. I just hope she's going to pull through."

I found John in the kitchen, also in quiet mode.

"No news, I suppose?" he asked me.

"No."

"Is it the flu, do you think?"

"I don't know. She seemed relatively well yesterday."

"She's too frail for that flu."

I began making drinks for Joe and Lianne. I was sure they'd not been thinking about their own needs.

"I've soup here," John said.

"I'll offer them some."

"Take some biscuits. Look, I'll put a few on a plate for you."

The bright-colored mugs seemed somehow inappropriate.

I was being punished. Mrs. Cook had been fine a day ago, and now she was dangerously ill. It had to be to do with me. The flu outbreak had cleared up. Everyone in the village was over it. I felt dreadful, and I knew this was just the start of something. I was on a downward spiral and couldn't turn back, heading for a gloomy place where I'd flounder, unable to find a way out.

****

Belle was a help to me. She was certainly motivated by her yoga idea. She frequently called to talk through her latest findings and ask my opinion. She was attending an advanced class to refresh her own abilities and to put herself in the right environment mentally. I was surprised by the amount of energy she'd conjured to pursue her plan. I'd never seen her take much interest in anything before, and definitely not for such a length of time. She was making use of her blog to gauge appeal. She had quite a number of followers and had started a poll to find out if there was a general interest in classes, what time of day people would prefer to attend, and whether beginners' classes would be most popular or more advanced options. Few of those responding were likely to live close enough to take part, but she thought the information would be likely also to reflect local interest.

"You'll be coming, I hope?"

"I've never tried yoga in my life."

"Perfect, I'll be able to teach you from scratch. You won't have acquired any bad habits."

"I'm not sure it's my thing."

"Oh, Lucy, I want you to be there for my first ever class. I'll do you a special rate!"

Belle was a difficult person to say no to. "I don't think you'll have a problem finding clients," I told her. "I'm sure you're going to be a natural when it comes to tutoring."

I would have loved to discuss the manor with Belle. If I could choose the right words, she'd listen and have some good ideas; she'd support me. George also, I'd have loved to speak to him, to hear his wise words. I held back. In reality, I was sure neither of them would want a thing more to do with me once they came to know the history behind my situation.

****

George's second archive show went ahead. Mrs. Cook was confined to her room with a chest infection, but the rest of the residents were excited about the event and gathered in the lounge well in advance of the start.

George was in good form, helped by the fact that he had become acquainted with his audience. He knew how to pace the show. He knew which of the residents to banter with, who would be able to hear him easily, and who would struggle; he knew which of them would see the show as entertainment and who would wish to be educated. George delighted in teasing additional information from the group. He stored it away in his memory for his own pleasure. I watched along with everyone else. It was clear George was building up to something, when near the end of the presentation, he revealed another image and stood back waiting for the reaction.

"That's me! That's me, George! You did it! I knew you'd come across me somewhere or other." George clicked to the next image. "And there I am again!" Bert had been revealed as a smartly dressed member of the Boys' Brigade and a proud member of the Boys' Brigade band.

"Look at the fine head of hair you had, Bert," noted Ethel.

"I know, pity it didn't last!"

"No wonder you're so good in Rita's sessions," said Lionel.

"Is it a cornet?" Marcia asked.

"Yes, I'm not sure I could play it anymore, though. Took a lot of breath!"

We spent time looking at the shots of Bert, and then Agnes asked George a question.

"George, do you have the pictures from the last show with you?"

"Yes, they're all loaded on the laptop here."

"Do you think we could have another look at the

ones of the school? They brought back such good memories for me."

"Yes, of course. There's a couple more in this sequence, and then perhaps we can have a break, and I'll set them up."

Mariana and Barbara provided tea and sandwiches along with carrot cake. Everyone chatted enthusiastically, remembering stories that had been brought to mind during the show. George beavered away, searching for the images of the school; he was soon ready to project them.

I sat with Molly, sipping tea, and while the others looked at Agnes in the picture, I stared fixedly at my own image and the image of Rosamund sitting quietly beside me. She seemed to be looking out into the room, straight at me, and there was something about the picture that nagged at me in a way that I couldn't quite grasp.

"Can you come in and see Mrs. Cook?" Barbara was suddenly in front of me, and she looked anxious.

I jumped up and went with her to Mrs. Cook's room. I was immediately worried. Mrs. Cook was extremely pale and seemed to be struggling to catch her breath.

"She's had all her medication?" I checked.

"Yes, everything she's supposed to take. She's not managed to eat anything."

"I'm going to get Joe," I said.

At home, I was finding it hard to sleep. Mrs. Cook's illness, the meeting with Miss P, the general pressures of my work, and the dilemma about my life choices all swam around in my head. I'd nod off temporarily, then wake abruptly. I'd stay wide awake for long periods trying to calm my mind and willing myself to rest. In the mornings, I wouldn't feel refreshed. I'd get up and try to carry on in the normal way, but my whole body felt tired, my head sore, and my mind full of anguish. As ever, Morsel helped me cope, but it was a big task for a small dog to have to take on.

\*\*\*\*

"Come in and sit down, Lucy."

Miss P had finally summoned me to The Flower Pot. We were in the lounge. I was on the reproduction sofa, and she was on a matching armchair. She sat on the edge of the seat, alert. I could tell we had business to discuss, but she began with some pleasantries. She'd made tea. She poured it out and offered me a tiny almond biscuit.

"The paintings came from the manor. You realize that. You could say I'm looking after them," she said.

"Oh, no, I hadn't thought about it."

"Nic wanted me to look after a few things. Items that meant something to him."

"Nic did? When he went to America?"

"Yes, some years ago. I didn't imagine he'd stay there for this amount of time."

"He intended to return?"

"I'm not sure, but I always thought he'd come back." We both drank a little of our tea. Miss Pickering then shifted the conversation on. "I visited him in Los Angeles two weeks ago."

"I did wonder where you were. Everyone was missing you."

"It wasn't my first visit, but I'll never go again."

"Did Nic ask you to visit?"

"He did. You see, he can't come back now. He wouldn't be able to manage such a long plane journey."

"It seems strange that he lives in America."

"I think it was too much for him here, too much responsibility. Reg wanted him to take over the business, and that went hand in hand with the family affairs."

"And he didn't want to return, even for his father's funeral?"

"His health wouldn't allow it. He has people in place to look after things on his behalf. I'm sure he would have wanted to come to the funeral, but in terms of the business side, his advisors look after everything. He trusts them."

Miss P went quiet. I felt I needed some sort of clarification. I took a deep breath and dived in.

"Miss Pickering, I enjoy speaking with you about these things, really I do, but I'm not quite sure why it's me you select to converse with."

She frowned in a way that I took to mean she didn't believe my statement. "Come now, Lucy, I think you have a good idea." I didn't respond. "Nic remembers you well. I'm sure it's reciprocal. You and he made each other some promises, had an understanding."

"He told you that?"

"Oh yes, many years ago…a long time before you arrived back in Steely Green."

"Really?"

"Yes. He told me a lot of things before he left the country. I suppose I was a confidante to him. And he needed someone here…to be the keeper of his thoughts and his intentions."

Inside I was getting excited. I felt hot and clammy and couldn't wait for the conversation to continue. "What did Nic say about me?"

"Nic never cared too much for the rest of the family, apart from Algie. I think he'd like to have had Algie go to America with him, but Reg would never have agreed to that, not during his lifetime, and it wouldn't be appropriate now."

Miss P hadn't answered my question. "Is there something Nic wants me to do?"

"No. Algie is looked after. The rest of the family will each have something from the will. Nic doesn't want to keep all the assets tied up together."

"There was a rumor about the will being contested," I said.

"Ah, Reg's will, yes."

"Are we not speaking about Reg's will?"

"No, we're speaking about Nic's."

I think something was beginning to sink in. "Is Nic…"

"Nic is very unwell." The variety of emotions I was going through was indescribable. My thoughts were churning from excitement to regret, self-loathing to self-importance; all were fighting for prevalence. "He's going to die, Lucy." I had to fight to hold onto some sort of decorum. "You met Fergus," Miss Pickering continued. By now, the inside of my head was out of control. Surely it was showing on my face. "He was looking into you. You know what I mean, making some checks. I think you knew that."

"The Scotsman?" I managed to say.

Miss P laughed. "He's an American, but obviously, you know who I mean. Nic wanted him to make sure you were still the right person, something like that."

I couldn't bear it. I sank my head into my hands.

"Lucy, come now. Nic doesn't want to cause you any distress. He wants the best for you. He loved you. Don't take this the wrong way, but he loved the simplicity of your life and dreams and your values. He could think of nothing he'd rather do, no one he'd rather help." I raised my head and saw Miss P's bright, intelligent eyes waiting to look into mine. "He's leaving you the manor, Lucy."

I was numb. Miss P came and sat beside me and took my hand.

"Now, at some point, hopefully, we'll have a telephone conversation with Nic. Until then, you must keep all of this to yourself. I know you can do that. It was part of my job to make sure we could trust you and that you would be discreet."

I sat dumbfounded.

"I'm going to make more tea. After that, I think you should leave and get on with your day as if we'd never had this conversation. In due course, I'll set up the telephone call, we'll all speak, and then there'll be solicitors to meet and various things."

"I'm to carry on as normal. Am I still being tested?"

"You mustn't think of it like that, Lucy. It wasn't that you were being tested, not really. Nic just wanted to make sure you were still the kind-hearted, selfless person he so fondly remembered. If you must see it as a test, you passed with flying colors!"

\*\*\*\*

For days I questioned every thought in my head. Why should I inherit the manor? It was probably all an elaborate trick, another punishment for me. I saw Miss P at Moonstones and in the village, but not a word about our meeting passed her lips. Sometimes I asked myself if I'd imagined the whole thing. Then I began to wonder if Miss Pickering was actually mad; it was Miss P who'd imagined the whole thing. Did she really go to America? Did she really know Nic? I continued to argue and debate in my head. Still, the two things that allowed me to hang on to the possibility the situation was real and the promise was going to come to fruition, were the mention of Fergus and the suggested telephone conversation with Nic. When I thought about Fergus, it made sense that he was checking me out in some way. I'd suspected it. Of course, that accent was American. It was the name that had confused me; I wasn't a well-traveled person. Nobody else seemed to have come across him, and I obviously remembered the time I'd spotted him coming from Miss P's cottage. I also remembered seeing him in the village in a car, in the dark, looking as if he was watching someone. Could that someone have been me? Who followed Belle and me after the carol singing?

All I could do under the current circumstances was wait. My head was in turmoil, but there was no alternative. I'd prepared for years for this; in reality, I'd been working on this outcome since I was a child. I had to be able to hang on for a little longer.

****

I was still able to engross myself in Moonstones. Candy and I were in the kitchen with John, who'd made a batch of scones. They smelled absolutely delicious.

"Are you sure you've made enough, John?" Candy asked him. John was busy transferring each one carefully onto his cooling rack and didn't see the cheeky smile she'd given me.

"That's the normal," he said.

"Ah," she exaggerated her disappointment.

John picked up on it. "You're hungry," he concluded with a laugh.

"I am for scones like those."

Candy and I were behaving like children, covetously ogling John's creations.

"There's plenty. Poor Mrs. Cook won't be having one," John stated, which made us feel bad. "Come on," he said, alarmed that he'd changed the mood. "There's more than enough. The old folk won't manage more than one each, apart from Mr. Pickering, that is. Those aside, if we earmark a couple for you two, there'll still be a dozen left.

"Phew," said Candy.

"Will there be butter and jam?" I asked.

"And cream?" Candy added.

"Good butter, the best strawberry jam, and local clotted cream."

"Roll on tea time," I said.

I thought a lot about Nic, how ill he was, if he was really going to die. I was relieved I didn't lower my standards further by looking forward to the latter. I could wait. I supposed I'd always liked Nic. It wasn't his fault his brother had destroyed the cottages in a fit of rage. He did lie about what had happened, but it was out of loyalty. It wasn't for his own benefit. He'd done it for his father and for Algie. He'd been put in a difficult position, and I sort of understood.

****

"I could smell those scones all along the corridor!"

said Lianne, arriving at the kitchen door.

"Sorry. I should clean the extractors," John said. "I'll do it during the week."

"I wasn't complaining, except possibly on behalf of my waistline. I was more angling."

"There's enough," I said. "John's made plenty. We've been checking."

"Thank God for that!"

Lianne and I poured ourselves tea and headed to the office together.

"The doc's coming again tomorrow," Lianne confirmed.

"I can deal with him," I offered.

"That would be good. I'd like to get into Melstow in the morning, and Joe's on the night shift. He'll be done for."

"That's fine. I'll get in early so you can get away."

"Are you all right, Lucy?" Lianne said. "You look tired yourself."

"I'm fine, but I've not been sleeping too well, it's true."

"I hope you're not coming down with something."

"No. I just have a few things on my mind."

Lianne gulped at her tea. "Do you need to share?"

"No, it's not important. Once I'm here at Moonstones, I forget all about it. This place is a great tonic."

"You know you can always talk to me if there's anything you're unhappy about or if there's anything you need to get off your chest."

"Thank you."

****

I took to getting up early again and walking before

most in the village rose. I thought if I thoroughly tired myself out with my walks and my work, I'd be able to sleep and have no time to think about the future. Even so, each day, I walked to the far end of the copse and looked across the land to see the tiny glimpse of the manor at the point where it was visible from the path. Some days I would sit on the stile, consider the friends I'd made in Steely, and wonder what they were going to think of me when they found out. Would they reject me? How would Candy feel? What would Lianne say? I supposed I would be giving up my work at Moonstones. Would Lianne think I'd taken the job under false pretenses? Would she be angry about all the training she'd given to someone who was soon going to walk away? I couldn't bear to wonder what Joe would think. What about Belle? She'd know I'd been hiding something from her. She'd begun to confide in me on all sorts of things, but she was going to find out I was keeping a gigantic secret from her and had been all the time I'd lived in the village. I concluded that everyone was going to hate me.

Staring toward the manor, I remembered the days I'd spent there as a child: times with my dad, the pictures I'd drawn of the furniture and the carvings. I'd never been into the downstairs rooms, apart from the staff areas. I wondered what they were like and what would happen to all the furnishings and possessions the manor had housed. Would they be left to Nic's brothers and sisters? Why had he given some items to Miss P for safekeeping? Did he not trust them? Was Vicky up there now snaffling the rest of the stuff?

I woke up in a sweat one night thinking about the village game, the treasure hunt. Surely I would soon be responsible for it. I'd have to continue with it. Imagine what the villagers would think if I failed to carry on the tradition. The thought worried me and I stayed awake trying to think of clues, wondering what prizes I should offer. Would I opt for a huge and decadent prize, the best ever? If I did that, the villagers would certainly love me, at least temporarily, but it would also set a precedent. I might be expected to repeat the standard year after year, or even better it. Another night I woke up worrying about money. The cost of looking after the manor was going to be immense. It would cost a fortune just to pay for the electricity it would guzzle. I would have to set up some sort of business straight away. The manor would have to pay for itself. My head ached from the worry.

Come the mornings, out in the copse, the warm sun on my face, and the glimpse of the magnificent building through the trees, I'd feel more positive. George would help me devise the clues for the treasure hunt, and I had already come up with rafts of money-raising business ideas. Even just letting out rooms would bring in an income if it came to it. Imagine worrying about money if you owned the manor!

Eventually, Miss Pickering beckoned me over to speak. She was in the lounge of the rest home with Bob, enjoying a large slice of the delicious fruit cake Larry had made the previous afternoon.

"Tomorrow. Five p.m., at The Flower Pot," she said, between mouthfuls.

"I'll check with Lianne. It should be all right."

"Make some sort of excuse if you need to. It will be difficult to rearrange."

"I'll be there, Miss Pickering."

Bob looked at us quizzically but didn't ask questions.

I drank a large glass of wine that night. I knew there was no chance of sleep otherwise. In the morning, I went out walking and then to work, aware that I was looking at the clock approximately once every five minutes. I'd told Lianne I needed to leave at four thirty, and it didn't seem to be an issue. It was impossible to sit still. Several times I strode round the home, to the lounge, the kitchen, each of the resident's bedrooms, the garden, the kitchen again, and back to the office. I couldn't eat lunch or make any meaningful conversation with anyone.

At last, four thirty arrived. I retrieved Morsel from Bert's room and set off to Miss Pickering's. I dropped Morsel off at home.

"Good girl, I won't be long, and when I get back, I might have some news." She pressed herself down against the floor, chin firmly on the ground, watching me with her dark eyes. She knew there was something going on.

"Come in! Come in! I've set the phone up here in the lounge."

"Thank you, Miss Pickering. I hope I'm not late?"

"No, you're just fine. The call will come in at seventeen fifteen our time."

"Do I need to know anything in advance?"

"No, but I'll take charge, so don't worry. I can pick up on things if need be.'

"Oh, I see."

"It will be a conference call. I'm not sure exactly who will be at the other end, apart from Nic, that is."

"There'll be others?"

"A number of advisors, I expect."

I felt sick. I'd thought I was going to have a phone conversation with Nic, not a conference call with a crowd of frightening American legal eagles.

"Now, let me get you a drink quickly. We can have a slice of cake afterward, and a bit of a debrief. Coffee?"

"That would be very welcome. Black, please."

I sat, then stood, then sat. I realized I should be preparing my mind, working on my greeting, thinking of questions, but I was beyond any of that.

Miss Pickering returned with a large porcelain pot and poured me a cupful of strong black coffee. I took it and clasped it tightly in both hands.

"Five minutes to go. How was everything at Moonstones today?" Miss Pickering went to the desk and came back with a box file. She took out an A4-size writing pad and a pen. "I'll make a few notes," she said. Nothing she did was making me feel any more at ease. Then the phone started ringing. She picked up the receiver. "Here we go." She laid the receiver at the side and pressed a button. "Good afternoon," she said. "Good afternoon, Prudence Pickering speaking."

I put down my coffee.

"Hello there, Pru," came a return greeting from a voice that seemed familiar.

"Fergus, hello! Good to hear you! I'm here with Lucy. We're on speakerphone. Say hello, Lucy," she instructed.

"Hello," I said in a whispery voice.

"Can you hear us, Fergus?"

"Loud and clear. Let me introduce our end. We have Giles Sooster, Nic's attorney."

"Good afternoon, ladies," said a slow, deep, strongly accented voice.

"And Delilah Zhar, the Lesters' trust and tax manager."

"Hi," said a bright, young-sounding, American female.

"And Nic, of course,"

"Hello, Steely Green," said Nic, in his unmistakable educated English tone.

Fergus took the reins, "Lucy, first of all, I want to apologize to you for the strange meetings I put you through over there in your village." There was a pause, and Miss P nodded to me.

"There's no need," I stuttered out, becoming aware the pause was left for me to speak into. Laughter came from the other end.

"Whatever did you think of me?" Fergus said. "I could never properly introduce myself or partake in any ordinary conversation."

"I thought you were just walking your dog, nothing else." More laughter.

The attorney began to speak. "Now, Lucy, I need to run through a few things. Are you ready?"

"Yes, I think so."

Miss P smiled supportively.

"As you know, Reg Lester, Nic's father, passed not long ago. He left the family affairs in the hands of Nic here, as was agreed many years back."

Delilah spoke next, "We've been working on the estate. It's not been entirely straightforward, down to a number of factors."

"We're not going to go into too much detail." said the attorney. "Suffice to say there's a large estate, and

Nic is not in a position to continue in his role for much longer."

"The Lester Estate is to be divided," Fergus stated. Again there was a pause, and I wasn't sure if I was supposed to say something. I looked at Miss P. She interjected.

"Do we need to spell the whole thing out, Fergus? Shouldn't we just let Lucy know her position?"

"Sorry, yes, that's our plan. Nic wants to say a few words now."

There was another pause before Nic began. "I'm just going to say that I've thought about this carefully, over time and also recently, and I need you to know, Lucy, that I very much want this for you, and for no other reason than I've always liked you, and that you were a good friend to me, and to Algie. You've remained in my thoughts all these years. I hoped to see you again, but that won't happen now." I heard coughing.

"That's enough, Nic," Fergus's voice interrupted.

"What about Algie?" I said, without really planning to say it.

"Algie is in no position to take on the family affairs, unfortunately," stated Giles.

"I just meant, how is he, and what's happening to him?"

"Typical Lucy," Nic managed to say.

"Nic always says you think only of others," Fergus said. "I also found that to be the case."

"Algie will be looked after," confirmed Delilah. "There's no need to be concerned about him."

"The family members will all be looked after in their own way, dependent on their needs. There will be no reason for any more controversy," stated Giles.

"And they won't get in your way, Lucy," Nic said before breaking down again in a series of alarming coughs and gasps.

"I think we need to speed on," said Delilah. "We're soon going to need to let Nic rest."

"Go ahead," said Giles.

"Lucy," she said, "we need you to confirm that you won't discuss the following with anyone, apart from Prudence that is, until everything is finalized. Can you promise us that, here and now? We'll accept your word. It is a requirement, however. I should make this clear. Can you make the promise?"

"Yes. I won't speak a word to anyone."

"Lucy, on Nicolas Lester's death, you will inherit Steely Green Manor. You will also inherit a sum of money, the amount of which will not be disclosed until the time of his passing."

That was it. Clearly, and in a matter-of-fact fashion, it had been stated. A silence followed. I felt all sorts of emotions at the same time. I sank my head into my hands, and streams of tears began to roll between my fingers.

Miss P spoke next. "Lucy is overwhelmed," she said. She came and sat beside me and put an arm around me. "Can you say something, Lucy?"

"I don't know what to say," was all I could manage between gut-wrenching tearful shudders and gasps of my own.

"No need to say anything," I heard Nic state in a now faint-sounding voice.

"We'll try to arrange a further conversation in a week or so," Fergus's voice came in. "In the meantime, that's all that needed to be said with everyone present. There'll be papers to read through and sign, as there will for you, Pru. We'll get everything over to you. Is everything clear enough for now?"

"All clear," Pru confirmed. "I'll call you about general matters in due course, Fergus."

"Thank you, Pru. We'll have to let you go now."

"Goodbye, and thank you," Giles said, and the phone line went dead.

Miss P continued to sit with her arm round me until I began to feel less emotional.

"There, there. It's a shock," she said. "Take your time. Take some deep breaths." We sat, and Miss P gave me support. "At least we got away with just the two legal chaps." I'd not been expecting any legal chaps. "You don't need to worry about anything. You did well. There's time to think things through now. Nic wanted that. He didn't want to go ahead and die and let you find out afterward. And trust you to think only of Algie! You prove yourself over and over. Everyone finds the same. Lucy, the woman who never thinks about herself. However did you manage to stay that way in a world like this?"

Later I spoke to Morsel, hoping it would be acceptable and feeling sure no one was likely to find out I'd told her.

"We're inheriting Steely Green Manor," I said. "We're going to live in a big, big house with an enormous garden."

I hadn't asked the obvious question, although I would have liked to. I wouldn't ask Miss P either. How long was Nic going to live? Was there a prognosis? In any case, I would carry on at Moonstones without changing my behavior in any way. I would continue to look after my appearance and step up on educating myself about the ways of people with assets. I wouldn't go anywhere near the manor, only stop to glimpse the building through the birch trees on my daily walks, but following the day's events, I would see that glimpse in a brand new light.

Chapter 25
I Own the Manor

I'd been scheming for years. Coming back to Steely, changing my appearance, everything was, in part, my preparing for the outcome that most of the time I couldn't believe would materialize but wasn't able to completely banish from my mind. Now I had a new set of challenges. Every time I spoke to a villager, I talked through a filter that represented my future. They must have no idea about what was to come, but I had to use the days ahead to bridge the gaps that might emerge when the new reality took over.

Each time I spoke to Lianne, I was thinking about the day I would tell her I was giving up my job. I desperately wanted her to be happy for me and for us to remain friends. As I spoke to John, I thought about him finding out that I was moving into the manor. Would he then see me as someone who'd changed too much for him to continue to associate with? It was the same whosoever I met. When I next bumped into George, I could hardly contain myself. I knew he could live in my new future. For a moment, I thought I could confide in him, and he'd keep things to himself, but what if he told Helen, and in turn, she told Dr. French. I so badly wanted to tell Belle, I had to avoid seeing her at times to stop it from coming out.

At home, I spoke to Morsel, who understood and

would never repeat a word of it. I discussed all the good things with her, but I also told her about my pain, because along with the elation came excruciating torment. I had duped everyone for a start. No one would believe I'd planned it all, but I'd always have to live with that knowledge. Most of my pain, though, came because of the unavoidable truth that I had betrayed Rosamund. As children, and in our teenage years, Nic had bribed me, and to all intents and purposes, I'd blackmailed him in return. I couldn't forget that I'd asked him for the immense recompense. I'd threatened to tell Reg the truth about Algie and been persuaded not to do so only by the offer of Nic giving me something in return. I'd let him know I wouldn't be happy with a small gift. I'd told him outright that it had to be the manor.

In the village, everything looked different to me, and in my eyes, everyone seemed to have altered. I was walking on Broad Street when I spotted Amber coming in my direction. How would I choose to deal with someone like her?

"Good morning, Lucy. What a beautiful day."

"Isn't it."

"Are you working today?"

"Yes, later on."

"I have a day off," Amber said. "I think I'll have a stroll beside the river."

"It's a lovely walk."

"Yes, and you see the village from another angle."

"I suppose so."

"I tend to think about the village when I'm out walking," Amber said.

"Don't let me keep you."

"I can't help thinking that one day everything in Steely Green will be as it should be."

We parted company, but Amber's last comment went on being said in my head. A strange comment, I couldn't help thinking. Did she know something? What had she meant by it?

Once again, I thanked God for Moonstones. I was brought straight back to reality. Mrs. Cook had deteriorated, and hospital was being considered. The other residents had wind of it and were concerned and agitated. Joe looked tired; Lianne was trying to deal with too many things at once and had been short with Larry. I had a role to play and threw myself in. I walked the corridor with Molly, reminisced with Agnes, played the sock game with Bert and Morsel, and sat and talked with Lionel, Lolly, and Ethel. They bravely attempted jokes and smiles.

"We could do with another slide show," said Lionel.

"I'm sure George is devising something," I said.

"What happened to the one about gardens?" asked Lolly.

"That's a point," I said. "I must catch up with Jenny on that."

"We weren't in the mood for bridge," Lionel reflected.

"Poor Mrs. Cook," Ethel then said, unable to keep her from her thoughts any longer.

"Joe is with her," I said.

Marcia was sitting near the window, knitting. She wanted to be on her own.

"Where's Bob got to today?" I asked them.

"Not seen him," said Lionel.

After knocking loudly I entered Mr. Pickering's room. He had his back to me. He was in his chair looking out across the garden. He didn't turn round.

"Is everything all right, Mr. P?" I shouted.

"Oh, hello, Lucy."

"Aren't you going to the lounge?"

"I don't think so."

"You prefer to sit in here? Is your sister coming to visit?"

"I'm not sure."

He did seem down. His usual twinkle was absent. I supposed it was to do with Mrs. Cook. I couldn't seem to lift his spirits. Later in the kitchen, Larry told me Mr. P hadn't eaten his breakfast, which was a first as far as I could remember.

"Do you think Bob is all right?" I asked Barbara.

"He's been quiet the last few days."

"He doesn't want to go to the lounge, but it might do him good."

"I'll work on him," she said.

Barbara was good at getting to the bottom of things. "Do you think he's worried about Mrs. Cook?" I asked.

"I'd say that's what it is, and something he said to me brought home the reality of old age. After Mrs. Cook, Mr. P is the oldest of the residents. It's hard to imagine being the oldest resident in a home for the elderly. I suppose it must make you think sometimes."

"Well, Mrs. Cook is still here, and who's to say we won't have older residents in the future?" I said.

"Yes, getting older doesn't have to be seen as a bad thing. Some of the residents are incredibly proud of their age," Barbara stated. "Bert certainly is."

"That's true," I said.

"But Bob's the older brother too. Perhaps that makes him sad sometimes. His sister is still living an active life in the village, and he's stuck in here."

I couldn't allow Barbara to start feeling low. "Barbara, I think you and I have to remain strong and bring everyone through this. The managers are tired, and the residents and staff are feeling gloomy. I believe you and I have the energy to get Moonstones back to its normal happy state."

Though I said this, and my head agreed with my statement, I found Mrs. Cook's condition difficult to come to terms with. As usual, I blamed myself—and this ridiculous inheritance I was about to be the beneficiary of. Every night I tossed and turned while poor Morsel tried to stay in place at the foot of the bed. One night I woke with a start. I'd been dreaming about Mrs. Cook. Bob had told Lianne that I was poisoning her. Bones was also in the dream, Fergus' dog. He was outside Bert's room, guarding the door, and wouldn't let me in. I'd been worrying about Bones during my daytime walks, Fergus being in Los Angeles. I tried to decipher the meaning of the dream. Did Bob blame me for Mrs. Cook's ill health? Did he think I could have done more for her? I wondered where Bones was, who was looking after him. Did Bones actually belong to someone else? Perhaps Fergus only borrowed him so he could devise an excuse to keep bumping into me in the copse. Or did Fergus acquire Bones especially, and had the dog by now been taken to a rescue center and abandoned?

\*\*\*\*

Miss P was visiting. I made straight for her.

"Miss P, I'm a little worried about Bob."

"Are you, Lucy?"

"He's been very quiet these last few days, and he's not wanted to join in with things."

"I'm sure all is fine. I'll see if I can get to the bottom of it."

After spending her whole visit in her brother's room, she came to find me.

"Bob is all right, Lucy, really. I know him inside out. I say don't make too much of a fuss. He'll be back to himself in no time. Just let him be."

"If you say so."

"Can we speak here?" She said. "No one will hear us, will they?" We were in the corridor, so I took Miss P to the lounge and found a corner seat. "I've had a further conversation with Fergus."

"Oh. I wasn't required?"

"No. I speak to him regularly. The paperwork is on the way via courier. If you come to the house the day after tomorrow, we can get it all signed."

"Do I need a solicitor or anything?" I asked.

"I don't think so. Do you have one?"

"No."

"We'll read everything through together and make sure you're happy. Come at five p.m. if you can?"

"Yes, that will be fine."

\*\*\*\*

I went to Belle's that night. She'd invited me for tea. Charlie had chosen the menu. We had various things on toast. Belle and I also managed a few large glasses of white wine. It was as much as I could do to keep from telling Belle about my coming good fortune, but I bit my tongue and repeatedly asked questions about the progress of the yoga business idea.

"I haven't seen George for a long time. How is he?" she asked, probably trying to change the subject.

"Yes, how is George?" Charlie joined in.

"I've not seen much of him lately," I said.

It transpired that Charlie would be staying with her grandmother in two nights' time.

"Would you come round to mine?" I asked Belle. "I could see if George could make it too.'

"And Helen?" she said.

"Yes, if she can, but George quite likes to get out on his own sometimes."

"I'd love to come…whoever else turns up," said Belle.

"Right. I'll make an attempt at some sort of food."

"If you do a main, I'll bring a pud?" she offered.

\*\*\*\*

Two days later, my mood had changed considerably. Mrs. Cook was on the mend. The doctor was happy with her progress, and hospital was no longer likely. We would have to keep a close eye on her. She wasn't strong enough to get out of bed, but she was spending less time sleeping and had been able to drink some soup. Bob was in a sunnier mood. Lionel and Lolly were a great help, welcoming him warmly back into their company in the lounge and thinking up story after story to cheer him up. I found the three of them in fits of laughter at one point during the day. They were laughing so much they couldn't tell me the joke. I went off to Miss P's cottage feeling positive.

"Come in, Lucy. I've made tea."

"Wow, is that the document?"

"I'm afraid so."

"It's so thick!"

"There are two copies. Let's take one each and go through it point by point."

I couldn't concentrate on the document and would surely have signed it without reading it at all if it hadn't been for Miss Pickering's meticulous attention to detail. She had me check the spelling of my name and address and make sure my date of birth was correct. She patiently explained some phrases and legal language that I could make neither head nor tail of. She questioned me a number of times, confirming that I fully understood the clauses relating to my rights. I wasn't to say a word to anyone about the inheritance until after Nic's death. On his death, I would be informed, and following that, I would be put in touch with a local solicitor who would handle the arrangements for me, the transfer of ownership of the property, and the sum of money, however much it might be.

"Why do you think I am also to receive money?" I asked her.

"Well, it's not cheap to keep a large manor house running," Miss Pickering said.

"I was thinking that."

"I will be here to help you throughout."

"Thank you, Miss P."

"I will be able to advise if you wish to employ any staff or carry out any works."

"Imagine!"

"Owning the manor?"

"And possibly having staff!"

"I believe you should also think of a business idea," Miss P continued. "I don't know how much money might be coming your way, but I expect you'll find you spend it rather quickly. You may need to make the manor pay for itself in some way…or you could sell it."

"No! I could never sell the manor! Believe it or not, I've already started thinking of business ideas. It seems preposterous, but one evening my imagination seemed to run away with itself, and all sorts of ideas came into my head."

"You're a clever woman, Lucy."

"Miss P, can I ask you one thing? Something's been nagging away at me."

"Go ahead."

"It's Bones. I always met Fergus with Bones, the bulldog. Surely he didn't take him to America? I was thinking about the poor dog. I hope he didn't have to go to the rescue center?"

"Heavens, no! I didn't realize Fergus had been walking him. He's Algie's dog, Lucy. Of course, Algie can't walk him. One of the staff takes him out as a rule."

"I only ever saw him with Fergus, never with anyone else."

"I think they exercise him in the grounds of the manor as a rule."

"What is to happen to Algie? …and Bones? Do you know?"

"There's an arrangement. Another property, I believe. Don't worry, Lucy, it will all have been thought through."

So I signed the documents, and Miss Pickering witnessed my signature. She was to deal with dispatching them. I went home to wait for Belle and

George and spend the evening trying my hardest to behave normally, and not to drink too much of the gorgeous wine George would bring with him, in case it over loosened my tongue.

The evening turned out to be just what I needed. We talked about yoga and about Charlie, about slide shows and Mrs. Cook, and about an area somewhere on the south coast that George was to make a study of.

Out of the blue, Belle asked, "Do you think you will always live in this cottage, Lucy?"

"I'm not sure. Why do you ask?"

"It's nice having you so close, but I wondered if you might try to buy a place…now that you're a manager and all!"

"Oh, I don't earn enough for that. You mean get a mortgage? I'd not even thought about it."

"Oh, good! Not that I don't want you to buy somewhere. It's just that I like it like this!"

We all laughed together, and George suggested a toast to the three of us…and liking things the way they were.

\*\*\*\*

All remained the same for approximately five more weeks until a wet and windy Tuesday evening in April. I was on my way home from Moonstones, tired and thinking of nothing more than getting inside, drying Morsel off, having my evening meal, and putting my feet up. A windswept Miss Pickering appeared on the horizon, charging along the pavement, trying to tame her long waterproof coat and over-large umbrella.

"Hello Miss Pickering, do you really need to be out in this awful weather?" She looked distressed.

"Lucy, can I come in and talk to you for a minute?"

"Yes. It's not Bob, is it? I saw him only a short while ago."

"No, not Bob, Lucy. The thing is, you see, we've just lost Nic."

It's hard to explain, but it certainly wasn't happiness I felt.

Over the coming days, several things happened. I was given a letter from Nic, written to me by way of an explanation. In it, he told me the sum of money I was to receive.

*Dear Lucy*

*I write this in the final days of the time I was given. My end is almost upon me. I know that you will continue to fulfill the demands made upon you and that you will soon receive the inheritance we've spoken of. The sum of money left to you is one million pounds. It may sound a large sum to you, but believe me, you will need to spend it wisely if you are planning to keep and look after the manor. I know that you are quite capable of making a go of this. You know how to do a deal! I will be thinking of you wherever I end up and hopefully looking in on you and encouraging your progress in setting up what I imagine will be an inventive and enjoyable business venture and also a warm and welcoming home.*

*I often think back to the days I spent with you, my brother Algie, and your dear friend Rosamund. I remember those happy days by the river and often wish I could turn back the clock and be there with you all once more. I have kept Algernon informed about the situation in terms of my will and the beneficiaries throughout and have always had his full support. He will be moving to Hurst End, where we have made the purchase of another property and have been adapting it to perfectly suit his needs. I should add that he would be interested in meeting with you at some point in the future if and when you feel ready. The remainder of my family will be looked after elsewhere. Each will receive something after my death, but none will have any property or business interests in the Steely Green area. No one will interfere with you or your affairs.*

*I wish for you that you are able to remain in touch with the gentle, caring qualities of your young and present self, the determination, the steadfast belief in goodness and the loyalty, and if so, Lucy, whatever else you do, you will be a major success and an asset to the community.*

*For myself, all I hope is that you will remember me with warmth.*

*Good Luck, Lucy*
*Nicolas*

The letter made me sad, not only because of Nic's death, but due to the loving description of me, that was so obviously wrong. Then there was the reference to my being able to do a deal. That didn't quite sit with the generous description. The only deal he could have meant had involved the betrayal of my dear friend. Even after death, Nic had left me in no doubt that we'd negotiated the resulting situation. So, here I was with a manor house and one million pounds, but what had happened to Rosamund? I knew I would suffer for it.

\*\*\*\*

I hardly remember telling a soul about my newfound situation, though I was free to do so after Nic had passed. Nevertheless, everyone quickly found out. I realized this the very next morning. The rain had blown over, leaving a crisp, bright day in its wake. I was walking on Broad Street when I saw someone rushing toward me. It was George.

"It's you, Lucy! It's you!" he shouted.

"Hello, George."

"It's you! You've inherited the manor. It's wonderful!"

"Shhh. I don't want the whole village to know."

"Why not? We should tell everybody. Let's celebrate!"

"Not so fast, George, please!"

"Here's Belle. Look, have you said anything to her yet?" He began waving frantically at Belle, who was walking in our direction.

I remember the look on her face when George revealed my news. It was one of pure delight. She was so pleased for me.

I'd wanted this: it was the realization of the dream that had burned inside me for many, many years. I wasn't sure I'd ever believed it could happen, but it had been part of my life, the way I lived. It was something that occupied my mind. Now it had come about.

I wanted to tell Lianne and Joe before the news seeped through to them. In fact, they were the only people I told; everyone else just found out. Joe answered the phone.

"Isn't it your day off?" he said.

"I need to speak to you urgently," I told him.

"Is everything all right? What is it, Lucy?"

"Can I come to Moonstones right now and speak to you and Lianne? In private?"

"Yes, of course. You don't sound yourself, Lucy. Whatever is the matter?"

"I'll explain. I'll be with you in twenty minutes. I'll come straight to the office."

I agreed to carry on working, though I'd cut my hours. I promised I wouldn't leave them in the lurch. The arrangements that would set up my new life were going to take time. We'd see what happened as the days went by and adapt gradually to the new situation. They were extremely excited and couldn't stop asking questions.

Later in the week, I was working a shift when Joe asked me if I'd pop down to the inn with him. It was late afternoon, and I was planning to finish up and walk Morsel. I thought Joe must want to talk through my situation in more detail now that he'd had time to think things through. Maybe he wanted to find a new manager. Lianne was on duty, and he'd prefer to get away from Moonstones for an hour or so, he said, so we could talk without being interrupted.

We walked into the saloon bar. The room was full. My news now being common knowledge, the villagers had come together and organized a party for me. They'd made a huge banner which adorned the wall, '*Congratulations Lucy, Our Lady of the Manor.*'

George rushed over to me and wrapped his arms around me. "It couldn't have happened to a nicer person!"

Soon, each villager was coming, in turn, to hug me and give me their words of encouragement.

"We're so happy for you," Candy told me. "Paul can't stop saying so."

"What a result!" announced Linda Hughes.

"It really is you," said John Crane. "I always hoped it would be."

Ange and Will said they could think of nothing to say. Jenny and Malcolm couldn't stop talking. Miss Pickering was in the background, but I could tell she'd played a part in the organization of the event. She smiled constantly and seemed to be busy answering questions about the situation. I knew she would be speaking with utmost discretion.

Mr. Peters then asked for everyone's attention. He was going to make a speech.

"Villagers! Villagers! Quiet, please!" He beat his pen against the side of his glass. The bar went quiet. "I would like to say a few words on behalf of all of Steely Green." While he was speaking, Mrs. Peters and two of her sons began to circulate the room with silver trays, offering champagne in tall flutes. "As we are all aware, Steely is an exceptional village. That means, over the years, we have seen some special times and have been given the benefit of meeting some incredible people. Rumors have been rife recently about Steely Manor. Everybody had heard something. Everybody was curious. I should know, being here at the inn and having to listen to it all!" The villagers laughed. "One rumor kept coming up. Lucy Short was to inherit the manor." He looked around at his audience. "And do you know, not one person had a bad word to say about that idea. Everyone embraced that rumor and very much hoped there was truth in it." The villagers cheered and whooped. "It is with immense pleasure that we have finally learned that this particular piece of local gossip was correct. Lucy is our new Lady of the Manor. And, Lucy," Mr. Peters turned to address me in person, "every one of us wished to have this gathering, to welcome you into your new position amongst us. We want you to know that we all support you, endorse you, and want to remain your friends and neighbors. You have the kindest heart, a selfless view of the world, a nature that wants only to give, and help, and love. We all appreciate this, Lucy. We wish only the best for you." He paused, and there was quiet in the room. "And now, without further ado, let's all drink a toast… To Lucy Short!"

It was hard to grasp the situation. I had to keep calm and speak meaningfully to each villager as they came to share stories about how they'd heard the rumor and what they'd been doing at the time. Each one told me how delighted for me they were. Lianne had arrived with Mr. Pickering, also Lionel, and Lolly. They'd wanted to come and represent the home and the residents. Barbara was looking after things at Moonstones. I spotted Belle, standing with David and Charlie. They didn't feel the need to rush up to me.

I went to them. "I'm a bit lost for words."

"I'm not surprised!" David said.

"You're the best person to have the manor," said Charlie. Belle nodded.

"Thank you, Charlie. What you think matters to me, you know."

Belle and David beamed.

"Will I still be able to visit you?" Charlie checked.

"Of course! You will all be welcome, any time."

"Wow!" Charlie said.

"Wow indeed," said David.

"It will be hard to keep us away!" said Belle.

"I'll need you all to help me too," I told them. "I'll have to make plans, and I'll want to discuss them all with you!"

George and Helen joined us.

"Congratulations," said Helen. "What are you going to do about the treasure hunt?"

"She's joking," said George.

"Oh God, I know! I'll have to have one, won't I? I hope you'll give me a hand with it."

Everyone was excited. I felt almost dizzy from the sudden release of years of secrecy, planning, and plotting. I'd made it to my destination, and what's more, people seemed happy for me. The negative thoughts were kept at bay. For the moment, I wasn't thinking about how I'd sacrificed my friend, blackmailed Nic Lester, planned my return to the village for this reason alone, and spent most of my life pretending to be a good and praiseworthy person. But, in an instant, my bubble seemed to be bursting. Daniel, who'd not made it to the party, pushed in through the door of the inn, breathless, an anxious look on his face. The room fell silent; the whole gathering looked over to him.

"It's the manor," he said. "I think it's on fire."

We all hurried to the door and out into the beer garden. We stared ahead of us into the distance, to the outskirts of the village, and sure enough, where the land rose beyond the fields, somewhere behind the trees, black smoke was billowing up to the clouds. George was beside me.

"It does look as though it could be the manor," he said.

I immediately knew that it was, and what's more, I knew what had happened. Something had finally come to me the night before: the intruder I'd disturbed at the house, the glimpse of their profile, the school photograph in George's slide show.

"It's Rosamund," I said. "It has to be. She's gone and set fire to the building."

"Rosamund?" asked George.

"Amber, Rosamund, same person," I said. "Do you have your car? We must stop her."

George and I scrambled into his 4 x 4.

"I hope I don't get breathalyzed!" he said.

"I'll take the blame. It's an emergency. Quick, we need to get up there. Algie could still be in that building."

George drove like a vanquishing racing driver. We swerved round the village streets, burned through the country lanes, and screeched past the gates at the manor entrance. We sped bumpily along the gravel drive. Flames, taller than I'd ever seen, blazed from windows; thick black smoke rose above the roof and rolled across the land, beginning to engulf the whole area. Amber's sports car was visible, parked ostentatiously right outside the main entrance. She'd not even tried to cover her tracks.

"We have to get inside."

"We can't, Lucy. It'll be dangerous. We won't be able to breathe."

"I'm sure Algie's in there. He'll be up on the top floor. Over there." I pointed. "Above the library." The fire hadn't quite reached that part of the house, but George now understood the urgency.

"Once it takes hold in the library…" he began.

I ran to the rear of the building, knowing that the best access would be via the back door I'd gone through with Dad years before. George followed. In the distance, we heard the sound of sirens. Someone had the presence of mind to call the fire brigade. We got as far as the old kitchen. A commotion met us: a barking dog, people making their way down the stairway, obviously finding it difficult to make progress. We found Amber. She was with a nurse, dressed all in white, and between them, they were doing their best to carry Algie, who was trying to assist but evidently had limited capacity to do so.

"Help us, Lucy," Amber shouted. "Please, I think the whole place is going to go up!"

George squeezed past them. He positioned himself behind Algie and wrapped his arms under his shoulders and around his chest to take his weight. The nurse, a young, strong-looking, dark-haired man, moved to the side and rested Algie's legs across his arms, lifting his feet high so that they wouldn't drag against the stairs. The group moved jerkily, a step at a time, trying not to jolt the passenger. Amber and I guided them carefully. Bones stayed a few steps above, making sure we were properly caring for his master. There was a loud crack, and a burning ceiling beam fell beside us. We progressed down, coughing, eyes smarting, through the old kitchen, out to the yard, and on round to the front of the manor.

"We must get away from the building!" Amber insisted.

We carried on to the middle of the lawns, where we finally stopped at one of the stone seats and helped Algie to sit down. There was sweat on his brow; he looked pale and shaken. Bones kept close by his side.

"We'll get you away from here as soon as we can," said the nurse.

Algie wheezed, struggling for breath, his thin-looking body bent in discomfort, but a glimmer of a smile came to his lips.

I looked toward the manor, my manor. The heat was almost too much, even at the considerable distance we were from the scene. Fire engines were arriving, yellow helmeted firemen jumping from them and running to find water for their hoses. Somehow, I felt almost nothing. Amber was standing a little way from me, also gazing at the building. I stepped over to her.

"I want you to know I don't blame you for doing this," I said. "I understand. You took the blame all those years ago for the fire at the cottages. No one stuck up for you. Your world changed. You suffered while the rest of us remained free to live our lives as if nothing had happened."

She turned to face me. We looked each other in the eye for the first time since I'd said goodnight to her in front of old Mrs. Benson's house, that summer evening almost thirty years before.

"What do you mean?" she said. "That's not what happened, Lucy. I didn't do this!"

"Victoria," wheezed Algie. He started coughing uncontrollably.

"I was on my way to the party," Amber said. "I was working up courage. I had an idea that you'd recognized me. I was planning to speak to you and congratulate you. Then I saw the smoke. I drove straight here, and what did I find but Vicky Lester, a crazed look on her face, barrels of petrol from the garages dragged out into the yard…some lying on their sides, already emptied. I knew what she'd done right away. She saw me and ran back into the building. I shouted to her, told her to at least tell me how to find

Algie. She didn't answer, so I rushed inside and started to call his name. I heard Chip here, shouting back to me from the first floor. Chip was trying to bring Algie down the back stairs, he couldn't risk using the lift, and the route to the fire escape was already in flames.

"I had to abandon everything," said Chip, who was crouched beside Algie, doing his best to assist him. "The wheelchair, the medication, all the specialist equipment...everything." He stood up for a moment, his face marked with soot. "And look, the flames are there now, in Algie's quarters. It will all be gone."

There wasn't much more to say, but we stayed for some time, watching as the manor burned.

Chapter 26
Wrong

I found out that Amber was the person I'd twice disturbed in my garden. She'd wanted to speak to me but wasn't sure how I'd react and had second thoughts. She'd become known as Amber as a teenager due to the color of her hair. She'd been married briefly, which meant that her last name was also unfamiliar to me.

It was two weeks later that she and I arranged to meet Algie on the grounds. It was a beautiful sunny day. Amber picked me up in the sports car, which had somehow escaped without damage. She had the roof down. I sat Morsel on my lap, and we drove to the manor. We parked outside what could still just about be made out to be the main entrance. We walked across the lawn to the same stone seat where we'd witnessed the recent disastrous event. Chip and Algie were waiting for us, Bones beside them. I bent and put my arms around Algie. He smiled, then moved his arms toward Amber, keen to embrace her as best he could. He was in a wheelchair, a replacement, I assumed.

"Algie was hoping you'd push him down to the river," said Chip.

"I'd like that," I said.

Algie smiled again.

"Go and talk with your friends," Chip encouraged. "I'll wait for you here."

I didn't know how much speaking Algie usually did. His voice seemed weak and his words few and far between. We didn't really know each other anymore, but it was clear there was something between the three of us. I took charge of the chair, and Amber walked ahead, picking out the best route. The dogs had left us and gone to explore. We came to a spot where the reeds parted, and the river was in view. Amber had brought a rug. She spread it out on the grass.

"Can you get out of the chair, Algie?" I asked.

He reached forward, and we maneuvered him onto the ground. We sat down too.

It wasn't long before we noticed an old rowing boat, upstream, lying upside down on the bank, tied with a rope to a tree.

"That brings back some memories," said Amber, suddenly excited. "Do you think we could…?"

"I'm not sure any boat would be safe on the water in that condition," I said.

Algie was moving his head back; he lifted his chin. He breathed in noisily. It seemed he had something to say.

"Rosamund…" he said. He breathed in again, struggling to inhale, "…shall have a b-boat." There was still a boyish cheekiness in his expression.

We all began to laugh.

"I suppose, in fact," I said, "I must own the boat…unless it's yours, Algie?" He slowly shook his head. "So," I continued, "I think, Amber, you should have it. Nic left me some money, I'm sure you know that, Algie. Why don't I have the boat restored?"

"Then we really could go out on it, row down to the bridge," said Amber. "Wouldn't that be like old times!"

"I don't know if the manor can be rebuilt," I told them. "They're looking into it, and the legal situation. Anyway, we can still meet here and enjoy the grounds. We can get to know each other all over again…if you both want to, that is. Whatever happened, happened! Algie, we seem to have forgiven you!"

After I'd spoken that last sentence, Amber uttered the words that surprised me more than anything that had been said in the whole time I'd been back in Steely, perhaps more than anything I'd ever heard spoken.

"Lucy," she said. The look on her face was one of amazement and concern. "You've got it wrong. It wasn't Algie. Algie didn't do anything. Is that what you've thought all this time?"

"How do you mean," I asked, "I was talking about the fire at the cottages. If we're all going to be friends again, we need to get everything out into the open. We need to be honest with each other."

She focused on me, her expression serious. "You think Algie started the fire at the cottages all those years back? Algie did nothing. I did it. I started that fire," she said. "I'll never know what got into me. Something snapped. Algie tried to put the fire out. He helped with the rescue. I'm going to have to beg Algie to forgive me."

I could not believe my ears. Everything I'd done and thought, every day of my life since the morning after that fire, my whole way of thinking and living was based on how utterly sure I was that Rosamund had been wrongly accused.

At that moment, Algie began struggling to get to the lapel pocket of his jacket. His hand shook with the effort as he tried to reach it, but he resisted any help. He eventually managed to push his hand inside, and when he drew it back out, he was clasping a small, round item. He slowly pushed his fist toward us, his whole arm trembling, and turned it palm upward, opening his fingers to reveal a beautifully painted pebble. It was unmistakable: the delicate blue butterfly, the reeds, and the flowers. He turned it over, and there were our names on the back, *Algie & Nic, Lucy & Rosamund.*

"Lucky stone." Algie smiled.

**A word about the author…**

Beth Merwood is a writer from the south of England. Her debut novel, *The Five Things,* is also available from The Wild Rose Press.

https://bethmerwood.wixsite.com/write

Thank you for purchasing
this publication of The Wild Rose Press, Inc.

For questions or more information
contact us at
info@thewildrosepress.com.

The Wild Rose Press, Inc.
www.thewildrosepress.com